Waiting for Cordelia

Books by Herbert Gold

NOVELS

Birth of a Hero
The Prospect Before Us
The Man Who Was Not With It
The Optimist
Therefore Be Bold
Salt
Fathers
The Great American Jackpot
Swiftie the Magician
Waiting for Cordelia

STORIES AND ESSAYS

Love and Like
The Age of Happy Problems
The Magic Will

MEMOIR

My Last Two Thousand Years

Waiting for CORDELIA

BY **Herbert Gold**

ARBOR HOUSE *New York*

For James Oliver Brown,
and our long friendship,
which has surprised us both.

I

1

A LONG BLACK LIMOUSINE, California license MK-1, pulls off the path and onto the lawn, crushing only a few daisies. Inside, through glass darkened by treatments against ultraviolet light and bullets, a young woman who would be pretty, were it not for other considerations, is peering toward the tents near the swimming pool. She is accompanied by her husband, Leopold Kirwin, a retired real estate developer and Certified Public Accountant, her public relations advisor, Adolph "Benito" Renfrew, a crushed tomato out of Yale and the Greenfield-Renfrew Agency, and her best friend, newsperson Calvina Muir, who shares avocational duties as advisor to both Benito and the nearly lovely young woman.

Marietta Kirwin is a Supervisor-Councilperson-of the City of San Francisco. The mind might connect Supervisor Kirwin, who hopes to be the first woman mayor of San Francisco, with the liberal tact of only driving front paws of pre-official Cadillac onto the daisies. Your typical boss politician would have barreled right into the festive tent up ahead, gathering evidence for an arrest, a harassment, or a strong issue in the upcoming campaign, when

San Francisco's reputation for permitting a scummy moral tone would surely be an issue.

Leopold, Benito, Calvina, and Marietta stare without discussion. Intimate friends, sitting on advance-party sentinel duty, need no unnecessary exchanges of politeness. They are communing silently with nature and vice. Benito has his Minox at the ready, hoping for evidence. There is plenty of nature, buzzing and humming out here, but the vice is so busy it has little time to display itself.

Like me, they are waiting for Cordelia.

•

Ah, at last. I miss her, I need her. Hands on hips, breathing correctly from the diaphragm, Cordelia comes to study the line forming outside her tent. A smile hiding her thoughts, she takes note of the Cadillac scout car. She is also observing herself, that inner life, which I seek to understand, fitting snugly and invisibly into the way she lives; she rests a moment; then time to go back to work.

I am the first speaker. "Cordelia, you look so good! What happened? You spent the weekend at the beauty farm?"

"No, Professor, I got interviewed—"

"That makes you beautiful?"

"—on *national television*."

"That makes you so beautiful?"

"The Mike Wallace Show, man! I got my fat ass on the Mike Wallace Show! I bet I'm as famous as Hugh O'Brian, Chuck Connors, or Peter Lawford, plus more attractively feminine in my ways."

"Well, you sure look fine."

Her face grew long and thoughtful again. "Of course, Sammy Davis Junior is more famous. Richard Nixon, too. I only got twenty minutes out of a possible sixty. But I'm really accomplishing something for the women of the world, especially those in the streets. So it's not just for me. That's what makes me look so good—a sense of mission, man, a fucking sense of mission."

There was one objectionable word in this speech which Cordelia flung out loudly enough to penetrate the ultraviolet and bullet-resistant glass of the liberal Cadillac. No matter; Benito's Minox had already drunk its full. The motor purred and Marietta's husband backed the wheels off the lawn, careful to hurt no more flowers than absolutely essential to the interests of moral regeneration in one of the great convention cities of America, where the hotels were really hurting because of street crime. If it weren't necessary to protect his wife from the security risks of contemporary American politics, Leopold Kirwin would have traded down to an American compact for the campaign. A Pinto would be more fitting to his wife's image: a touch of the old-fashioned Puritan values, plus care for the ethnics, the downtrodden, the plain economical. But the old Caddy certainly was comfy when you had a lot of friends and colleagues aboard.

"Fucking snoops!" cried Cordelia.

But the scout Cadillac with its crew of live witnesses and Minox-wielding campaign advisor was bumping down the path, slowing past elements of the wedding party, very aware that a lovely young candidate for mayor is always in the public eye.

"I'm not sure they heard you," I said.

Cordelia shrugged. "Makes no difference, that was just an expression," she said. She looked into my face—a blast of happy sunlight across my eyes—and socked my shoulder like a pal. She gave me one more instant of radiance. Then she ducked her head and dove back into the surging, wavering, shimmering heat of the tent, sun above, bodies below, an accumulating battery of solar and copulatory thermal energy. There were bird peeps of girls. There were hippo roars by male guests. It wasn't fair to let her ladies do all the work while Cordelia gossiped with the professor. I strolled across a path of grass for natural-food carrot cake and organic apple juice from La Maison Magnolia Thunderpussy.

I stood in line for healthy sweets; I stood apart on a little hillock with my goodies; what trouble would Marietta Kirwin try to bring upon Cordelia? These two powerful contemporary women had uses for each other as enemies. Marietta—her bill-boards called her only "*Marietta*," as in Mother and Mayor—needed to show her sense of traditional moral values to overcome the accusation of coddling welfare, union, and minority elements of the population. She had boldly declared herself in favor of women's rights, abortion in cases of rape, and non-sexist equal employment. A crackdown on vice was just the turn of the dial to calibrate her program. As I recalled that pinched, pretty, tea-party face, I was sure she had another powerful emotional weapon in her anti-prostitution campaign: *sincerity*. It was not just a vote-getting invention by Benito Renfrew and Calvina Muir. Chauffeured by the old husband, that was a Cadillac full of honest moralists.

Adversaries, but why enemies? I could see hatred on Marietta's face.

As to Cordelia, she needed renown as some need love or power or freedom. She needed love and power and freedom, but to get them, she needed fame. And she didn't mind the trouble Marietta might bring, if it helped to bring the women of the streets and the upstairs hotels together in Cordelia's great dream, an inter-national union of all free-working whores.

I didn't want Cordelia to go to prison. I didn't want her to fail in her mission. I didn't want to mess up my thesis.

I finished the last of my carrot cake, slid the plate into the litter can, and tried to forget my worries. I've been chronically anxious ever since I gave up my happy psychopathy, thanks to court-ordered psychiatric treatment. More about me in due course.

The only way I could get close to Cordelia was to be attentive without annoying her. While I worried, I would try to appreciate the wedding party. I would rather eat carrot cake than fire.

The fire-eater over there would rather eat fire at this wedding in a meadow of Hillsborough near a house modeled on the Petit Trianon. Jugglers juggled. A comic Master of Business Ad-ministration from Stanford, a cousin of the bride and a patron of Cordelia, announced and consequently performed his famous tennis-ball juggling act: one pink ball in the air at several times. Cheers. Funny remarks. Laughter. His audience included a tame squirrel with a peanut balanced between two paws and muzzle. A chamber music ensemble played its Mighty Mo Suite, an accoustic rendition of the Eine Kleine Nachtmusik. One of the classic San Francisco rock bands played the classics of rock, plus "Hello Hello," a forgotten classic. The ushers wore matching fat ties and described themselves as "best men," although the real best man wore, in addition, three-inch cork heels and a large yellow happyface button. The one-ball juggler was an usher, judging by his tie.

"How come that fire-swallower is so skinny?" asked Colette, the cellulite-plagued manager of Tops and Trowsers, Ghirardelli Square branch. "He's slim and lovely. I thought there's calories in fire."

A Prince Faisal—one of three—offered a plausible argument in favor of plump thighs. It seemed plausible to Colette for awhile; then she remembered the pants she sold and said, "Listen, Prince, go wait in line for Cordelia. You're wasting your time with me."

Food and wine were served by European exchange students at little French picnic enclaves. Straw baskets crackled. Red-checked tablecloths were revealed. Children ran and played in perfect safety. Bees buzzed, alighted, curled their bodies deliciously, carried off the nectar of flowering bushes. The graceful suburban hill and meadow sloped and bulged and cost a lot.

The grandmother of the bride was carried from her Humber by her chauffeur. Both grandmother and automobile resembled bulldogs; the chauffeur resembled a black man. Lovingly he placed Granny in a wheelchair and wheeled her through the crowd. By respect, the one-ball juggler caught his ball and held it extended in his quiet paw until she passed. After her death, the property would be subdivided. The squirrel, astonished at the sudden stillness, ran up a tree. He was tame but nervous. The fire-eater belched a few forgotten flames from a recent snack.

Everyone tried to bring a wedding gift appropriate to the occasion, their friendship, their talents. The groom, a lawyer, had defended street artists and won them the right to partial possession of the sidewalks. The rule was: a person could sell the fruits of his own labor. The groom received nearly fifty belt buckles with tooled leather belts. Most of them were made in a factory in Tijuana. They were the fruits of somebody's labor. The bride received enough macrame to satisfy her macrame needs in the foreseeable future. Books, recordings, paintings, sport gear, silver heirlooms, comic roach holders, Third World craft items. The father of the bride brought money.

Immediately after the ceremony, everyone's friend Cordelia had installed herself in a tent near the bathhouse, near the pool, with several of her girls, including Black Barbara, Rose Ann, Blossom, Sharon, and Cybil. A sign lettered with child's crayon on cardboard said: CORDELIA'S COMFORT STATION. A linen supply house had brought in plenty of pilowcases, towels, and soap. Garden hoses led into portable tubs. Cordelia always insisted on adequate sanitation.

As her wedding present to the happy couple, Cordelia and her girls were taking on all comers. Bees susurrated in the rose garden nearby. Human beings splashed in the pool. The cries of private, acoustic ecstasy were inconspicuous among the amplified public merriment. A fortune-teller in her tent only tells fortunes. Cordelia was giving good fortune.

Prince Faisal was impatient. His father couldn't wait to visit the Mosque of Omar without the Jews in Jerusalem. Thirty-two out of thirty-six of his brothers shared this passion. Personally, it muttered little to the Prince. He had his Maserati. He had his other ideals. But Cordelia just said: "This is a democracy, buster, so either take your turn in line or pay me a lot of money."

"How much?"

"Today I'm only taking Israel bonds," she said.

She didn't mean it. She closed the tent flaps, saying, "Wait. Be nice."

When the grandmother departed in her Humber, she carried

Rose Ann back to San Francisco, a wounded, bee-stung wedding gift, allergic, needing repair, repose, and benedryl. Cordelia redoubled her efforts on behalf of her fallen colleague. Marietta Kirwin would never understand this trade-union comradeship. The fire-eater extinguished himself in Cordelia's tent. Faisal staggered forth, fond of democracy. Distracted, drunken, adventurous young men entered. Calmness, repose, and sleepy grins emerged. A putting out of the holy fire—or of furtive flamelets—was the fruit of Cordelia's labor. Due to the sanctity of the institution of cross-sexual marriage and the holiness of the occasion, lesbians were turned away. Cordelia apologized to a concerned bulldyke citizen. There was a lack of facilities.

Looking for my thesis, I found it at last in the social consequences of non-victim crime; subdivision: social deviance; subdivision: prostitution. I had been waiting for Cordelia without realizing how many problems she could solve—my tenure at the university, my tenure on earth. The work had more than academic significance. I had spent too many years in my graduate-student apartment complex in the Berkeley flatlands, waiting to grow up. Those who expected so much of me (clever student, sudden felon, newspaper celebrity) now needed me to perform an act of Sociology. My department head, Professor Jarod Howe, accused me of coasting on my reputation as a bank robber. This was not entirely true. But I had been tuckered out by premature notoriety and Sixties relevance, a little like Mario Savio. I needed to find a useful task which would also justify tenure at the University. I needed to fashion a midnight conversation with my fellow persons, something to occupy me as more than a tuckered-out bystander. I needed perhaps to give something to someone else. I could even learn to take a little better.

My undeveloped truth might be revealed to me through (a) work, Science, and promotion, and (b) true love. Well, I'd settle for three from Line A.

Cordelia's tent billowed slightly, sailing through the universe, although the breeze had fallen. She had hung the poles and ropes with tie-dyed banners, symbols of her craft. Balloons. Undies. A classic red light done in collaged felt on a background of the zodiac and sliced bananas. Bodies folded together like Gemini, unfolding.

I stood there, folded together within myself. "What do you like?" she asked me.

"I just want to talk with you."

Like any other john, I wanted to slow down this hurtling through eternity.

"You'll have to proceed to the end of the line. Can't you see I've got a lot of wedding present to deliver?"

"When can we talk? I want to talk about the Union."

"In Union there is Strength," she said. "What if we picketed the hotels? What if they had to arrest johns, not just us? Deprive this city of our services and see what happens to the tourist business. You want to come work for us?"

"Marietta is going to use those pictures. She's going to light a fire under the cops."

"Let 'em cook."

"I can't explain it all at once," I said.

"Neither can I," she said.

Her upper lip was damp. Her hair was dark, rich, and clean. Her teeth were squarish and strong. There were chevrons in the tender eyeflash. Her eyes at the corners reaped the harvest of many smiles. Eternity was large enough to contain her.

"Just hang out, puss. Later, when there's time, I'll try to give you what you ask."

I knew most of the members of this wedding the way you know your neighborhood when you are either the kid who cuts out of school or the truant officer. I had seen them as I flew by, the Sausalito bargeoisie, those who hang out at night, the forever young of North Beach, Union Street, and Noe Valley, the watchers and waiters and drinkers and dopers, the seekers of a simple (but undisclosed) truth. The once and future singles. Henry Garrett, the not very smart lawyer, was there, so you couldn't say it was just delightful people. No. But Lester Jones, the bisexual brown bartender and goldminer, was helping things along with his smiling presence. And Jeremy Jensen, sweet and delicate; and Florin Schultz, who built highrises; and Cody, the painter who was so anonymously prominent in Dr. Kinsey's first report; and Fred Ellis, my tennis partner and stockbroker, a man who needed more love than even the Summer of Love could provide, back in 1967, but he was still looking for it; and Luigi Mendoza, the smart old lawyer who wore his Phi Beta Kappa pin on the swim trunks and his Legion d'Honneur on his velvet jeans suit and his belly kept spreading, because nobody is as young as he used to be and some eat more—Luigi was heading into the tent with Rachel, but he would prefer Rose Ann, a fresher whore; and Piero Grandi, another middleaged hustler, I think he had a travel agency; and Karla and John Rowe, who both loved black women and good design; and Arthur Pesche, the North Beach novelist and silent thinker; and FitzHugh Gross, the accountant, lawyer, and accused Peeping Tom (misdemeanor charge, dropped by popular request); and Sam Bowers, the record producer who was definitely not involved in narcotics except as a hobby and sometimes to help out his friends; and Danny Doomsday, another lawyer—the groom was a lawyer, so naturally he knew a lot of the same people. Sandy White. Shel Silverstein. Kitty Desmond. Margo St.-James. Some older women with flowered hats, like real estate salespersons. Michael McClure with a wolf-faced violet in his lapel. Michael Stepanian, the champion rugby player. Oh, so many others whose names make news in San Francisco.

Odd quirk of selective focus. She was very important to me. I was discovering a way to become important to her. My eyes quickly adjusted to the sun-filtered canvas dusk of the tent. I now saw only Cordelia, and a glimpse past hanging silks of a leg of Cybil, a gleaming, goose-pimpled torso of Black Barbara, a sliding, turning, mouth-open head of Sharon on a small pillow covered with a towel. The men were transparent wraiths, partners of smoke. Perhaps if I blinked they would become visible again.

I blinked. They emerged sheepish, chop-fallen, heading for elsewhere.

The guests of the wedding were busy using ten percent of their brains and one hundred and ten percent of their pleasure domes. This California mathematics might come out okay under the mild sun of Hillsborough. The synapses crackled nicely, quadraphonically, at each other under the heads of straight, whitish hair, the heads of straight, rich, brownish-red hair, under the long curving skulls of California people. Everyone looked pretty today. Everyone felt healthy and sweet in their appetites.

It was not always a happy job for Cordelia. Jeremy Jensen, a cornsilk lad, fresh and clean, came gasping in her arms; and speaking of the bride, said only, "I loved her."

Then, like everyone else, he returned to the carrot cake and apple juice stand run by Magnolia Thunderpussy for some of that wedding carrot cake and apple juice. It gave good karma and vitamins. "What's your sign?" asked Magnolia of each supplicant. Jokers answered Texaco, KLH, or Mastercharge. Zodiac truthtellers answered Pisces, Capricorn, Cancer.

"You're getting your act together," Magnolia said. "Careful of those paper plates, they bend."

"Oh, yum," said the man who was mourning the loss of his only true love.

The frosting on the carrot cake was a protein and ascorbic-acid-rich combination of nuts and orange juice bonded together by one hell of a lot of sugar. Walnuts floated on frozen dextrose waves. In the shade of the willow nearby, sheltered by a canopy of green, surfeited with goodness, guests with sweet lips crushed poppers underfoot and inhaled eagerly. None of them took amyl nitrate for the angina.

The smells outdoors, beyond the willow, were of flowers and trees.

In Cordelia's tent, of day-old bread and week-old cake, a bakery heat.

Near the pool, of chlorine.

Near the fire-eater, of gaseous fire.

Near the rock band, of grass and grass.

Near the watered sod, of greenhouse fertility.

Near Cordelia, in her busy tent, of punk, bread, cake, sobs. And the pile of used linen and towels grew like a compost heap at the entrance of this temple.

Before white men came to California, also women to gild the rush for gold, there were so many flowers that you could walk practically noplace without crushing thousands of petals. The low-tension hum of bees occupied the air for thousands of years, and birds pecked and sang, and snakes curled in the hot places of rocks. Oh, a nice time to be a flower, bee, bird, snake, or sun-baked flat rock. You could have eliminated millions and millions of flowers and still hike a thick carpet of blossom across the territory. There were also Indians, lakes, rivers, and stony mountain peaks.

Californians changed all that. "Eureka, we have found it!" But on a day like this, near the house copied from the Petit Trianon, with managed gardens, balloons, and banners, the sun shining, redundant fertility in the air, I remembered, for once in my life, that there had been a history in El Dorado beyond my brief career as tenure-seeking assistant professor of Sociology at the University of California, Berkeley.

"Hi, Cordelia. Another break?"

"You waiting for me?"

"Not necessarily."

"Just taking in the sights? Hey, gimme a hit of that apple juice, this is hot work. Better I should have brought them a Ronson table lighter, I know a place you can still get them."

"Mostly they don't use table lighters anymore."

"They're not so good at what we're doing either, Al. These are not a satisfied people. For sound orgasms and seeing the Buddha I never did count on Stanford boys. All that *thinking*. They don't ride with the flow. They're into worry a lot. They're worse than some of my sad old married men with false teeth and false wives. The moment passes them by."

"Maybe they don't think it's important."

"For them, everything unimportant is important. Buying shoes is important. Where are the priorities, Al? What makes a Marietta think like she thinks? I run an honest whore house. It's for enjoyment and business, not for show."

"Do you think, because I'm a professor, you have to be a philosopher? I'm the lowest ranking professor. I don't have tenure."

"Talking nonsense with you is a rest and a treat, Al. And I do love a nice value judgment in the morning. Oh, man, if there were only ice cubes in the apple juice, I'd like to suck me an ice cube."

"That's better."

I liked Cordelia to say what was really on her mind. What she said, it was only a part of her mind. She tricked. She hid her self in play. That's only one of the great things about her. If she hadn't learned to play so well, the dark side might have taken over. I knew there were things that scared her; I didn't yet know what they were, but they weren't the usual frights. She had the power to make life scary for others. She chose to use that power for comfort.

Now she broke the secret of the confessional, where a lad lay counting his throbs like beads in her arms. "See that john over there? Blond kid? Holding the wine like a can of beer against his tummy?"

"Frat boy," I said.

"You're hard on people, Al. He thinks of only one thing. The girl he lost." She licked her lips, which had two small red perforations in the lower left corner. Someone had bit her, or an incipient herpes simplex, due to fatigue and fret, was working its way in and out. It dwells on every lip, awaiting its chance. "I learn from my johns, which is why I don't have to worry about the freebees. I never lose. Nobody loses. Making love to a whore is like winking at a girl in the dark. She doesn't know you're doing it. You take no chances. You lose nothing."

"Gain nothing."

"Rah-eet," she drawled. "Right, Al. And it's got a business side to it. In return for letting you wink at her, and she twists and twirls, she gets a commission. I'd like her to get some benefits, like any other worker. Do you think I'm just painting bubbles?"

I shrugged; she made a kissing motion in the air which would barely break a bubble. She wanted to help me begin to understand. At the same time, as usual, she wanted to throw some glitter at the world. Well, don't the sun and sea, fog and clouds and pollen in the air, don't they all do the same? What's false about glitter?

"Who's that over there?" Cordelia asked.

"Sam Bowers. You don't know him?"

"Um. Sam Bowers."

That music producer in skinny bootjack jeans, tooled Texas Ranger musician boots, with a two-color suede, purple and tan jacket, Sam Bowers, was trying to look like a music producer. Succeeding. It was he who discovered and promoted the Epitomes —Sisters Three—and the art of Sibling Rock. Good skinny long legs, true. But I didn't necessarily like him too much as Cordelia meditated on his being.

"Falling in love is not the only agreeable occupation about love," she was telling me. "For some, falling out of love is all they trust. It seems real. And hurting love. For those who need to degrade it, we serve. For the man whose wife disappoints him, brings not life but a chill, to do dirty things gives him more than pleasure. It gives warm dirt, which is what he requires. We supply dirt when needed."

"What's that these days?"

"What a person thinks. I'm ready to let a man name his filth and dream as ugly as he likes, which he gets his joy of."

"And you?"

"The hooker has a hook. Money."

"That's all?"

"Well, Al, me personally, I want justice for my kind. We'll make the Union. We'll strike. We'll blast them out."

"You better see your lawyer, Cordelia. Marietta has that missionary look. She is dangerous."

"I see him all the time. Luigi's one of my all-time favorites. He says I can't be a legal hooker, but I tell him I can't stop doing what's right."

"Going on strike is a way to stop."

"Oh, you're so smart, Al. A short statement right to the balls of the dilemma."

I absorbed that as best I could. "You like to tell me the truth, Cordelia? Because if you tell me the truth, maybe I can do something, too."

She looked into my eyes. She hadn't expected this much from me. I didn't expect it, either. When I was crazy, I had few doubts. Now I was cured and dubious. But for once I had said the right thing.

"Well, Al, me personally, as I was telling you, I like to understand. People want true, deep, profound communication and love, it's as natural as a good shit. Sometimes you can't have what you want. You learn to want money. Or understanding. Or strength. I always get *something*, Al. I come out okay. Some people build their lives on sand."

"And yours?"

"On clay."

She was laughing. We both knew what happens when you pour water on clay. For Marietta Kirwin, intelligent, quiet, raging, once a mother and now hoping to be a mayor, was determined to wash out corruption and degradation wherever she found it within the limits of the city and county of San Francisco.

2

CORDELIA IS ONE OF THE MADWOMEN of San Francisco. They could not exist without the madmen, among whom I count myself. As a lad in 1967, just a lonely college kid afflicted with anomie, the stylish disease of the late Sixties, sort of like cellulite, I robbed a bank and got middleclass punishment—psychiatry at hard labor, incarceration in the real world, probation. Now I teach sociology at Berkeley, and most people expect my great work on Social Deviance and Victimless Crime to be more scientific then the history I'm about to share with you. Jarod Howe—who made full professor at thirty-six—says being black taught him to be practical. I'm not black and I am not practical. I'd like the goodies Jarod likes, but a certain dimness in me needs to be lightened up first. We'll see. Crazy like Cordelia would help. Cordelia wants to end oppression in the world and also to make herself comfortable.

How can she do both? Well, to begin with, this is California.

And this is my chronicle, in lieu of thesis, of the valiant, clean, and militant whores of San Francisco, California, plus their colleagues in the sex business—the police, the customers, the lonely, the deprived, the philosophers of desire. Some are pretty and some are smart and all are a little peculiar, even as you and I. It would be falsely democratic to pretend they are the same as everyone else. They are different. Marietta Kirwin, for example, was a sincere politician. She sincerely wanted to earn respect for womankind and sincerely believed that Cordelia practiced a reactionary and degrading trade and sincerely wanted to get elected to as high an office as a pretty, serious, hard-working thirty-eight-year-old member of the Board of Supervisors could imagine. She wanted to be mayor so bad she could have tasted it, if she hadn't had a recent tastebudectomy (slight allergy to cigarets, causing a mild set of tumors). Just as she had given up smoking with the help of a hypnosis clinic, so she believed prostitutes could give up their destructive activities and find useful careers for themselves as salespersons, clerical aids, or homemakers, with the aid of strong public action against Cordelia.

I suspect myself of bias in favor of Cordelia. She founded WOO, the Whores' Union, to protect her good sisters. She became first a cocktail waitress and painter—acrylic weeping American bombs and aircraft—who happened to earn additional rent money by renting out her body; then she became a law student, whore, madam, and union organizer, in about that order, because she was unjustly arrested on a charge of prostitution.

Unjust?

Well, this vice squad cop, Sergeant Boger, seemed so nice. They had a chat at the bar of the Fiesta Club. She discussed some of her theories about the cerebral tantric unity fuck (a hundred dollars and a lot of eye contact), but it was too deep for him. Then she discussed how to ride with the flow for fifty dollars, with a really groovy person, but he wanted something more specific. So she invited him to her place on upper Grant for a drink and a cuddle. He asked her to perform an unnatural (later, natural) act, and she felt like bringing a little happiness into the world. Afterwards he offered her money, and since he was so generous, and seemed to have lots of it, and she didn't have so much, and needed money to support the art of acrylics, she said: "Yes, thank you, I'll just put it in my little box here."

"Sergeant Boger, Vice Squad. I have to take you in, Cordelia."

"No!"

"Yes. Don't make a fuss, Cordelia. My partner's in a squad car— look out there."

She ran to the window and then ran back. Her breasts, running, were one of her nice qualities for Sergeant Boger. Shrieks of pain and outrage. Her breasts were heavy, firm, and milky-white except where the sergeant's beard had speckled them with a pink rash. Or maybe that was just gratified desire. He had enticed her; it was love at first sight; the money was his idea; oh, pain and shame.

"Resisting arrest would be an additional charge, Cordelia."

She calmed down. "May I wash first?"

"Yes. Take a toothbrush."

"Don't you want to wash your little dingie, too?"

"Never mind. My wife understands."

"What about the boys at the station house?"

"Smart talk is the same as resisting arrest, Cordelia. That would be an additional charge of malicious mischief."

He let her clean up (sophisticated Frisco) while he rearranged his clothes and pulled his belt up a notch. He sighed. A long evening's labor. He had to listen to her tantric philosophy plus take all this rub-a-dub-dub. And they booked Cordelia on a prossie charge. Her lawyer, Henry Garrett, a Greek with too much white collar showing above his jacket, didn't get her out till ten o'clock the next morning. She barely slept, eyes closed, cockroaches rustling, the Ommm in her chest choked off by resentment and chagrin. Just when a girl needs an Ommm, it's not available.

Marietta Kirwin made a nonpolitical statement to the press. "I do not believe in harassment of these poor women," she declared. "I have never said that North Beach should be cleaned up by wholesale sweeps of the vermin in that area. If only people would learn that our community standards here in this lovely City and County of San Francisco are just as high as those elsewhere, we could have a Renaissance comparable to none. Of course, now that the matter is in the courts, with the arraignment of one of the most flagrant offenders, it would be interfering with the process of justice for me to comment."

Calvina Muir commented, however, in her column, "My High View," in the San Francisco Chronicle. Adolph Renfrew commented. Even Leopold Kirwin, as silent and dignified as a man who has been a chauffeur of Cadillacs all his life, and not a tiger of condominium development, a retiree and husband, commented to a few other well-off senior citizens. "Poor creature," he said, "must be sick. I bid three no trump." He felt sorry for his friends who had neglected to marry women much younger than themselves. Not for him an old age full of disuse; Marietta's passion, her power, her integrity, her candidacy. Leopold could help. He put his haggard shoulders to the steering wheel. In another day he might have employed Cordelia personally. Now—the shrewd old codger agreed—they could still use her.

Cordelia's friends, such as me, mobilized themselves to protest unjust pig aggression everywhere (late Sixties) and pack the courtroom. The judge, Barton Shoubstein, who owed his seat on the bench to a now-defunct party boss, was a moral man who had emigrated in his youth to San Francisco from Daly City, where standards were higher and he remembered a person could be safe from temptation in his own home. By what law or equity should a person like him, who went to the non-denominational church of his choice, be obliged to sit still for a person like Cordelia, with her big teeth and wide gums? And why was she always smiling? But it would all come clear in the day's judgment. He tried to listen and focus his eyes, and found that anger focused the eyes nicely. "Quiet in the courtroom or I'll have the bailiff clear this courtroom!" Other men were at least busy with black revolutionaries; he had to content himself with this creature, Cordelia

Celtic, twenty-six, probably older, a vagabond, who had no reason to be so happy.

He didn't even tune in on AM disc jockeys and here she brought these FM deejays to talk about her character. Judge Shoubstein could recognize dumb contempt trying to pull wool over his eyes. The wool itched.

"Quiet! Now witness, accused, take the oath."

Cordelia was a tall strong person with a wide mouth and a large nose and sleepy eyes and good hair and a fake name. Without looking masculine, she did not look feminine, either. She looked monumental. She had hips and breasts and teeth; they were all large and powerful. If there were any malice in her, you would say she was a dangerous person to have on the opposing side. But she had no malice in her. It was not established what she could convince Judge Shoubstein of, but she looked convincing. She was not a girl. She was a woman.

Now she was on the stand, on the opposing side, explaining once again how she happened to be arrested for soliciting, performing, and collecting for an act of lewdness. "I liked him," she was saying. "I still do, he's kind of cute, but now I'm sore at him. I hope he gets the clap."

"Quiet! Quiet! Contempt!" cried the judge.

"I hope he suffers for his entrapments," said Cordelia, lowering her eyes in a modest blush. She appreciated homosexuals, lesbians, senile slobberers, boyish impatients, midgets and pituitary dwarfs, religious fanatics, protein-packed professional athletes groaning under their steroids, journalists, actors, dope dealers, commuters, visiting Japanese businessmen, Peninsula electronics industry personnel, North Beach bar owners, even some cops, but she hated euphemisms.

"The witness may proceed. The contempt citation will be reviewed at the conclusion of sentencing."

"Thanks a bunch, Your Honor."

The testimony wore on. A day in court is made elastic by boredom and anxiety; it stretches. Yawns accompany the voices which accompany the hum of fluorescent lights. Sinus headaches; stomachs awry; digestion tilts. I remembered my own trial for anomie and bank robbery. Cordelia had to do without the psychiatrists my parents rushed up from Santa Barbara.

There is a shortage of flies in San Francisco, but as the hours passed, the steady buzzing grew louder in my ears. It may have been an acceleration and perfection of fluorescence, it may have been the thickening blood seeping through arteries; we were sitting too much. Sleep rolls its snug blanket over present company. The questioning, prosecuting, and defending all took time, and time also makes us sleepy.

A Mrs. Rowe from Marina Boulevard explained she had bought paintings from Cordelia to hang in her front hall. (This shows another source of income.)

A recently-divorced KRON television producer told how Cordelia had decorated his apartment, buying carpets, drapes, and furniture, and she also chose the attractive shade of yellow for his kitchen; many compliments from his friends. (This shows another source of income.)

Piero Grandi, silent partner in the Awful Apple at Columbus and Broadway, forty-nine percent ownership, explained that Cordelia was a weekend cocktail waitress. (This tended to indicate that she had a source of income other than using her body to provide direct-sale carnal pleasure for retail consumer use.)

"Next witness, please."

Cordelia's lawyer, Henry Garrett, proud of his arguments, sure of his evidence, and confident in the expanse of Dean Martin collar which framed his throat, smiled becomingly and gave over the witnesses, each in turn, to cross-examination by the prosecutor. The prosecutor was not taken with the idea. He let them go. The witnesses shot Cordelia their timid, hopeful, helpful smiles, and gathered up their things, and went out. Each was buoyed by a happy altruism. Each was sure he had won the case for her.

"Next, please."

The prosecutor reappeared before Cordelia, steadying himself with the fingers of one hand spread on the table. In an earlier life he had been a tripod. Cordelia was wearing a matronly hat, a purple purse, and a skirt recently lengthened by a strip of pink ruffles. She was overdressed for comfort and charm; beads of wetness on the upper lip. She was nervous, anxious, and smiling with a fixed high beam on this curvy, tricky highway. Indolently inquired the prosecutor: "When was the first time you took money for the act of, uh, love?"

"Love?" inquired Cordelia.

"Whatever you call it, Madam."

She ignored the sarcasm. She opened her mouth to the flow of feeling. "Everyone needs sex so they can get an idea what it's like to be seized by a power outside yourself. Mystical religion or vomiting—"

The prosecutor raised his hand to interrupt, but decided to let her hang herself. Henry Garrett was immobilized by his low I.Q.

"Mystical religion or vomiting gives the feeling of being a vehicle, you are seized by forces outside yourself, or within, but not everyone these days believes strongly in God or regular throw-ups. Almost everyone can do it."

"Do *what*, Miss Celtic?" the prosecutor purred.

"What I mean is pour yourself out through the eyes into another human being just lying there. Become a, a river, two streams pouring into each other, a waterfall, a bloodfall—"

"With force and violence?"

"—a tumble of blood, sir, just looking through the eyes. A bunch of reasons to live which shoot through the heart. A pleasure." The smile went into low beam on life's highway. "That'd be about a hundred dollars." Her smile was affectionate, thoughtful, and absolutely alone in the courtroom. It was a god's smile. Judge Shoubstein, the prosecutor, and Henry Garrett didn't understand a word of it. I wanted to applaud because I understood, but I couldn't be sure, either.

The judge was troubled by the need to make distinctions; the prosecutor restated his question: "When did you start doing it for money?"

"Never! Never!" She raised her hand to swear to heaven. "I never turn a trick just for money!" she cried, and there were tears of sincerity in eyes which somehow had worked it all out.

There were tears of semantic rage in the judge's eyes, too. People who don't turn tricks don't say, I don't turn tricks, any more than a person who was not a crook would say, I'm not a crook. The judge's robes billowed about the gasses seething within. Did he ever have a foretaste of the word Guilty in his mouth, in his brain, in his heart, in his soft plump behind spread warm as cream on the fragrant felt of the bench? Sometimes he could smell the word Guilty rising in his belly like a child's happy milkburp. Unlike a child he must keep it back until the appropriate time. But he knew, the prosecutor knew, the bailiff knew, the recorder knew, everyone but Cordelia and her lawyer knew she was guilty. And would be so found.

I thought to myself and Jean-Paul Sartre in that courtroom: The whore becomes a whore because she is called a whore. Before that, she was just earning a bit of money doing something she likes which happens also to get a man through the night.

"I would like to point out," said Henry Garrett, pointing out something that only made the judge more impatient, more eager for the taste of Guilty. Dumb Henry with his healthy cheeks and spacious collar. "And furthermore, may it please Your Honor—"

Something pleased His Honor. His inner life was satisfactory. "Yes, yes, yes, Counsel."

Cordelia was winking at me from the stand. She thought she was doing fine. She liked the attention. Soon, she believed, she could return to her interior decoration, her painting tears on bombs and airplanes, her waitressing, her turning tricks just for love and small tokens of affection, such as a few dollars. She made love available to the ugly, too. Why should only the pretty good have it pretty good? She supplied love for the specialists, for the diversely troubled. At last the nations of love could form a true democracy, thanks to money.

Sweet Cordelia, the good sister. She had the trick of understanding how lonely men dream. They dream of warm indulgence, soft music, a tongue; they dream of no worry, just please yourself, no additional dues to pay, no tomorrow; they dream of sliding through, and a smile at the other end.

Most of life doesn't offer this easy farewell to loneliness. Cordelia, out of the goodness of her heart and the hunger of her purse, did. Are you sad, baby? Don't be sad. Don't be sad. You like this, baby? I do too. I do too. We'll be lonely together, baby; it's our problem, baby; just now, everything is all okay, isn't it?

She had many lovers before she learned her simple innocence.

•

Police Officer: "She took me into this room full of all sorts of, of, *equipment*."

D.A.: "What sort of equipment?"

"Swords, whips, vises, clothes."

"*Clothes?*"

"Well, all different things. The, uh, crotch was cut out on this, uh, leather jocky short, this brief. This item." (Holds up Exhibit 7-A.) "The, uh, straps on this corset. Um. This stuff."

"And what did she suggest?"

Objection!

"What did she say?"

"She said: *What's your hobby?*"

Order in the court!

"And you answered?"

"World affairs."

"And she answered?"

" 'Groovy. Me too. Especially Transylvania.' It's in my report."

"And you understood by that?"

"A kind of radio. I don't know. She offered to bite my neck.

She claimed she had an arrow dipped in the river Jordan, but she didn't show it to me."

Exhibit 9. Arrow. Mark it.

"It's an Indian arrowhead from a Seminole reservation in Everglades, Florida." (Turning it over.) "Marked Souvenir of Everglades. Made in Osaka."

"She lied."

"She wasn't under oath," remarked the judge, "but nevertheless it goes to the question of her character."

Cordelia lifted her breasts at the cop as if to throw them at him and explode the bastard. Then she drew her finger slowly across her jugular vein. Henry, her lawyer, said Shush, as if she had made a sound, which she hadn't; he patted her hand and arose:

"Your Honor. The testimony is irrelevant, immaterial, and unworthy. My client is a freelance painter and interior decorator. Naturally she keeps certain items in stock."

"These certain items," began the prosecutor.

"Certain items which are sold openly as props or decor in adult bookstores, Swedish catalogues, and for medical purposes only between consenting adults. The defendant respectfully submits that the witness come to the alleged commission of an alleged crime."

Cordelia's breasts, aimed and primed, looked more dangerous than anything to be found in a Swedish shop or an adult catalogue. Her smile menaced with pleasure; the big teeth would give a tooth job to whatever meat got in the way. The eyes were brown, flecked with yellow, and calculating. The nose was mighty and straight. The lips were chapped: nobody's perfect. She was born of man and woman, and grew up in a small town, and drank cod liver oil, and longed to be beautiful but was not, and made friends easily in a way she first explored fully at age eleven. She discovered she could make friends with women, too, at age nineteen. This came about because her chief male friend, a ski instructor, had a Swiss lady friend with dirty underwear who liked Cordelia for her American charm. Yoost cuddle, she begged. They yoost cuddled, but due to her preoccupation with completeness in everything, Cordelia took the older lady in an impetuous rush, just an innocent American child violating a diesel from Zurich who liked to pretend she was a femme.

"Daddy," she asked her father later, "am I queer?"

He looked up from his copy of Barron's Weekly. "What you been doing?"

"Nothing," she said.

He sighed and returned to his magazine. "Then I guess not," he said, pursuing Alan Abelson's analysis of President Eisenhower's most recent thoughts on relieving corporate tax burdens.

Henry Garrett, Cordelia's lawyer, a man with a hairpiece, capped teeth, and a changed name, believed in telling it like it is and advised Cordelia: "Just tell it like it is." He told how the sergeant had borrowed her aerosol deodorant can and sprayed under his arms with his shirt and jacket on. He told how the sergeant had asked if she would do something really dirty and she had answered, *What?* and he had told her.

What did she say, Officer?

Let's snatch this brief moment of happiness on the wing.

Guilty.

•

And so, at a difficult junction in her life, out of revenge and the desire to get rich, and also to pay her legal costs, Cordelia took to the world of small business. She selected a company of pretty girls who hated to share the money with pimps but would share it with her. She began to work out WOO, a future union, a syndicate of working girls. She would ask the help of Piero Grandi. She would dump poor Henry Garrett and get a first-rate attorney, Luigi Mendoza, with whose desires she was familiar. She would consult the media. Due caution keeps a girl out of more serious trouble when she's making both love and war. She became a landlady. She ran a house of entertainment, an artistic and coital salon for those who ask Who Am I?

Who-Am-I is a disease which occurs when the question is asked. On fall days, when the leaves shrivel up and there is music in the air and blood in the veins, or on winter nights, during a holiday season, and also in the spring and summer, the epidemic question kept Cordelia busy. For those who need brief, inadequate answers, and whose metabolisms reject drink and drugs, Cordelia provided a tickle, a thrust, a distraction. She sold affection. Will buyers never cease. Divorced men, unmarried men, widowers, ugly men, sad men, ordinary men, extraordinary men, distracted men—these, in general, were the sorts who craved Cordelia's service. Religious fanatics tended to avoid her, except under unusual duress. Cops adored her, since there was no danger in making arrests or collecting the payoff, depending on the proximity of elections. Doctors and lawyers thrived. Businessmen found commerce eased. She harmed no one. She was a helper. She helped the seekers. And since what she did was illegal, even those who were not interested were strangely interested. She crossed party lines. Even Marietta Kirwin understood something, although what she understood about Cordelia was incomprehensible. She had prominent teeth and gums, but this didn't prevent her smiling a lot. Did she have reason to smile? She did. Marietta may have had plans for her, but Cordelia also had her plans.

Men dream of being kissed by lovely film stars named Nicole or Rosemary, and women dream of Dicks and Tommys who truly care and are very thoughtful. Instead they found raucous in Cordelia's various residences. Ah, it's so sad, Cordelia told me, because she too wanted what men and women want, she wanted more than most other men and women, she wanted everything. And she was desired by those who had fantasies of strange, or liked mere strength, or by cops and sociologists, and they don't count. Ah, sad Cordelia. Here we are in the Seventies, where Valium is the drug of choice. But: she seldom allowed herself to be sad. Thoughtful, strong, and considerate is not the same thing as sad. Fresh flowers in every room and sweet rock music most of the time and good food and dope are not the same things as sad. Cordelia, making out okay, wanted to help others do the same. And then she would make the best move for herself and for hookerkind.

So here, in the notes of a gloomy sociologist, a failed psychopath, is an accounting of a woman who, unjustly accused of whoring, became a madam. Not walking the streets is a better way of life. My aim is understanding and sharing. However could this unaffiliated business agent and organizer bring trade unionism and fellowship into the world of artful lust? We're all feeling our way in this thing. Even Cordelia, confident Cordelia, nourished herself with doubts. Her clients felt safe in the tender chaos of her embrace. I'll watch. I'll listen. Cordelia's friends—Lester, the brown bisexual bartender and goldminer, Jeremy Jensen IV, just crazy about Victorian houses and Eurasian girls, the happy Rowe couple, subjects of gossip by petty minds, Avigdor Malchik, the Soviet agent who defected into the custody of a San Francisco brothel because in a police state he couldn't get the really stylish abuse he craved, Piero Grandi and Florin Schultz, imperfectly tempered johns, Cody, the distinguished painter anxious for a new experience in the Now world of homosexuality, Luigi Mendoza, the top-quality barrister, Sam Bowers, record producer with skinny legs and nearsighted former lover of a trio of black girl singers, Rachel, the sullen Jewish whore with a liberal social conscience and a spoiled temperament, Black Barbara, who wore leather and administered punishment, Al Dooley, sociologist specializing in Deviance and Victimless Crime—will enter to speak their pieces and give the news that they too have immortal souls.

Even Marietta Kirwin, who seldom moved without her little group, Leopold driving, Benito advising, Calvina Muir judging, Cadillac casting its shadow, was convinced that to have a soul is necessary. She thought soul happened because a woman cared enough about her ideals, about herself, and Marietta did. I think she cared enough to tear Cordelia limb from limb.

Cordelia was building her life and fame, Marietta was building her life and fame, two forces of womankind were approaching mortal combat.

Cindy Celtic, that sad child up north. Souls form a part of history.

Now may I please rest in the story as it flows.

3

"THAT'S OUR CORDELIA, queen of all she keeps waiting," said Lester, whose fancy flew. "That woman is so *much*. I'm happy to be alive and gay on the same planet."

"Me too," I said.

"You alive?" he asked. "You more like doing a *survey*, man."

But his smile, eyes, and teeth were caressing ones. There was no offense meant on this November evening at the Feroce, a not exclusively women's saloon on the Barbary Coast in North Beach, where people were having conversations with Lester Jones, the bartender, B.A. Illinois (Circle Campus), M.A. in Sociology at the University of Chicago, under special scholarship on an affirmative action program for bisexual brown men. Lester was only a part-time barperson, but a full-time goldminer. Also present: Me, Albert Dooley, sociologist, Berkeley, ungay, passing the time with Lester while waiting for Cordelia, President of WOO, a militant trade group.

"She's the Harry Bridges of the Tenderloin," Lester said, "if you remember your history, that's our Cordelia, and she'll be along shortly. She got so much mimeographing to do, man. And the girl runs her addressograph ran away with a detective. He was indicted. To Brazil. And look at Sandy and Maggie over there, but don't turn around."

I disobeyed; it was the only way.

Sandy and Maggie, two pugnosed diesels, wearing unironed blue work shirts and hair in short pigtails, were having an intense discussion at a table under the Hell's Angels poster. They were talking out the problem. They both wanted Kim, the slim and delicate femme sipping her Dubonnet over chipped ice at the bar. Winsome Kim looked away. Her fitted jeans were appliquéd by a loving Levis machine: PEACE, plus a pink hand clutching a choice cut of buttock. She looked through the purple wine to the crowded mirror behind the bar and her eyes filled up with longing at what she saw reflected back. She was skinny, soft, young, and hoped to be a good wife to some resolute diesel, but it wasn't up to her to decide. Elfin Kim could go either way. She could go with Sandy or Maggie. She could go with Cordelia. Someday she might go with a husband too, carrying all she had learned in those eyes that filled up like saucers in the rain with memory of the empty past, with hope for the marvelous future. The blessings in store for a girl with patience and sweetness and skinny hips are (she thought) a definite plus. Happy was all she wanted to be, and what's wrong with that? She would bring this person her gift of peace, her hands, her buttocks. When you're an elf, you wait for what the rains bring.

The voices of Sandy and Maggie grew a little louder. I noticed that Sandy had P.O. pants on and Maggie had a blue P.O. seal on her shirt, so they must be colleagues of the zip-code sorting crew.

The voices of Sandy and Maggie grew disputatious. There were specific themes, such as "cunt" and "who says?" and "when you were just an Oakland dyke." But that was only language, mere details. Hairy bitch, skinny twathole, dry noodle—an adversary courtship. The substance of the discussion was who knew Kimmy longer, who had taken good care of Kimmy after her abortion, who spiritually had been her guide, who picked up the pieces when she was so down, who brought her out of the closet.

The burden of the discourse was, goddammit, immovable force meets immovable force on behalf of movable object and both Sandy and Maggie, goddammit, wanted Kimmy. Each felt ready to face the challenge of a difficult karma. Outside, the winter fog was streaming down the gulch of Broadway.

I listened to Lester. These other persons were skilled interpersonal communicators, huffing and puffing muscular charmers. They were not ladies of few words. Their still waters rippled along at top speed. Argument, argument. Epithet, epithet. Lester kept a wary eye on the situation.

"This is not one of your lesbian bars," patiently re-explained my friend, bartender at the Feroce, a lesbian bar. Lester also had an honorary degree in Post Office Management, but he preferred the harmony of explaining to the chaos of mail-sorting. "Your true lesbian bar is a bar for girls who like girls. This is more for men who like girls who like girls. It's a concept."

"I understand," I said.

"Concepts are for understanding," Lester said, wiping away the wet with easy circular sweeps, "but do you *feel* it?"

This was California, wasn't it? I had memorized the Feroce—pool table with fems and non-fems clicking their heavy marbles, Hell's Angels poster with two hairy, tonguing monsters soul-kissing each other, announcement of the Sappho League Spaghetti Feed (on these premises every Sunday afternoon, two hundred ladies can be found twirling their spaghetti in mess kits like infantrymen getting ready for combat), flocked wallpaper and gold carpet and raised stand on which Amoebic Runs, an all-girl band, sometimes rocked. Yes, this was San Francisco, California, which used to be a wild place where folks sought to find gold and themselves and never settle down. Now there was lots of soft leather and good dope to settle down on, relaxation from the worldwide cares of the day. They needed Cordelia to keep them settled and unsettled.

"Thank Mary, single parent, no problems of an owner for me," Lester said. "Marietta Kirwin wants to clean up Broadway, you heard? What'd people do if they clean up the streets?" He shook his head with incomprehension of what he understood. Heavy feet walking on humankind. Marietta's feet might be small and dainty, but they were heavy when they walked on a person, on a whole way of life.

Two sailors were hunched whispering to each other at corner stools. Lester called this corner Scared Space, where the foot-dippers hung out. The sailors didn't know why they chose their spot. Fate chose it for them. In his usual seat a plump bald fellow with a short-sleeved placketed shirt sat watching; this was a man who had a usual seat. A black player in white denim suit, wide lapels, rosette of the Legion of Honor, white straw hat with a tri-color ribbon, white shoes, white girl, swung through the door and down the short tunnel of gaybar velvet. He headed for a Good-will couch with his girl.

Lester said: "She been a good girl all week, so he bring her in here for a little R & R."

"I was meeting Cordelia," I said.

"I know. You a friend. Cause if it's business, she always on time."

"She's a friend," I said

"She got lots. You a special friend, Al?"

I couldn't answer that. How special was it never to go to bed with Cordelia for love or money? How many say, Oh, I just talk with whores for my research? Tell me, honey, you ever come with anyone but me? Do you ever inter-relate with any other sociologist? Who else wants in on the sticky paperwork of a hookers' craft guild?

"That's her great pleasure, discussing," Lester said. "Man, in that case, she be *very* late."

Maybe this space of waiting is what is known as a culture gap. Lester answered politely, fully, thoughtfully, and with that marvelous concentration on friendship which is the habit of your typical lonely bisexual who never quite finds your individual soul-mate.

He helped a girl to a beer, draft.

He helped another girl to another beer.

The girls looked away, lit cigarets, looked in the mirror, looked around, finally looked at each other. They already shared a common background in draft beer.

Lester wiped and waited.

My name's Linda and I'm a secretary, one said, and the other said, Sharon, and I work at the telephone company, what a shitty job. Yeah, yeah, said sympathetic Linda, I have a boss who farts while he dictates, but at least he isn't a computer.

Linda and Sharon picked up their beers and headed for a table together. One tight behind with the command SMILE; one relaxed behind, issuing no embroidered orders. Lester's brown face crinkled in a happy rictus of the person who is doing the work of the world and the work is going well.

While I waited for Cordelia, he kept an eye on Sandy and Maggie, who were having their difficulties about Kimmy, who sipped her Dubonnet. Since I had no special troubles to confide, he could tell me his hopes and dreams, which are usually what bartenders keep to themselves (professional ethics) and it makes them edgy. Lester was no longer a graduate student or, in his heart of hearts, a bartender, except for the bread. He was a goldminer. He was an entrepreneur of modern Klondike discovery. There was gold in the snowy tundras of Alaska, but white men can't find it because the Eskimos won't tell them where. The Eskimos know, but they're only interested in caribou, seal meat, drinking sterno in Fairbanks, and maybe a bit of warmish nookie now and then. They don't care. But if they like a fellow, they'll help him help himself to the gold. They like Lester. That's not a mere detail. It makes the whole quest comfortable. "Even in a time of revolution, man," he said, "it's important to feel comfortable with the Eskimos or Maggie and Sandy. But that Kimmy really could be called a troublemaker if she wasn't so nice—right, Kimmy?"

"What you say, Lester?"

"I hope you're not sleeping, Kimmy."

"Just dozing a little, Lester."

Lester had bought the sure-thing geological map of buried treasure from the proprietor of a Black Muslim bookshop in Seattle. The dude just kind of took to him, and himself, he was too busy with politics to bother.

And so each spring, time of thaw, Lester hustled up the fare and packed his pan and his Geiger counter and his compass and some hardtack and dope and a few paperback books for the Arctic evenings and hurried up north. Oh-oh, they'd say, he's come again, the schwartzeh prospector. Lester spoke a little Yiddish, learned from the graduate students at Chicago and the pawnshops of Fairbanks, where they helped him out when he needed a ticket back to San Francisco. They took from him the pan, the Geiger counter, the compass, and the hardtack was all gone, and some Eskimo kid had the paperbacks, and the dope was all smoked, and Lester returned to bartending and planning the next season's seduction of this somber, mosquito-haunted El Dorado of the north.

Broke he returned to North Beach, and broke he begged the nice dykes for his job back at the Feroce Bar, and the nice dykes hired him at a little less than the last time, no allowance for inflation, because Lester would rather chase his dream than theirs. That's the definition of unreliable.

He saved his tips for the next gold-hunting season. Lester's solitary obsession freed him to be sane elsewhere. He would be a rich man someday, which is power and love and fabulous and white. And so, with the foretaste of his success, a memory of the happy future, he was a cheerful ombudsman at the Feroce. Success improves character, especially a cheerful character. The great tycoon in the bye and bye smiled, listened to people's sad stories, and pulled his frostbitten thumb when he had a moment to spare.

"I think I'm wasting my life," I said. "I thought I paid my dues that one time I got in trouble, but now look at me. Just collecting the data, like everyone else."

Lester dropped the cloth into the sink and rubbed a little

Jergens Lotion into his hand. "Wasting your life, I know what you mean. We bartenders are prepared for that very question. I have some words for you from my long experience as barkeeper, goldminer, sociologist, brown man in America, plus polymorphous outsider considered in some circles to be a faggot." I waited for the words. "Think petty," he said. "You want true love? Don't be so ultimate! One step at a time, or maybe a half-shuffle, you be tired. Get it in little chunks, a twat here, a conversation there, a suck upstairs, a chuckle in the Safeway parking lot." He poured me a complimentary glass and intoned with a juicy false baritone, like a Responsible Negro Leader, "To the day be true, my man."

"I'm just waiting for Cordelia."

"That's the truth."

A couple of girls came in with a poodle. A couple of girls came in without a poodle. Cody, the painter, was reading in a corner and didn't look up. I wouldn't greet him first. K.B., a pimp-in-training, came in with his girl and joined the other pimp and his girl, like Frenchmen on a picnic, two straw boaters on the bench together, ribbons. As a youth, K.B. had parked cars in a lot on Turk Street, but now he was seventeen.

The tongue of one hairy Hell's Angel on the yellowing poster vibrated perpetually like a mandolin pick into the mouth of the other Hell's Angel; the poster had been there, pasted to the wall, curling at the edges, since 1967. After someone took a red Magic Marker to the tongue, Linda, partner in the bar, shellacked the paper against additional graffiti. "She's so femme," Lester explained, "a lovely boss to work for, a great little housekeeper, considerate to the help."

"You're considerate, too," I said.

"Bartenders and goldminers need to be. The Eskimos appreciate it. So do the sailors and whores and the soft femmes you get in here. This is not one of your butch joints where the bartender got to pour and swizzle and once in a while hit somebody with a pool stick. No, man. Linda is lovely. And so's her guy Brenda, who hides out in back, does the accounts, ruins everything with her bad vibes when she comes up front. But that Linda. Oh, nice. I could use her myself if I wasn't just the help around here."

I envied his ease. I envied K.B.'s ease. I too wanted to be easy. Originally I had come from Santa Barbara to study ease, which is essentially the same subject that others name jump-off-the-Golden-Gate-Bridge or Martini, two of the traditional pastimes of this city. And Lester was a smart version of what I sought. He was not one of the walking wounded of North Beach, the screaming meemies of Noe Valley and Castro and Polk, the psychiatric outpatients courting each other on Union Street, the frazzled stockbrokers and insurance men of Montgomery, the coffee-drinkers and grass-smokers of Sausalito—oh, all the Beautiful People who were also studying suicide and alcohol and ease. On that point of desperation Lester had found his balance. "Natural sense of rhythm," he said, wiping the oaken bar and agreeing with my analysis.

"Thank you."

"No, I got it, not you."

"But thank you for flattering my mind, Lester, which is filled with theories."

"You better get Cordelia fast."

"She's a friend, I don't make it with her. I'm doing research on victimless crime."

"Pal. You better get Cordelia *plus* another friend fast."

It wasn't the same need for him. All I had were my fantasies of data, which didn't complete my life. I would do a half dozen papers, a book on deviant behavior; I'd have my promotion. But Lester had his private jet, his harem of boys and girls and a few more boys, his memory of riches to come. He did not think petty. "Ah'm a Fubi," he called himself, "a Fine Upstanding Bisexual Individual. My story will be called 'From Coon to *Tycoon.*'" And laughed a rich, masculine, charmed laugh at the pleasures of being fully alive in a place where it was permitted.

"And now I got to take care of my other most favorite cus-tomers," he sang out, still joined with me in spirit. "Cordelia sure be in soon, Al. Really. You wait, hear me now?"

Cordelia sometimes hung out at The Study, with its lovely young fems, or at the Saturnalia at Valencia and Duboce, with Karla Rowe, where the going gets tougher, or at Kenny's, on the 200 block of Turk, above Kitty's, because there was a lot of loose cutting edge around. But the Feroce was best. That's the soft, fierce heartland, the place of forever springtime, with all its nostalgias of time passing and johns hoping and girls making the best of what they are put through during this our life on earth, of earth, returning to earth. Old North Beach, the Barbary Coast, and memories made it mellow for her as if it were still the hamlet of Yerba Buena with its sweet-smelling weeds on sand dunes.

Outside the Feroce, grit and bus transfers swept down the slope of Broadway as the evening fog cleared before the night winds. The Chinese women who worked the treadles in the sweatshop next door had gone to bed; the meth lab behind the sewing estab-lishment was bubbling away, attended only by two alert kids with Master's degrees in Chemistry and gauze masks over their mouths and Swiss bank accounts. Bruce and Teddy would later relax over a beer at the Feroce, study the girls for taste, firmness, and style, and decide whether to pick out two friendly ones or go back with each other. One of the nice things about getting a rush from each other was it gave them freedom of the will, which they defined as independence from the charms of women.

Cody, the painter, melancholy and middleaged with his modi-fied gray Afro, sat in the deep Huey P. Newton wicker throne, flipping the pages of "Frisco," a monthly pamphlet from the Tavern Guild, the association of gay bars. I heard he had split with his last wife and his daughter was in trouble in Italy; hashish, maybe. Such is success. He may be the most famous painter in the Bay Area, and he's listed in all the "Under Fifty" lists of the best artists in the country, and here he is alone in the Feroce, passing the time till he can sleep. Cody wasn't talking. Working his splayed artist's thumb on "Frisco," an official journal, that's what he was doing. Hard times for old Cody. When I see a man who wants to be alone, I let him achieve his goal.

The Hell's Angels' tongues lay entangled year after year. "Who Says America Is Getting Soft?" A Mona Lisa poster with a Florentine roach holder around her neck. The pool table clicking away. Ferns in painted Crisco cans. Akron Tiffany lamps, nice soft light, everyone forever young, even Cody. A smell of beer and leather and anxious women. Maggie and Sandy disputatious still. A pinch-faced woman pulled her railroad watch out of her jeans; she had left her kids with babysitters and didn't want to owe too much if the evening wasn't going to pay off. "Deviant Behavior & Victimless Crime in a North Beach Modified Gay Women's Bar (Some Considerations)" could be published as a paper, separate from my book. I had hold of something here. Maggie and Sandy disputatious about Kim.

Lester was back at my end of the bar, talking to me but thinking about Maggie and Sandy. "This part-time guy was trying to off his girl by bringin' her in where there was more girls, pretty girls, and she didn't mind making it with a girl now and then, like some do, but she didn't like how he was doing it to her, treating her like a thing in his very own dream, nothing to do with her soul, man, her I-Thou *soul*. So she bent down and I thought she was whispering to him. His face was bleedin', man. She was a scratcher—with a *knife*."

"What'd you do?"

Lester was frowning. "Normally nothing like this is permitted. That was the worst thing I ever saw here, except for Sandy and Maggie right now."

Cody looked up suddenly. His eyes were off his own troubles. The pimps and the girls looked.

I looked.

Oh, my. That cracking sound was the neck of a Coke bottle

against the tiles on the floor near the Hell's Angels poster. Sandy had done it. She put this jagged weapon snugly in her palm, thumb extended to brace it. Maggie shrieked. My god, it was rage, not fear. What manner of women are these? She wasn't frightened of the jagged glass; she was mad at the advantage it gave her rival. I registered it in slow motion, with this failure of feeling. Kimmy stared through her glass of Dubonnet. She avoided taking sides. She awaited developments. The two sailors grinned and swiveled. Lester grunted. He thought he still had a moment to act on the can of Mace he kept with the bottle cloths and brushes. The two alert chemists yawned and decided to go back to their lab behind the sweatshop. This was so uncool, ungroovy; this older generation of fighting diesels was beyond their comprehension; but the world doesn't need to be comprehended if you can manage your metabolism up and down nicely through life. Through the velvet curtain, ripples; and they didn't look back.

Maggie yelled. Sandy yelled. Tarzan territory shrieks. Jane, her consciousness raised, shrieking for Cheeta. Two P.O. colleagues didn't want to slice and cut each other over Kimmy unless absolutely necessary. They opened their mouths and let the jungle out. Lester counted on this hot period to act as a cooling off period. Kim raised her glass to sip the purple sweetness, glancing at the other femmes, the ones with the spade pimps, to see if they registered how well a girl alone could be fended for if she just rides with the flow a little.

Maggie had a switchblade. It was flashing onto the table. She just put the knife on the table. Okay, there was a sheared bottle, there was a knife with a button on it. Christ, this is probably illegal, I was thinking: Lester, Lester, do something!

Good old goldminer was springing over the bar with his dog-repellent can in hand, and his boot caught Kim's glass of Dubonnet, and she made a bitter mouth as it splashed on her cork sandals. That sweet wine really stains. It was Lester's turn to yell and he yelled something that sounded like *Wait, Wait, Wait, Wait, I don't want to, Wait.*

"WAIT!" shouted Cordelia at the door. She pulled aside the heavy purple curtain which guarded the entrance, and stood there, draped imperiously: "Maggie! Sandy! Lester! Kim!"

She took it all in, didn't she?

"Oh, children," she said. "Oh, people. What is this foolishness? What is this violence—this *potential* violence?"

Lester, feeling unnecessary, retreated to his station behind the bar. He poured Kim a fresh Dubonnet, but without the slivers of ice this time. Warm Dubonnet—he must have had things on his mind. He wiped the mahogany. There was a spleeny Caucasian gray under the healthy brown of his cheeks. Sandy and Maggie stared at their boots. Maggie twisted her foot and studied Vibram soles. Cordelia's gaze swept the room. "Ladies, ladies, ladies," she said to all of us. "A little thought, please. A little care. Ladies, try to think, a little judgment!" Her eyes on mine were bold and important, though I was responsible for nothing, hardly even for myself. "Ladies! My dear friends!" The pimps were smiling. White folks sure get in trouble sometimes. The pimps' holiday girls were holding their wrists in a touching, baby primate gesture. Bushbabies with long lovely fingers. Cordelia, imperious, was working toward a just anger, but there was no hurry about it. She was insulted. On behalf of truth and sex, she was concerned. She wore a large-brimmed felt hat, a suede miniskirt, and her breasts overflowed the blouse. "Hi, Al," she said to me in a lowered voice that didn't interrupt that other flow from her lips. "Do I have to watch all of you *all* the time?" she demanded. "Even after I'm dead and gone, which isn't due to come for a long time, I still won't forget what this looked like when I entered a nice room, expecting sisterhood, and what did I find? Thisssss," she said, a hiss of chagrin, and making everyone feel sad because Cordelia had to carry the memory to the grave. "What is the struggle for existence about, if it doesn't include comfort?" she asked. "How can you old whores and dykes make the revolution of taste and manners if you can't even make yourselves be nice to each other? Maybe I ought to just go back to Elko and settle down. I'm sad, my fellow sisters."

"Don't," said Lester.

"Amen," said K.B.

She withered these interruptions with haughtiness. She took off her hat, dragging a pin through her hair, and threw it down on the carpet. She put her foot on her hat!

"Sandy, Maggie, how can you disgrace your sisters in such a manner? Don't you know? Can't you see? You are bringing us *down*," she cried in full voice. She ground her high cork heels into a mass of writhing felt which now represented sisterhood. "I've just been talking to Marietta Kirwin. You know what she might be? She might be the next mayor of San Francisco, and I didn't get anyplace with her, not yet I didn't. And you know what else she's after? She's after our ass. So do I have to remind you to keep a clean behind, goddammit? Behave! What chance is there if I can't point to the sweetness in you? How can I protect the nice bulldyke hookers if they don't know how to live with finesse? Are you listening to my questions? Is this a pigsty? the Tenderloin? a massage parlor? a bath? *There are gentlemen present!*"

It was enough. Shame does the trick with Americans and the sisters of Biletis. With dexterous hand Maggie was rewinding the rubber band on her pigtail. Sandy waited, and then shook the same hand like a good sport. Cordelia was right. A scandal is bad for the whole world, like the Viet Nam war and Watergate and lost special delivery letters. Sandy and Maggie were doing the Power to the People thumb squeeze. In the end, a free femme, Kim would have to decide for herself.

"Hi, Al," Cordelia said cheerfully, "sorry I kept you waiting. I don't think I ever met a lady didn't like me, except my mother, but now I met one. Marietta. It made me late. Trying hard, Al. That little clan of hers. Oh, man. I'll make it up by being gladder

to see you 'n if I hadn't done my chores first. Hiya, hiya, hiya,"—
and she touched the back of my hand, tickling the tracery of
veins.

She was worried after the meeting with Marietta. I could see
she was worried and wouldn't tell me very much.

"Cordelia buddy," said Lester, "I knew you were coming and
that's the better way, and anyhow—"

"You're saving your strength for the gold fields," she said
soothingly.

"Well, those Eskimos trust me, but they're not sure. And it
gets cold and buggy up there. But I'll find it, next season I'll
find it!"

She patted his arm, too. "I know you'll find it, Lester. And you
did good to wait. Anything else would be sexism."

"I'm no sexist, Cordelia."

"You're a nice boy."

He beamed like a happy child. Cordelia was here, who makes
war and also makes peace. A hat-wasting woman of real and com-
passionate power is the main treasure this side of an imagined spot
in Alaska, buried in snow and ice and ferocious swarms of mosquitos.

Lester prayed out loud: *Lord, help me with my mighty sword;
Lord, it ain't so mighty.*

Those were the words I was searching for.

4

I was sitting with Jeremy Jensen in the front of C.F.W., Cordelia's Fine Whorehouse, in a quiet residential neighborhood of Twin Peaks, which oldtimers used to call "Twin Titties" when the milk carts clattered up the cobblestones, pulled by desperate, short-lived horses. Now Cordelia performed hospitality therapy in improved clinical surroundings. "Erections probably don't cause brain damage," she said, "but what if maybe they did? Then we'd have to cure them." She catered this salon for healing the risk of brain damage. The house was endowed by a benefactor who liked to run with her in the park. Her will was strong. There was a yin-yang sign planted in flowers in the garden. Near the yin-yang sign grew giant sunflowers which had sprung from seeds spat through the lips of two star running backs of the Forty-Niners.

Jeremy and I passed the time of the evening, waiting patiently, as men might, when they are waiting for something they want and are sure of getting. It was good to come together in peace and fellowship in yin and yang. The sense that we were miners returned from the goldfields and somehow, at the same time, poets who crossed the river from Montparnasse to visit Montmartre, made us feel not twiceborn but thriceborn. And besides these sentimental memories of a past we never had, we could get our rocks off without having to be polite about Chinese food, first-run movies, and babysitting arrangements. A few doors away, a do-it-yourself husband was nagging at a nail in a garage. Tick tick tick tick—not us.

Jeremy Jensen, lank-haired lawyer, whose grandfather was reputedly an honest mayor of San Francisco—therefore assassinated by an irate, corrupt citizen—had managed the job of becoming effete in only three generations. He conserved his capital; he wore shell glasses and three-piece suits from London; when he laughed, he showed white teeth and emitted a nervous giggle. Thinness was his religion, but his blood was not quite so watery as it seemed. His great-grandfather, the murdered mayor's daddy, had controlled a thin strip of land, too narrow for most uses, which ran from St. Louis to San Francisco. It was wide enough to build a railroad on, which old Jensen had done. He employed Chinese coolie labor, and some had been beaten and shot like the buffalo and the Indians if they forgot their proper places with picks and shovels, twenty minutes for rice, on the thin strip of land. The descendants of the survivors lived in little Chinese towns in the Delta, Suisun City, Birds Landing, Rio Vista, and told awesome stories in perfect English about J. Jensen, Pres. of the Company, and his son, J. Jensen, Mayor of San Francisco.

J. Jensen IV, lank-haired lawyer, belonged to California Now, the Sierra Club, the Friends of the Earth, The Foundation for San Francisco's Architectural Heritage, the Victorian Alliance, the National Trust for Historical Preservation, the Committee for 2000 (this had to do with water, fish, and fishermen), Save-the-Bay, the Committee for Green Foothills, People for Open Space, Save the Redwoods, the Russian Hill Settlers, the Russian Hill Improvement Association, and the Russian Hill Dixieland Band, where he played the cornet. He attended meetings of his block group at the Telegraph Hill Neighborhood House. He spoke on the need to guard traditions at the Miraloma Park Improvement

Club, the Merced Manor Property Owners Association, and the Alamo Square and Cow Hollow Societies (penetrating comments, wry humor, rousing summary statement). Also he could only make it with oriental girls. This was not so specialized as it seemed, because by oriental his soul included Chinese, Japanese, Hawaiian, Vietnamese (communist and non-communist), and even certain Eurasians if they wore slit skirts, worked at Trader Vic's, and had that nice, friendly tinkle in the voice. And, without bragging too much, he admitted that he not only made it with them, he made it good. One of his Eurasian series, Nanny Norton, spoke French and Russian, attended Vassar, and her father was a member of a large firm back east. So it wasn't that he needed a degraded or declassée lady.

Of course, Nanny did have that tinkle in the voice, a slit skirt, an epicanthic fold, and she abused him with a small dildo in both French, which he understood, and her Vassar Russian, which he did not. Afterwards, it was fun to talk about prep school viciousness (Milton Academy) and Simone de Beauvoir's theories concerning the subjugation of women. That was a good summer vacation for Nanny, too, a work-study program in Cordelia's house on Twin Peaks, which Jeremy often visited after a nervous committee meeting. He served the community along with Marietta Kirwin, and would have been able to support her for mayor, if she didn't suffer her peculiar twist of conviction. But from dealing with Marietta in her world, he needed Cordelia's world. I told him I needed it because of my book on victimless crime and deviant behavior in a modern metropolis. "Oh dear," said Jeremy, "still lying to yourself."

I chose not to take up that offer of conversation. Instead, I admired the eight-foot sunflowers. I told Jeremy about where they came from—a cellophane package, two protein-starved gridiron heroes. Cody, sketching in the parlor, glanced up from his pad.

"Where's Cordelia tonight?"

"In her room. Migraine."

"Migraine?"

"Sick headache."

"Sick headache?"

He squinted at me, that dumb echo-says. "She got a call from Cindy, it always brings her down. I have a daughter, too. Mine is in Italy."

She got a call from Cindy?

"Children are not always the joy I paint when I try to paint joy. I painted my last Paternity-Maternity-Kiddies triptych in fifty-six. I don't think even Picasso got so much joy from his paternities...."

When he broke through, he talked. Cody was a melancholic. Despite the healthy pink cheeks and the flat slaty bristles of careless beard, he was not the happy king of North Beach. People thought he had it made. He didn't have it made. Mostly he didn't break through. While we fenced together, I strained for a look at Cordelia, there down the hall, and she only waved at me on the way to an empirin. That worn, maternal look of grief. The kid gave her a hard time, just as Cody said, being far away, and yet she couldn't bring her here to live. Cordelia's face looked gaunt, as if the healthy weight had sunk into her chest, and her motives were slipping away.

She appeared. "Make yourself at home. Coffee, tea, or them. Sorry, Al, I got the blahs today."

"What's wrong?"

"The blahs."

"If you can't be with the one you love, honey, love the one you're with."

Cordelia smiled. White lines of forcing at the corners of her mouth. "There are two kinds of men, Al. One can quote songs and one can't. You can't." She patted Cody on the arm. "Here's a great artist and he can't either."

Cody blushed. Even on her way to an empirin, Cordelia could bestow laurels upon men in need. It was one of her enduring gifts. She too was a person in need. She pretended to need money. She pretended to need power. She thought she needed love. She needed to find the trick of enduring in her own skin. Like others, like me since the cure of my psychopathy, she knew grief, the blackness; longing, its emptiness; desire, its sleeplessness. She swept the flood from her door. But when she stopped, was alone, paused, the grief, longing, and desire came back like an engulfing tide and she feared she would drown. She would die of the emptiness. In the middle of the night she sat upright and thought: Hold me, someone.

Sometimes there was a someone to hold her, but she wanted the same thing anyway, as if the man were not there. "Whuzzit?" he asked sleepily. "Whuzzit, Cordelia?"

"I got a kid up north—" He started to come awake. "—just a little girl of mine with my mom."

He subsided back into his gratified sleep. Herself, she lay awake sometimes, she told me, although she wouldn't tell me with whom.

She can give me her facts for my book. I need something else to penetrate Cordelia's secret.

"What do you talk about with the girls?" I asked Jeremy as we sat in the front parlor together. Cody sketched to protect his silence.

"It's easy," Jeremy said.

"What do you have to talk about?"

"Pesticides, noise pollution, solid wastes, shoreline regulations, the ozone exchange—"

"I'll bet they're more interested in zero population growth."

"As a general thing," he said, tossing his hair in that handsome, girlish, overbred gesture. "I got Nanny to join Spur. The other girls, well, they're close to the earth, but they're not exactly birdwatchers. When I took Blossom on a picnic, she wanted to bring non-returnable bottles instead of a thermos of wine. But Al, she really cares for me."

"How do you know?"

"She says she digs me. Wouldn't talk like that if she didn't mean it. She licks me all over, Al,"—spoken like a young banker accounting for a good credit risk. "I'm teaching her not to litter. Last time we had our picnic on Mount Tam, she made it so nice afterwards—no paper napkins, and even the fieldmice liked her. We saw a little garden snake, and a lot of chipmunks, and we picked some blackberries. She ate them out of my navel. Actually, she's quite witty, Al."

Jeremy was not so kinky as he seemed, exactly as he was not so straight as he seemed. If only a blonde California matron could put into words and deeds the notion which Nanny and Blossom and the other pensive, tinkling Asians and Eurasians presented for his consideration, they might also live together forevermore in the house on the Belvedere Lagoon with 2.6 children: *You're the best I ever had, you're the only I ever want.*

But Sharon or Cybil would have to mean it, and the thought never occurred to them. Whereas Blossom could mean it sincerely and easily, simply because she had a short memory; even better, she didn't have to say it. It was in the air she breathed from his shoulder. Her hand uttered the thought as it touched him like a butterfly. Her fashion of passing through the universe was a survival from older ways and times.

The parlor was filling up. When a door creaked, Jeremy stopped and looked around. Lovers are impatient, and he was a lover. Florin Schultz, builder of highrises, cleanser of neighborhoods, an alert figure in San Francisco real estate, ambled in and lit a cigarillo. "Hiya, hiya, fella," he said to both of us. "Waiting for Cordelia? She's not feeling so good. Aw, that's really rotten." He was reputed to have bankrolled C.F.W., a little hobby of his, Cordelia and her works, peace signs on the coffee tables and matted photos of the girls in prize-winning positions with men on toilets, art, comfort, and incredible plumbing facilities, all things thoughtfully arranged, and a touch of wildness in the sunflowers blowing in the breezes. It was probably true. He had the look of a proprietor: beefy, striations of fat, good health, confidence, many successful battles against citizens and zoning. "Jeremy," he said, "hey, you notice I sent in my twenty dollars to the Save Victorian Houses League?"

Florin preferred a touch of sadistic whimsy to help pass the time in the war of life. He stood firmly and thickly, legs apart. The earth was partly his. In his office he kept a photo gallery of old San Francisco wooden buildings which he had replaced with aluminum shell skyscrapers that maybe won't shatter and dump shards of glass on the folks in the next earthquake. Also he had a few goofy California offhours preoccupations, which caused him to finance Cordelia's enterprise and buy the name Florin. His real born name used to be Stan. He sent away to a little hamlet in Ceylon, where lived a guru with a P.O. box, to find out the name which Krishna wished him to bear in his dealings with American-Standard, Kaiser Aluminum, the Fiberboard Corporation, and the Crocker Bank. *Florin not Stan, Schmuck*, was the burden of the answer he received for his love donation and humble plea.

Florin believed in good conversation, serious talk between equals, a certain amount of philosophy. That was his dream for his investment in a whore house. What's this crap about a Union? he asked her, but he didn't stay for the answer. He felt it was trouble. He didn't expect a normal rate of return from Cordelia; he expected truth and style. Knowing I am an academic figure who once robbed a bank (an error of my youth: probation), he squared his shoulders to do battle in what he called social metaphysics. He was a businessman, a doer, but also a thinker. He wanted to explain his truth to someone who had a use for understanding and, perhaps, the capacity.

"Everyone is perfect," Florin said. "Hitler was perfect. Now he's perfectly dead. Nixon is perfect. Marietta Kirwin is perfect. I'm perfect. You're perfect."

"Either that's nonsense, tautology, or merely semantic," I uttered.

He blinked twice. "Listen to me. Nobody listens with genuine humility without ending up agreeing with me, not really listens. Have I got a deal for you, Al. Listen with humility, I beg you. Perfection means you are what you are. Trouble comes when your parents don't realize you're perfect. If they love you, you accept your own perfection and you can love others. If they don't, you strike back. Hitler, for example, struck back. But for what he was, he too was perfect."

"Oh, come on, let's talk about something else."

"If this bores you, I'll stop. I don't want to impose my thought on anybody. But if your questions are sincere, I seek to answer them. How do I define perfection?" he inquired (had I asked any questions?). "That which is its own nature. How can anything *not* be perfect? My son, he's in Synanon now, I didn't realize how perfect he was, I was just selfish, but they saved him from materialism. He took a lot of dope and speed. Now he's perfect, too, though I wish there was a little more love at Synanon—"

This man's name was Florin and he also builds condominiums. He used to be named Stan, until he sent away to Ceylon for his Perfect Name. The check cleared the bank before the name arrived. "I want to thank Hitler just like I want to thank my son for being perfectly responsible for their own space, being where they are. . . ."

A pale young man in a brown suit had slipped silently through the door and sat tending to concentrated cigaret business—pack, match, flare, inhale, exhale. We put him immediately into the cop file. His suit, his shoes. No matter; this is San Francisco; he's hiding nothing, so it's okay. He kept peeking at me to see how I took Florin's explication of the universe; cops adore clues. Finally he cleared his throat. "I'm waiting for Cordelia. I thought I was first."

"That's all right, sergeant," said Florin, "that's perfect. I just have to ask her to sign something and I'll be on my way. I had my bath already. A deed of trust—that's a technical thing, just take a sec."

He drew a long envelope out of his pocket and smoothed the

paper in triplicate, with carbons, as if it were a kitty with a splendid tail, and included the sergeant in our conversation. "Now you take your normal workaday whore girl out there on the street: she thinks she is *flawed*. That's her innermost self-derogatory thought. But if she believes in herself, her immortal soul, and acts in keeping with her beliefs—"

"She could be as perfect as Hitler," I said.

Sadly he shook his head. Academic smartasses are the worst. Sometimes even money can't buy them when they're on planning boards; they are illogical and unpredictable. "Don Sheean," he said, "this is Al Dooley," and smiled radiantly. The sergeant just looked morose that Florin knew his name and rank. Well, he was a taxpayer and the vice squad is public servants, too.

Jeremy had the jitters. Blossom never kept him waiting without good reason. He hated those good reasons.

Sergeant Sheean looked intently at Florin. "I'm here to help out a little. One of the girls has an, uh, emigration problem—"

I thought he said "irrigation," but it didn't matter, we lost the train of thought, because oh God, here came Karla Rowe, the distinguished architect's wife. She made too much noise as she joined the other men for no cigars, no brandy, while they awaited the ladies. Karla wanted hers. In a laudable ambition to service all citizens equally, without regard to race, creed, color, or sex, so long as they had the cash, Cordelia kept leather-covered Barbara on hand for the likes of Karla. Mrs. Rowe had a large, wide-lipped mouth which looked empty despite the usual furnishings, tongue, teeth, palate, saliva, words. It was especially full of words, and yet it brought to mind a cavern. Karla liked to get her rocks off with the men, to pay her money like a man, to betray her husband like a man. But now she wanted to discuss her theories, too, while Sergeant Sheean blushed and Jeremy fidgeted and I remembered everything as best I could. Cody was turning the pages of the pad in his lap. He meant to be absent. Florin and Karla could make beautiful philosophy together.

The architect's wife swayed back and forth, chiming in her Indian artifacts as she demonstrated the eternal flow with which some do not yet ride. "The trouble with Israel," she said, "is they're uptight. If they would just flow with the energy, you know, like Uyeshiba and Magda Proskauer teach—just ride."

"What problem would that solve?"

"Everyone is so hostile. Nixon"—he kept coming up—"was tense. People were so tense about him. You have to just..." And again this sea-breast rocking in front of the canape table as she demonstrated how a body can escape trouble. Souls and nations can do it the same way.

"That's the answer?" I asked her.

Her eyes grew large and loving. "You can just *disappear*," she said. "The trouble can go. Your body goes. You're just *there*." She had been a beautiful girl, and now she was an attractive advertisement, in her Mexican dresses and jewelry, for how the Change can bring another creative time of inter-relating in a woman's life. Hot flashes colored her face with para-psychological insights. She blew her nose in a broken swatch of Kleenex, noticed a richer prize than she expected, and gave over the results to an ashtray. It was thick and damp enough to stifle the butt smoldering there. "I feel," she said, "I feel...stiffness. Here. The back. The center. Uptightness I feel, all around me." Her eyes glittered. "Barbara gives such strong massage."

Karla had strong bones and opinions. To my taste she lacked compassion, except for herself, but compassion wasn't her line anyway. Maybe Barbara knew something else about her. Barbara (a coincidence that she is black?) cleaned up the debris with which Karla's husband clotted her. She helped her with the ambition to just disappear like a Japanese fighting master. They normally don't disappear clanking with a full carload of Native American and Inca artifacts.

When Barbara, shiny black leathers against shiny black skin, came out with a smile and said, "It's AM-FM time on your local clock radio," Karla stood up in a trance and followed her away. The rest of us were relieved by the presence of this absence. She had filled and overfilled the space. Now she was gone to have some fun.

Pale pink meat Sergeant Sheean looked at his hairy wrist, where there was no watch to study.

Jeremy nervously bucked in his seat, long legs shooting.

Both of them were waiting, and it was easy to figure: both of them awaiting Blossom Los Altos. Cody had slipped away. Like Lautrec, he did his business and departed, low-profile. Florin Schultz was pretending to read his perfect documents. I was doomed to move my project forward.

Karla, suddenly silent and shy, how demurely she followed Barbara into the hallway. How love makes us children. How I wish I could be a child.

Cordelia, show and tell. Is Luigi scaring you about Marietta and all the little Kirwins?

Blossom appeared and made a little peep. "Oos!" she said. She was not prepared for conflict. She stood in the doorway where one customarily says hello, saying Ooosss. It was Friday. Was she on a Tues-Thurs schedule with Jeremy, Mon-Wed with the sergeant? What had gone wrong? The point of jealousy's triangle jabs each one in the belly, here, below; it turns, oh it hurts. And yes, I've been a child, too. I'm not cured of that, no matter how it hurts.

Blossom peered into the room. She frowned. Despite all the Tiffany splashes of color and light, she saw through to the impenetrable darkness beyond. She was only nineteen. She was slim, with straight black hair, long straight lashes, a firm, small mouth, with breasts like newborn kittens under her blouse of shimmer fabric, with downcast eyes. She lived alone in a jungle, surrounded by beasts, snakes, and dangerous wild men. If you look at them, they only get stirred up.

Sergeant Sheean looked at Jeremy. He could give her legal immunity, treatment by reliable doctors, Kaiser medical insurance, the steadiness of Christian marriage between a cop and a whore, a pension plan. He loved her.

Jeremy's eyes unflinchingly met those of the sturdier person. He too could give her reliable doctors, specialists at French Hospital, plus culture, money, interesting associates, a weekend house on the Russian River. He loved her.

Probably they could both give her devotion, and they knew it, and their soulful gazing stated this brotherhood in the essential fact. They equally needed to be cherished by Blossom. They wanted to fit their lives into her soft hand. They needed her support services. Jeremy might give her gestalt therapy, but Sergeant Sheean could offer a less demanding world of other policemen's wives to share troubles with, fruitful participation in the Police Athletic League, good work on ghetto playgrounds; Sergeant Sheean would be happy with standard lovemaking. Jeremy might be changeable, interested in saving the redwoods and a great deal of oral sex. And yet they both cared for her, and this should bring pleasure, a rose to Blossom.

They offered themselves.

In this silent contest I wished I were elsewhere, but was glad to be present.

The grandfather's clock ticked. It was Florin's Christmas gift to Cordelia.

A phone rang far, far away.

Blossom sobbed and ran, and both of her visitors jumped to their feet. They followed; they collided at the door, and somehow Jeremy's knee caught Sergeant Sheean in the belly, *oof.* "Oh I'm sorry," he said.

"It was an accident of destiny," said Florin, "I saw the occurrence. Nobody meant anything, I'm sure, sergeant."

"I'm really sorry," Jeremy wailed, "that was entirely—"

"Our coordination is perfect in a perfect world," cried Florin, determined to make peace, which would become war if someone didn't shut him up, "but in an imperfect world—"

"—entirely *inadvertent!*" cried Jeremy, using a word of art and feeling.

Doubled up, gasping, the sergeant, who had studied karate, said, "Oh, I know, sir, never mind, oh, oh."

Thank God they had no reason to fight. Only Florin had reasons for them to fight, and he didn't know what they were. Men fight over money and power in this world, women even fight over women, but for men to fight over women takes us back down memory lane. Saving the redwoods, or raising children for St. Anthony's School in the Sunset, shows a progress in male thinking. Sergeant Sheean wouldn't break Jeremy's collarbone with a single short chop—he would not.

In the doorway stood Cordelia, monstrous and grinning in her chenille bedspread for casual after-bath wear. She looked pink and bruised and happy, as if the whole Forty-Niners team, including substitutes and coaches, had tackled her on home ground. "Sergeant!" she called.

"It's all right, I've handled it," Florin said. "Don't worry, Cordelia."

She paid no mind to her benefactor. "A bit peaked this afternoon, sergeant," she said. "Come in for a cup of tea and leave these two lovebirds to their songs, won't you, darling?"

Sergeant Sheean was breathing in the manner he had been taught for recovery from a sudden blow or smoke inhalation. Careful; count; in and out.

"Right *now?*"

Sergeant Sheean obeyed.

Jeremy looked at Blossom and then at the empty hallway with its fluttering beads. He had inadvertently fought the good fight. By mistake his gangling knee had made him her hero. Her tears dried slowly on her cheeks. Fate and Cordelia had uttered their views of the matter. Cody had already gone. I followed him noplace.

•

Mrs. Blossom Jensen, accustomed to service, organized her own canape catering business. Jeremy is active in promoting the national park on Alcatraz. Sergeant Sheean helped arrange an outing by police boat for a few friends of the Jensens, who were examining the possibilities of using the abandoned dungeons to make a statement about the human quest for freedom. Karla's husband wants to design a monument to the Unknown Lifer. Florin will make money out of the contract for tourist facilities.

Cordelia's friends in the police department informed her there was a limit to how long they could forbear, Marietta impatient, Marietta running. Marietta was a popular Supervisor. Even Jeremy said she was on the right side about the environment, the old Victorian houses, the freeways.

Cordelia's mother said Cindy was growing glands, growing difficult, and what was Cordelia going to do about it?

I thought I was interested in finding the truth and in helping not only myself.

5

LONG AGO daddy was very nice. He kept sugar cubes in his pocket, wrapped in paper, and pulled away chuckling when Cordelia reached in his pocket. And when she ate the sugar. And when she licked the grains off the scraps of paper that said Jack Frost.

Long ago, this daddy was probably very nice, and they didn't quarrel, and they played, and it was hard to remember him now. So she remembered him as in a story.

•

Babies become children become grownups. They marry, have children, grow older. And then they die.

Cordelia was different. She had never been a baby; always Cordelia. This was not true; it was how she felt. She had never been a girl. She had always been Cordelia. And she would never marry, have children, grow older, and die. She would always be Cordelia.

Probably this was an incorrect way to think, since she already had Cindy, but it helped to arrange her life as she planned it. She lived by her plan, and she thought it right to do so. Because the world seemed to tell her: Yes, you are Cordelia. These are the facts.

•

When she started doing what the guys in her high school wanted, she decided this was the future and the past wasn't worth having. She would have a lot of present and future. She would be her own mother and father, her own lover, employing others as required. As necessary. Sometimes they are necessary.

Cordelia learned to make her life lively. Since few others seemed to have this knack, she thought she might make a profession of teaching them.

Something happened between her and one of the guys on the high school basketball team which surprised her one night. She felt a swelling pleasure, a seeping warmth, a sudden explosion. It taught her modesty. She thought she would teach others, but there were things for her to learn, too. All the more interesting. The first time she did it with a man in her own bed she felt the mattress buttons through the sheet. Not nice. So one of the things she learned right away was to buy a mattress cover from Sears, and then later other nice things—oils, jellies, silks, satins. She needed stores and money. She could use information. She was ready for change.

•

Once one of the high school boys got sore when Cordelia refused to do what he wanted. He had scrunched up over her in the car like some kind of goddamn body mechanic. He had grunted and churned. He had lowered his pants and there in the light his dong was hanging out, erect, bumping her nose.

She started to laugh.

He hit her.

But she knew what to do about this. She socked him back, a little harder than he had hit her, and got out of the car. She stood talking to him from the parking lot. "Listen, sluggo. I can hitch-hike home. But it's more convenient to drive. So are you gonna drive me or do I have to do what's less convenient?"

Her strength made him contrite. He drove her home.

•

Cindy was not a New Age, Whole Earth, Aquarian child. She was raised up north by a grandmother in a post-World War II tract house. Cindy's grandmother had been in office as a loser so long she was the Incumbent Loser and thought she had a win. She looked like a boss and acted like a boss and nobody obeyed. Closest to obedience had been her husband, Cordelia's father—long dead now. He cut life. Cindy only cut classes so far. She was an old-fashioned child. She nagged. She nagged her mother. She would have nagged her father—gimme, I wanna—but she had no father, so she nagged her mother twice as much; and her mother wasn't around for the gimmes, I wannas, so her grandmother had to take it from her in regular shitloads of forlorn, greedy, adolescent yearning and anger. Well, nobody's perfect. Cordelia tried to keep in touch with her.

•

Cordelia wrote poems when she tried to remember. Her father used to smile at her from behind a pipe and touch her hair—or maybe that was a father in a movie. Her mother didn't cry when her father died. She didn't remember very much about her father. She remembered stories and movies about fathers. Jack Frost sugar cubes. She remembered a long childhood in a place where it rained a lot. She was waiting for the rain to stop. She was waiting to grow up. When she grew up, she bled and her mother explained that now she would know the pain of being a woman.

She intended to know the pleasure.

She explained that she was taking a chance by giving me the poem. I asked if I mattered that much.

> If I want love,
> What do I want?
> An end of troubles.
> A flower of joys.

If I want marriage,
What do I want?
Steady today and tomorrow.
Yesterday of treasure.

If I want children,
What do I want?
Exceptional truth
—like everyone's.

If I end my life,
What do I want?
The only thing
I know I can give.

Sometimes Cordelia remembered her childhood and felt turbulent. "Peace," she would say.

Her mother.

Her daughter.

Peace.

Her past.

No Valium; just a few laughs; that's the ticket.

She would remember she was a little girl. She remembered she would be an old woman. Her teeth, her gums, her wrinkles, her leathered skin from the good feeling of sun on skin. The guys who paid and were so shy. Who made love and drove away in Buick Skylarks.

Peace.

Peace.

Peace!

Her wars never ended.

•

Cordelia asked: "And what do *you* want from me?"

I wanted to be dim, as usual. Professional. Collected. Recovered from my crazy times. But from beneath the gray waves a cry boiled up: "Cordelia! You're all I have!"

"What do you mean?"

"I don't know."

"Stop mumbling."

"You connect me with my insanity. With you, doing this, I'm still what I was. I'm still me."

"You're mumbling."

"No, I'm speaking clearly now."

"Ah. It doesn't make any difference, clear or mumble. You're a useless one."

"Cordelia, don't laugh at me." But I think she then said she liked me better as a professor than trying to be human and I said, Okay, that's what I'll be, and I sent my real self under again. But secretly, anyway, I was connected through Cordelia to that nutty fellow I was. And even that heart thump of desire below my belly was welcome. I was feeling something and Cordelia was leading me back.

•

"How lonely people are. But you have to pretend they aren't. And then with some—the difficult cases—who aren't lonely, it's necessary to pretend they are."

Cordelia doled out her mystery. I have no right to complain if she gave it to me so cautiously. What was I giving her other than my adoration?

6

"Hey, Joe, where you going with that horse and four other dudes with those horses?"

"To the horse-house, man."

"You some cowboy?"

"No, some western plantation owner. My birthday. I'm getting married."

"You got them three reasons to do this silly thing right in the streets and all?"

"Yep."

The cop did a quick decision therapy on himself in the sight of these five easy-riding scarecrow colored gentlemen on horse-back in the park. After all, they were still on the horse trail. After all, he was a San Francisco park cop, fresh from a two-day seminar in human relations, so long as the nice niggers are not mugging or molesting—he was no tac squad crowd-control freak. Dressed as they were, in Three Musketeer velvets, they probably had some good reason for following a white man's sport. They were too tall for ordinary people. The cop was alone, could use his radio, but what the hell. Peaceful community understanding welled up in his heart, and he said:

"Then go right ahead, Joe. What kind of horse is that, Joe?"

"Honda."

"You putting me on, man, or that some Japanese horse?"

"I ain't got the time to bullshit with you no more. Got this team of good men to take care of, honor of my birthday and wedding."

And on rode the five.

Thus, upon a San Francisco winter afternoon, it happened that five not quite seven-foot-high black basketball players came riding, riding, riding out of Golden Gate Park, clippity-clop, white Hertz rental horses, right up to the door of Cordelia's Twin Peaks establishment. Horseback was a whim of traditional elegance, and the lumbering rumps left a steaming trail of horsedroppings; as in olden times, instinct alerted the picky sparrows; and memory brought back those fine days of yore, when black men were shorter. The team's center, Leroy Howard, whose concept they were carrying through—a shrimp at six foot seven but an idea man—was kind of bookish. Perhaps his tiny size provoked this clowning-around prenuptial sport he had thought up.

"Welcome, welcome!" said Cordelia.

She heard their hooves, and had made her arrangements. She installed a hitching post and a parking meter only the week before. The equine basketball team was loose, clean, and exceptionally stylish in velvet knickers (Leroy), doubloons and morning coats (Freddie, Hastings, Calvin, Elvin), white ruffled shirts, basketball shoes, and sweatsocks (everyone). They only looked seven feet tall; they varied. They were brave and fearless men, smelling freshly of horses, and they wanted to get laid pronto.

The appointment was set up in advance. Black Barbara took the day off to panhandle for her hobby, sickle cell anemia, since her attendance would smack of tokenism. Five other girls, including Rachel, a freelance masseuse and assassination conspiracy researcher, were mobilized to service the elite ball-passers of Merritt College.

"Howdy," Cordelia said at the door. "You boys sho am hot stuff."

"This is an engagement party," stated Leroy Howard. "My friend here's fiancée has a rich white daddy and he's paying."

"Very thoughtful, I'm sure," said Cordelia, sensing the order of the day. Not too much kidding around. "Do you prefer anything in the sex line that I should know about?"

"No, sir, absolutely normal," said Leroy, "except I'm the center and I lead off, then the girls face us in formation as I begin to dribble and we all do it together, moving up and down the field in normal fashion, nothing freaky, but trying to get it in the basket at the same time. Nothing special."

Cordelia made a barely audible professional sigh. How to explain basketball to the girls, who weren't fans, when it didn't even follow basketball rules? Well, she would just say they were freaky, only not so it hurt. "A room big enough for five," she murmured. "Well, I guess it's the grand ballroom for us."

"My father-in-law said he can sure count on you," said Leroy's friend here. "He's white, also."

Leroy said, "We get him married soon, have this little party soon, cause we hear Marietta Kirwin gonna close you down. That's the word on the street, man. She gonna ride to the top on your shoulders."

"She's got a fight on her milk-white hands."

"She ain't gonna let you organize. She gonna protect the good honest people and children, I guess that means us. Woman, you better watch your ass." Leroy Howard had a pouting littleboy look as he said this. He didn't like to see his womenfolk messed with.

"Marietta's got a theory she's right," Cordelia said softly. "Thank you, Leroy. She's building toward the election. She wants the nomination. I read the papers, too. I realize she's dangerous. And now?"

He rubbed his pink palms together.

"You can cooperate in another way, fellows."

Just like real folks, sometimes white people improvise. Cordelia asked the team to help her move furniture before they acquainted themselves with the girls. Thump, thump, and they got the table she used for meetings shoved into the corner. The chairs were stacked off the court. Tables and lamps were carefully lined up along the wall. Good. Cordelia surveyed a meadow of maroon carpet. Excellent. Upstairs, warm waterbeds bubbled away, but these lads deeply preferred no frills. They were originals with excellent reflexes. Some were phys ed majors, might go pro; others would get jobs in the Community. Good boys. A horse whinneyed outside. Cordelia liked catering this special affair.

One of the young men, Leroy, carried a whistle. He blew it to signal the opening of play. He kept on his white crew socks for warmth.

Such a man, Cordelia decided, might be big, black, powerful, and dull, but he would never be wicked. Socks and whistle were all he was now wearing. The rest of his clothes were heaped on an upturned chair. With Rose Ann, Sharon, Cybil, and Rachel, the freelance urban guerrilla and newspaper clipper, Cordelia completed the pentagon of girls herself.

"Now where shall we begin?" she asked.

It was like an hour with a psychiatrist, except that most psychiatrists don't signal the hour with a whistle. And with a psychiatrist it takes fifty minutes or more to effect a cure, but with what ailed this team, twenty-five minutes did fine, except for Shorty Elvin, under six foot five, who required special mothering and fathering and brothering and sistering before he could howl like a real tall player.

Cybil was saying to Shorty, "Hey, there's a nice space around you. I kind of like your karma, fella. Wow, that was a terrific energy in your thrust. Shit, keep that up, man. Oooh."

"Shut up and let me work."

"Boy, you're not very verbal, are you? Personally, I'm turned on by conversation. For example, if you say, Ooh, fuck me hard, I like that. Why don't you try it?"

He grunted.

"Well, okay. I'll pretend you're talking to me. I'll pretend you're a KSAN deejay. I'll pretend you're whispering sweet nothings to me." She was pouting and tossing slightly and had her thin arm thrown back behind her head. He could have hit her in the mouth if he wanted to, but he was a nice basketball star who released his aggression on the court. He was having trouble releasing his aggression on Cybil-girl. He wished she would be sweeter about things. He wondered what had got him into this. He wondered how he could get out of it. Since there was only one way, he ground his teeth and barreled through.

Cybil said softly, so it wouldn't disturb him, "Oooh, ooh, ooh," expressing her own dreams.

Rose Ann, Sharon, Rachel, and Cordelia felt more comfortable with their solvable problems. A nice thing about the profession is that generally you get results quickly. Rachel, thirdworld polarity therapist and small-weapons enthusiast, unlike Cybil, could occupy her mind with thought. She was into brains. She was also a childcare clinic reformer and sender of anonymous mutilation collages to environmental polluters. Some people treated Rachel as a dilettante, but an occasional whore assignment kept her in touch.

Sharon thought about her old man.

Rose Ann tended to business, and didn't know as how she thought about anything.

Cordelia felt the invisible rock behind her buttocks as she did her job for the basketball team. It wasn't all just preparing the Union, building her legal protection against the trouble Marietta intended to bring down on her. A madam should never lose sight of the working conditions down in the beds, on the rugs, against the walls and shower nozzles. Whore Administration majors might treat this as business. They had a theoretical view of the market economy. Another labor organizer might forget to practice her trade. But Cordelia knew to keep in touch with the product, and her girls respected her for it.

She tried to recall which member of the team she was engaged with, the captain or the center, she forgot, one of those positions, and his name, too, which also slipped her mind as she drifted off into rocking motions—maybe he was both the captain and the center—and instead tried to emit life-fortifying ideas. On the whole, she succeeded. She also thought about kindness, generosity, sweetness, and trust. These were somehow abstract ideas for Cordelia as she lay there, professionally pulsating, but nonetheless complete in her mind. And she sought to give good value for the team's money, but not to think too much about cash flow and her taxation problems, the criminal code, trade unionism, and her coming conferences with legal counsel.

She thought firm.

She thought friendly.

She thought squeezing, rhythmic, and warm.

She thought such thoughts as she performed a skillful, somewhat abstracted, athletic twist-and-twirl for a man whose smoothly shaven brown chin kept bumping hers. "Careful of the teeth," she said to him with a smile.

"Uh, uh, uh."

She echoed his sounds, uh, uh, uh, to make helpful emotional vibrations. She smiled her friendly big-toothed smile at the distraught young man. "You show me what to do," she said. "I haven't fucked anybody since Monday." He didn't seem to hear and her horse smile stretched itself over the large teeth. She enjoyed lonely jokes. This was only Tuesday morning. The house creaked underfoot. The sun glinted on slats. Children played outside—nursery school kids home to lunch, peanut butter and jelly sandwiches on the way. Cordelia sometimes offered munchies to the kids. A car went erk. The basketball star came.

Cordelia gave him a pedagogical pat. "That was nice," she stated.

"Hey, this is only Tuesday morning," he said.

"Just a sec, peepee and I'll come back to make conversation with you."

"Aw," he complained, but put his arms behind his head, resting on powerful long muscles, not unwilling to doze a few seconds. Sleep was disturbed by curiosity about the continued labors of his teammates. Toilet echoed in distance. Cordelia appeared.

"Voilà," she said. "See, I said I'd be back in a jiffy."

"*Voilà?*"

"It's French for back in a jiffy. Listen, you're a terrific stud, I don't know why you need me."

He grinned. "Shee-it, we thought it'd be fun, the horses and all. That Florin Schultz paid. Roy's marrying his daughter. He's a nut. I think he likes publicity."

"I've heard of him," Cordelia stated. "So it was Florin's idea, was it?"

"Life can change on you," the basketball star said. "You feel good for awhile, everybody happy, you got your scholarship, and then there are some bad plays. The coach gets yucchy. You feel like shit. They take away the scholarship. I've seen it happen. . . ."

Cordelia had noticed this about men. Afterwards they got either sleepy or philosophical, or sometimes, as with this long-legged generalist, both. At least he wasn't talking about love.

". . . only thing helps," he said, "you find a good woman. Like you. Hey, you really the boss around here, this your whole damn place? You the slumlord and everything? You control the cash? You the big man around here, woman—?"

"You can call me Cordelia," she said, "since we did it together."

"—until Miz Kirwin shut you down?"

"Want a French job for ten?"

She didn't have a normal price, but French would certainly go for more than ten. Anything to shut him up, however. Cordelia met a lot of nice men in her business, not to speak of the wonderful women, but she preferred the dawn patrol melancholics to this cheerful morning gaming. "Ten?" she said. "This? Cause I really like you?"

"Okay," he said. "Uh, uh, uh,"—starting his chant as she

started to think of the Baskin-Robbins Maplenut Fudge cone which would pass the time while she did her job.

The neighborhood children were quiet now. The brief sunlight had disappeared. It was a cold day of fog on Twin Peaks, a cold low day, with a touch of Pacific salt in the air, so the kids went inside quickly as they got home from morning day-care. They were probably in mother's kitchens eating delicious peanutbutter and jam, peanutbutter and honey, or peanutbutter plain sandwiches. And Cordelia labored on a cold low day, thinking about the nice kids, thinking her job wasn't as neat as so many seemed to think it was because she seemed to think it was, especially when it was morning on a cold low day and this was a basketball star with less love in his heart than he thought he had. And then blamed herself. It was her idea to shut him up for a mere ten dollars because he went into that male philosophizing which she hated to hear too often, early in the day, with a long stretch of living ahead before she could rest.

Cordelia, passing the time: Something which I say isn't true. "Any real love is good love" is a thought that keeps me happy, but it isn't true. Because there isn't much real love. Not much good love. I'll keep on saying it because I hate to be sad and other people don't like it, either.

With time and effort, Cordelia completed her task. She surveyed the local debris, bodies of boys and girls, whores and basketball stars. She blinked and patted the corpse nearby.

"Okay, men," said the captain. "Score your goal as expeditiously as possible."

"Hey, what's that?" asked a P.E. major.

"In and out like a flash of fire."

"That ain't me, man."

"Then don't be you. Be whitey."

"Yippy-yi-yo," said a very fast dribbler. "I win?"

The medium-tall captain, Leroy, looked up, sweating, and merely grunted. He wouldn't stop to explain what the dribbler had done wrong. Beating out your friends is not the essential task. Eeeek! went his whistle, which Cordelia had playfully wrestled from around his neck, blowing and tickling with her breath to convince him to let it go. Blowing against purling sweat makes a fellow ticklish. Eeeeek! Eeeeek! "Time's up!" she cried.

The boys went to the showers together, finishing off with a little snappy-towel game. The bathroom had good tiles and drainage. Essentially, they were good boys. The place could be wiped clean in a jiffy.

The girls wore terrycloth robes and sat around a low table, drinking Japanese tea. It simmered, a quiet bubbling. The girls didn't say much. There wasn't much to say. They were tired, but not unhappy. They were unhappy, but not too tired. They were sleepy. Rachel was thinking she would like a bowl of her mother's mushroom barley soup. Next time she visited ma, she would get some in a jar for Cordelia.

Then the four girls plus Cordelia huddled together on the front porch, waving goodbye, bye bye, bye, as the relaxed young court stars leapt into their saddles and headed back to the stables in Golden Gate Park. A dozen sparrows had found their way to the steaming attractions on the street outside Cordelia's house. Cordelia sighed and hugged Rachel. Just like fine old times.

"Why'd you give him French for ten dollars?" Rachel asked.

Cordelia shrugged. "Noblesse oblige."

7

IT's ABOUT CORDELIA, but here I still am. Benito Renfrew telephoned one day to say Marietta wanted to see me, very important, wanted to talk to me, very confidential, and I asked why, and there was a click and she got on the phone and said, "Professor Dooley? Let's cut right through all the red tape. Won't you please come for tea and we can speak very frankly, heart-to-heart, all of us?"

A frank heart-to-heart talk with Marietta was a miracle I wanted to see. I turned up a few minutes ahead of time, parking in front of her house on Jackson Street, a modern redwood submarine with CB antennas, the Cadillac submerged in the garage. From where I sat, waiting the five minutes until I wouldn't be early anymore, I regulated my surprise at the splashy paintings visible through the bars on the window. She was security-conscious. I wondered if she had anything by Cody. I had known from her transportation that she collected money (Leopold's), but I was surprised that she was also a collector of art.

Chimes. Welcome. It was Marietta herself, like Cordelia greeting a john. Politeness and thick carpet, over which an elderly, elegant Oriental rug had been laid, so that there was a heavy, luxurious wading to my place in the scheme for the afternoon. "Do sit down"; I did.

And there we all were, Marietta, Leopold, Benito, Calvina, sunk in armchairs, lounging against mantels, moving like deep-sea animals in this submarine-shaped Pacific Heights house. I love the way people do things who know what they're doing. Tea, wrapped in a pot, wrapped in a cozy sock; cookies from Just Desserts, caramel with a chocolate foundation, blueberry muffins, fresh from the oven. . . . She really meant it about tea. "Would you like a drink?" she asked. "I have some Dubonnet, don't we, darling?"

Before Leopold could answer, I said, "Tea is really more nourishing."

"Then we can talk," Marietta said. "I'm so pleased you're as forthright as I am. . . ."

"Al," I said.

"Al," she said. "Marietta."

I nodded. Cups clacked their saucers. I bit into a cookie. Too much tension in my jaw: a little shooting pain. I put both cream and sugar in my tea to prove to the world how nourishing it could be. What did they want with me?

Benito looked at Calvina, Calvina looked at Marietta, Leopold looked at his shoes, they all looked at me. Benito cleared his throat and Marietta spoke. "We have done some investigation, Al, and we have found that you are not involved in the prostitution racket."

My cup clacked.

"Or, to our knowledge," said Benito, "at the present time, other rackets."

Calvina smiled encouragement at me. "It is our information, Al, that you are hoping to write a sociological study of a madam."

"That's the information I have, too," I said.

"So therefore, since you are interested in science and we are interested in the public process of conserving ethical standards," said Marietta, "it seems that we can be of assistance to each other. I trust you are able to keep your objectivity—"

"Our information—" said Benito.

Calvina cut him off with a glance. Whatever he wanted to say about my objectivity she didn't want him to say. He didn't say it.

"There are a number of questions which I'm sure concern you as well as us," Marietta said. "Naturally, as a partisan of the woman's movement, I—*we*—believe women must take charge of their own bodies. But does this mean that suffering and misguided women have the right to abuse their own bodies with narcotics or with men? Where is the free choice for an addict or for a woman who has been influenced young, by sickness or want, to destroy her human potential? There are many issues here which I needn't argue. The essential point is simple. Prostitution is illegal. Cordelia seeks to establish the grounds of legality, and furthermore, and here lies her admitted originality, which we grant, to expand and exploit this legality through public organization of prostitutes. Now I don't doubt that she knows what . . . scratch that," she said. "Cordelia is a woman who seems to be in control of her own destiny. It gives her a certain power. Marietta Kirwin responds to that, also. But do the changing sexual mores of the time require that such a woman, a woman with such views, comes to speak for others who are not yet certain? Does society need the trouble and weakening in its fabric of instant and public gratification for hire? Why should a liberal public person like myself, Marietta Kirwin, be treated as a reactionary because I ask certain questions, not about religion or morality as such, but about whether the City and County of San Francisco needs always to lead the pack in the most dangerous moral shifts—it was LSD a few years ago, Al—"

"Snuff movies!" Benito cried. "I hear she's going to show snuff movies in her parlor!"

"Shush," said Calvina. "Professor Dooley wouldn't know about this, would you?"

"Never heard of it."

"Made in Africa or Brazil. Where the girl climaxes, excuse me, and then they cut her throat, on camera—"

Marietta severely did nothing. Benito felt her lack of action or word. He shut up.

"We here are all deeply concerned with the problem Cordelia represents for this community," Marietta said. "I intend, should I be asked to run for mayor, to make morality a prime issue. It's time those of us on the left, relatively speaking—that's only how I phrase it on this occasion—the liberal democrats, coopt, if that's your word, the issues which really trouble the people out on the Avenues, in the Districts, the honest family people of this city. We are not what people say we are—an elitist enclave. We are a city of both Toyotas and Cadillacs. I, Marietta Kirwin, happen to have a Caddy for security reasons, that's all, but I adore the new American compacts. Anyway, to get back to our subject, there might be a way we could help you and you could help us, Al, we could participate together in each other's projects. I understand your position as a scholar. You must explore the subject. Objectively. We, on the other hand, need information and insights which only an objective scholar such as yourself can supply. If your study deals with morals and politics, surely you will want to reflect our views, the community standards, and we can clarify them for you. At the same time—"

"Names, addresses, telephone numbers, backing, payoffs, who stands behind her," Calvina said.

This time Benito looked baleful silence at Calvina. These friends and advisors just rushed in and said it. Only Leopold seemed peacefully patient to let what will be be. Marietta was not merely the center of this little web. She was the pacer, too.

"I'm sure you are concerned with the implications for our politics of our public morality, Al. Not just for the general population, which suffers the mistakes of its leaders, but also for your own personal development. Isn't there a book by Kropotkin, the anarchist, which I read at Stanford, called 'Mutual Aid'?"

What was she offering me? A job in some future administration? Did I want to be city librarian, sociologist in residence, member of a commission?

"You have paid your dues, as they say, Al. You have rare qualifications, an exceptional history for an academic person—"

"I'm not really a convicted felon anymore," I said. "I was discharged with psychiatric care. It was diagnosed as, oh, adolescent turmoil, a kind of fugue, plus perhaps some temporary mescaline psychosis. I'm running okay now."

Nervous still.

"I remember the whole story. It's in our files. Don't worry about that. It's not important. You have obviously made a tremendous and exemplary effort at rehabilitation, if only you don't get mixed up in your life, slide into ways which—you're intelligent, I believe—"

"Thank you very much."

"And thoughtful, too. Perhaps you have suffered in your own family. How do you respond analytically to the fact that Cordelia has a daughter whom she rarely sees? An adolescent child who will surely hear of her mother's fame, since her mother is determined to be famous as a prostitute, as a spokesperson for the trade of prostitution? Is this heedlessness a model for her crazed, perhaps psychopathic, surely very exceptionally irresponsible role in our city's life?"

"I'm not sure I follow."

"Ah. Sometimes I let myself run away. It flows in front of large audiences, but we must learn to be more precise here, where it's one to one." Benito's eyes narrowed precisely, Calvina's lips the same. She whispered so I could barely hear: Cindy, a reminder. Leopold was looking over their wall furnishings, paintings, a tapestry, a window, a glass door which led to the dining room, which perhaps led to a door which led down to the bulletproof Cadillac. Leopold was a gray, sad, thoughtful person. It occurred to me that Cordelia might help to relieve the burden of his constant melancholy preoccupation. Marietta was lecturing me a little: "I only hope you see what a degradation she represents for womankind. You are a man, but not without feeling. Beneath that facade of, oh, cleverness, there is pure manipulation. She is profiting. We should march forward together, men and women, but Cordelia wants to keep the same old ways, only to her elitist advantage. It's not just money. She is putting a modern and contemporary gloss on what is simply a malady. I'm not just talking about disease. I'm talking about the destruction of the dignity of women and Woman, Al, and men are crippled by this, too. Is there some way we could go over your research and get a glimpse of how it can be treated in a rational and institutional manner? I don't want to hurt anybody. I don't even want to hurt her."

She waited for my answer. And while she waited, she spoke almost gently, as if she were comforting herself as she reassured me. "I recognize Cordelia has a dream she wants to impose. She has a powerful dream and she is selling it. Well, Marietta too has a dream. I am very determined, Al. My dream is different from hers. I am thinking of what will help this community. And with the cooperation of your good will and that of others, I *will*— impose is not my style—I will make my dream real. All I ask is your understanding and help, for the good of everyone. I think that's not too much to ask of a man with your credentials and background."

I am influenced by what people say. Since she said it, perhaps Marietta didn't want to hurt Cordelia. Perhaps she only wanted to use her by killing her. Perhaps she loved her like a sister.

And why does authority still frighten me? I could feel the bullet-proof car in its lair beneath me as I sat with her teacup in my hand, and the four pairs of eyes drilling into my intentions. Marietta had some power. She would get more. What attracted me to Cordelia also pulled me to Marietta, but with dread. Her dainty fists were clenched. Her simple gold band (Leopold) must have hurt her fingers. I could imagine the fists pressing on the inside of Cordelia's knees to push them apart, or on her nose to break it. She was clenched and clotted with desire. She was dangerous.

"Oh, well," I said, doing my debonair act, "when I have something worth showing..." Ah, that was cowardice; it wasn't even cunning; it was transparent. "What I mean, I have notes. I'm writing something. So far, I'm not sure which way it'll go, and also—" A rising slide of hysteria as I tried to say what I meant. "And, and, and, Mrs. Kirwin, I have to be honest with you. That's the only way. I like Cordelia very much."

In that Cadillac-bearing redwood submarine there was silence, silence from Marietta, silence from Benito, Calvina Muir, and mournful old Leopold Kirwin. And within the silence my heart thumped away.

"You don't judge her at all?" Marietta asked gently.

"Yes. I do."

And that was all I could say. She waited for more. It didn't come.

"Then the lines are drawn between us," Marietta said. "You're part of the problem."

I tried to make a joke from Berkeley. "You mean I'm not part of the solution?"

"Enough of you,"—a cold voice from the periphery. "You're nothing for us. When it comes time for me to write about this in my paper—"

"Shush, Calvina!" said Marietta. "*So far* was all he said, my dear. So far he is very involved with Cordelia, and I understand that, loyal, she is his source—so far. He doesn't want to cut off his options, do you, Al? It's not necessary to think in terms of enemies. Hopefully, at least, as I always say when I deal with these matters on the various commissions, we must not prevent our apparent adversaries from returning to the path of right when they see it is where their permanent interests lie.... You will return, won't you, Al?"

She stood up to help with my standing up. I followed orders.

"Calvina, you're too goddamn hard on people openly," Benito said.

"I'm not a politician. I'm a person and journalist. I write what I think."

"Oh, dear, all our dirty linen," said Marietta, smiling at me. "You see, we have our differences here. Even Leopold and I don't always see eye-to-eye. I have a democratically-run organization, if you can call it that—*stop it, Benito.*"

Calvina smiled thinly at him. "So far I've only been hard on you behind your back, Benny. You'd like to start something else?"

Intense negative charge passing between the two. I felt invisible hairs being drawn out of my chest. Benito had piggy little pink, scared, and yet uncaring eyes. So he was Calvina's lover. So what.

Leopold came awake with the wisdom of his age. "This is all confidential, of course, Professor. You came to our home as our guest. We trust you."

I was backing out. Courtly old Leopold was showing me the door. Marietta still had something to explain. "What I was asking, what I need, is help, information, but nothing to violate your academic prerogatives. I have no shame for representing the cause of women, of all women in the Movement except perhaps a few ...Romantics? Extreme radicals?...If you have any questions..."

I backed, backed.

"Don't limit your options, Al. These days many learn that limiting one's options is a mistake. This could be your case, too."

She had no power at the University, did she? She had little to offer me, even if she became mayor. Did she? Was she threatening me? Only a little. Yes, she was. What the devil was she hanging over me? Unpaid parking tickets?

Nevertheless, because she was a woman of power, she had access to my warehoused anxiety.

Ah. I knew the harm she was threatening. Harm to Cordelia was on her several minds.

At the door, on a sunny dry day in Pacific Heights, Marietta was smiling. The others had disappeared in our wake and they were silent. They would wait till I was gone to have their conference. "Give our discussion some thought," said Marietta. "I consider it exploratory in nature. If you have some ideas to present, or if you merely want to discuss, I hope you will feel free to contact me either at my office or here at home. You have the numbers. And I hope and trust, Al, you will have some thoughts." With a gentle smile she began to shut the door. "Of course, I expect you to mention this meeting to your friend. I'm not so foolish as to ask you not to. Whenever possible I prefer to be direct and honest—that, plus decency and integrity, is what Marietta offers the people of this community."

Door shut, Marietta gone. Everything is supposed to be of value if you are fully alive. But of what use is this grief to Cordelia?

8

"WELCOME TO THE HOUSE OF HO," said Black Barbara, gleaming in her leather, vinyls, studs, bellychains, sweat, and youthful high spirits.

"Is what?" Avigdor looked wary. She sounded like a case of adventurist nationalism, and he had not taken this leave from other duties in Moscow to fall into a den of Maoists.

Barbara translated into the East Oakland. "De Ho House," she said, snapping her fingers. "De *ho* house."

Vig beamed. He understood. "Where all them bourgeois cats roll down the pebbles," he said.

It was Barbara's turn to suffer across a language gap.

"Rocks off," I explained, fresh off the Bay Bridge from Berkeley to share in Cordelia's new obligation. She was proceeding with due caution about the Union. She needed to build a firm place in the community. She needed to straighten up the legal situation, the public relations situation. She didn't want to become a sitting duck for Marietta Kirwin. The Soviet spy could give her a bit of international class.

Everybody was smiling; hands across the steppe; cultural exchange. Once more communication, the miracle of humankind and dolphins, was gracing the universe. Here in the house on Twin Peaks, where civilized care was taken, thanks to Cordelia, our guiding spirit, we were all delicate brutes together.

Avigdor Malchik ("Call me Vig, buddy") was everyone's favorite Soviet journalist, trial balloon inflater, KGB informer, stool pigeon, and bon vivant. His English and French were adequate for international travel, and when he dug into his Levi bell-bottom jeans—worth over a hundred dollars on the Moscow black market—he pulled out an infrared photograph of an English Foreign Service defector doing something dirty and colonial with a Tartar boy, a letter of thanks from G. Gordon Magruder "for many interesting encounters at a certain point in time," and an American Express credit card. He flashed the card when he really needed to make an impression.

"Wow!" said Cordelia. "I used to use Bank Americard till they stole it. They canceled me. Hey, could I borrow that snapshot? We'll blow it up for a poster over the fireplace."

"Very soon," said Vig, replacing his goodies in his wallet, his wallet in his pocket. He didn't seem to know that jeans are supposed to be too tight for a wallet.

Vig's pockets, filled with goodies, were unique in the world of current events. He also carried from Moscow a collection of ikons to exhibit for private sale to the sophisticated elite who surrounded Spiro T. Agnew in the lonely mansions of Frank Sinatra. He was in charge of a group of underground paintings ("Soviet Union is so modern, actually uptodate, you see, in art"); he had a letter from a Birmingham newspaper, accrediting him as its correspondent in Moscow, although the newspaper had been amalgamated into Popular Mechanics during the last credit crunch ("I write for press about doings, goings, and comings"); he had a wife whom he mistreated in traditional Russian family style, with an occasional punch, slap, or icy stare.

Now Cordelia had found him traveling unescorted in the higher reaches of the lower depths of San Francisco. His thyroid was turned up to maximum. The light gleamed off his octagonal gold glasses. Frankly, he possessed a notebook. "I am on interesting assignment from Moscow paper," he stated by telephone. "I am studying to groove. I was given your name by reliable person. I will be here, dear friend, at the downtown Hilton for precisely two weeks or a month. To meet?"

To meet. Charm is everywhere irresistible.

Cordelia asked me to join them for lunch. I had to send my reader to give my freshman students a pop quiz. Cordelia sought to broaden my conception of the hard life of a hooker-in-chief. It's not just fun and games; a woman is called to improvise on deep needs. "Man," she said, "this crazy Russian dear friend of mine. He wants to meet a Mafioso and I get him an Italian ravioli maker with an interest in a bar. So he talks to him about executions, man. Then he wants to play card games with some Chinese and he loses a bunch of dollars like you never saw. Then he wants to get loved by a Jewish whore on silk sheets—a travel guide he's writing—and I'd like a little company as I show him around. I don't want to sit at a matinee of 'Deep Throat' with this Soviet john, not all alone. He's *weird*."

"Cordelia, he's adventurous. Do you realize what he is going to write about San Francisco?"

"It's my city, right or wrong. I put my faith in hospitality."

"He's going to say the place is crawling with Jewish whores."

"It is not! I had to make seven phone calls."

"Does he know that?"

"Listen, I gave them satin sheets and he didn't even know the difference."

"He's a creep, Cordelia."

"Says he's America's best friend—loves Big Macs."

"I'm sure he's complicated."

"This best friend is more than *complicated*, man. Kinks? Oh, kinks. Rachel's signing herself back to Napa. Says she'd rather be nuts than deal with it anymore. Definite kinks, man."

Homespun America unrolled before a glamorous, pudgy little Soviet journalist, his rosy cheeks, his curly hair, his gold-rimmed glasses, his giggle, his charm. A happy stoolpigeon, a man of the world, the joys of San Francisco were his—Enrico's for lunch, parties in Pacific Heights, an interview about Soviet Men's Lib in the Chronicle (Calvina Muir). He seemed to avoid contact with his consulate. "Bureaucrats," he said, his eyes rolling mischievously. "Nice people, fine people, hardworking people. But for fun? Nyet."

As an intellectual, a scholar, cultured, a professor at the University of California, I would understand that Nyet means Who needs them? His eyes emitted microwaves of complicity.

I was a spoilsport, stamping out little flamelets of amity. I told Jeremy Jensen how he helped entrap artists into illegal currency exchanges. "But he knows Barbara Walters, and I'll do anything for CBS. They're so good on the environment," Jeremy answered. I told Arthur Pesche how he planted lying tales about Solzhenitsyn in the foreign press. "Well, I suppose he's got his faults like everyone. But cultural exchange is a must. Are you opposed to détente?" I told Karla Rowe he beat his wife. "He try something like that on me, I'll have his ass. But he's been a perfect little gentleman. Him and John just talked about Finnish design. Spacesavers and indirect lighting. I think Rachel tuckered him out."

So I too might as well enjoy his company. Cordelia invited me to a party in Vig's honor at her House of Ho on a cool slope of Twin Peaks. Valet parking available; no credit cards; earthquake reinforcement. I recognized the car parker in his white carparker's coat. He was a cousin of the bride in Hillsborough, an MBA from Stanford, and he was on probation for dealing cocaine. "Hey, you drive a stick shift VW?" he asked me. "Far out. Me too." He took my keys. "I'll have to put it in the bus zone, but Cordelia has a little dealie with the cop. Say, you introduce me to the Commie later? I always wanted to know one of those."

I swore I would, and left him with my non-tenured assistant prof's blue VW.

Hi there, Jeremy Jensen IV with your lovely Eurasian playtoy.

Hi there, visiting filmmakers from L.A.

Hi there, black Barbara with your whips and spurs. "Where your kid?" "White one or black one? I got two kids, man. White one home in Monterey with the orphanage folks. Black one here with me."

Hi there, Cody the painter, morose as usual, hoping for a viable answer to the problem of heterosexuality.

Hi there in the long mirror, Al Dooley, the snotty but intense sociologist.

Hi there, Rose Ann, Sharon, and Cybil, three ladies all in a row. Hi there, Lester Jones, bartender and goldminer—still bisexual, man? "I will be, pal, till you find a way I can be tri." "Tri harder." "Haha. I used to be witty, puns, shit like that, but at my age you want to get serious, man, so I'm going up to Alaska next week find my gold, really get it together this time."

Hi there, friendly hos and pimps and a couple of exhibitionist tennis pros and Cordelia's friends in the Union, and probably one or two informants for the police and Marietta.

"Vig," I asked, "you doing okay?"

"I always knew Frisco would be like this," he said. "Listen, our Moscow is beautiful, wonderful old churches, restored with such care into godless museums, good friends, Moscow nights singing of our sweet Soviet nightingales...." He leaned forward confidentially. "Not so groovy, nevertheless, as your dear Frisco, my friend."

"Groovy is about ten years old," I said.

He whipped out his notebook. "What would you say this year? For philological research—flash, fly, cool, tell me?"

I meditated. Ommm. "Neato."

He wrote it down. He nodded vigorously. "Detect derivation from 'neat,' meaning 'in a pleasingly orderly condition.' Very good. Frisco, neato. In Russian, many vowel end-rhymes, which is also why our Russian language is so rich. And this is Rachel," he said, producing a girl who had been tearing up her cigaret butt like an ecological veteran, rolling the paper into a pinhead and distributing the tobacco on a large ashtray as if it were a parade ground.

"We've met."

"Rachel, my dear friend, my pigeon, my dove, she is Mosaic person, we have many happy Jewish in my homeland, also."

"You have a happy family, too," Rachel said, chewing on her cuticle.

"In Soviet Union we have family problems resolve. Of course, love still exists."

"For export?" Rachel asked.

"Haha, joke, neato," said Vig. "However, to explain. True, my wife is beautiful redhaired former Komsomol person, all heart desire. However, is cold. I beat her, is still cold. I shout. Is Cold! I say: you are Party, I of course am artist-journalist, non-Party, but marriage is beautiful, my darling. She say: Very busy today. Personality more strong than party thoughts . . ." His voice trailed off with a familiar discovery which made him sad once more, as if he had just turned his wife over in the night and discovered the coldness, like a toad on his pillow, for the first time. "Is sad. Is morbid. I work hard, therefore. I travel far and widely. I have American Express card, perhaps only Soviet citizen to do so." He brightened, and there was an odd effect: the beveled gold rims and the glasses glittered, while the eyes remained a clouded, glaucomic blue.

Rachel took a cautious position on his story. "I know some Russian girls in Berkeley," she stated. "They're okay. They live in a women's commune."

Rachel was slender and might have been pretty, with her lank dark hair and large eyes and long narrow head, but there were sunken pouches about the eyes and a tranquilized slackness about the shoulders which put me in a mind of great age despite her twenty-seven years. She was merely going through the motions of sexy. It didn't fit. In the same manner, she was into revolution. She smoked too much and slept too little and had cold sores on the lower lip and didn't speak with her pig parents. Her sign was Capricorn and she tried to be an aboveground underground urban guerrilla. To be lovable was not her first priority.

Vig pinched her bottom. She wrinkled her nose at him and lit another Winston. Then she pinched his bottom, using skinny fingers and an expression of bared teeth. Nicotine stains.

I wish I could love more people. I wish I could love Rachel. I wish I didn't need mystery and magic.

Cordelia, towering in her platform boots, came up behind them and put her arms about Vig. She was wearing a many-colored patched leather skirt, an old Brooks Brothers man's shirt (Florin's?), and her gums were showing in that smile which held nothing back. "Hey, Mister Spy—you know people say you're a cop?—what do you think of our wonderful country now?"

"Spy, spy, all Russian is spy. Nonsense."

"Well, aren't you?"

He glinted happily. "Well, little bit maybe."

We all felt warm and good.

"But more I wish to describe my wonderful trip. Is marvelous fun corrupt neato bourgeois state."

"And we got rock and roll, too," said Cordelia.

"Ahah!" Vig's finger went up. The glint of light on his gold ring reflected the glint from his glasses. "Question!" he said. "Your rock and roll, which we hear even now, is especially for brothel entertainment?"

KSAN, the FM rock station, was playing its Grateful Dead festival, a weekly nostalgia event. Cordelia had turned it up and there were speakers all over the house. Vig turned his ears this way and that to attend to the speakers, which were also placed this way and that.

"Is for everyone," said Cordelia.

"Is piped from central rock-and-roll depot?" Vig asked. "In Moscow, all heat, all steam, such facilities, come from central depot. Is most efficient for continental winters."

"Our winters are less cold," Cordelia said.

"Is factor of warm coastal currents," Vig informed us. "Is obvious reason. Russian explorers discover California long ago, note climate with concern. Would now hope to observe whips and scourges for flagellator bourgeois."

As Cordelia led him away to the Outrage Room, Rachel said, "Shit, I've had it with that creep. I'd call that wife of his in Moscow—he's into *dominance*—but who needs that kind of phone bill?"

"Didn't Cordelia ask you to play nice?"

"Sure. And I'm not sensitive. I do my job. I even moved in. But anti-Semitic fucking is really out of my line, Al. You probably can't understand that."

"I can," I said, "but maybe not fully. I personally went to a parochial school in Santa Barbara, St. Ignatius', and the Protestant kids used to yell at us sometimes. Crossback. It's not quite the same thing."

"You're cute," said Rachel. "Wanna do something mean and dirty after I get my bath?"

"I'll bet that's just conversation, Rachel."

"I want to wipe that Russian off my soul, man. I don't care if he's a famous journalist and spy, he's a jerkoff creep which gives me lumbago."

Rachel was sad. Sorrow, I've noticed, only makes people behave with generosity of spirit after they reach a certain age. She was too young. She resented her general sadness; she resented any particular incentive for sadness along the way. Vig would have been better off being careful.

I took my leave. I required a clear head for my Introductory class, Criminology 101, a nine o'clock for beginning majors which I hope to eliminate when my research is appreciated among the scholars of deviance and non-victim crime. Cordelia's party had turned into a salon in which I recognized some of her standby whores, patrons, voyeurs, masochists, folks with limited inner resources. Jeremy, Piero, Florin—oh oh, someone brought Sam Bowers, he's usually too busy in the recording studio, since most of the bands like to work at night—FitzHugh Gross, Danny Doomsday and a bunch of other lawyers talking law and cocaine,

Fred Ellis. Not Cody. Cody was going through a bad time. Personally, I was developing some inner resources, thanks to hard struggle in the frontier science of Sociology. Long-legged Jeremy and Blossom looked loving and engaged, leaning on each other. Lately Cordelia had been too busy organizing the Union to have a large get-together. She did this for Vig.

Vig should have left town. Vig-buddy stayed around. Gradually he moved out of the Hilton Hotel and into Cordelia's place, first his body, then his plastic suitcases and his funny Russian typewriter that made the girls, particularly the Mexican and Oriental ones, giggle. They are an easy giggle. His soul seemed to move in. His inner resources moved in.

One afternoon I brought a questionnaire for Cordelia to fill out, the Wesleyan Timed Frays-Bronstein Psychopathy Quiz. A little history, a few snappy depth judgments. "Aw, Al. I know what Psychopathy means."

"Everyone's got it to a degree," I said. "Look, it's very contemporary, like sinus drip used to be. I was one of the champs of my year, 1967. I made all the papers with that Crocker bank deal. I'll sit with you, Cordelia."

"If you weren't so nice, and if I weren't a publicity hound. The union above all."

"In my opinion you're going to come out beautiful."

She blushed. "I'd like that. Nevertheless—"

"Anything that socializes the Life is good for you, Cordelia. You can't get trade union acceptance until you get legal acceptance, and this depends on the fabric of society accepting your option. . . ."

Fog, fog.

"The world's oldest profession has to be recognized as a craft and art. That's not a demotion. Smile, Cordelia."

"Okay. But you should pay me for filling out all these forms. Can't you get a grant? You see my point. You're a different kind of john. You use my body and mind, and those things take time, which is money, for profit."

"Cordelia, this is a new person. You never used to talk to me like this. Since you went with Avigdor you're more distant. You're cold. I take that back. You're, I don't know how to say it, you . . ."

I thought it best to let her reason herself back to her true character, which was generous in addition to power-crazy. Should I have thanked her for being her, for sharing her resentment of me, for maximizing her space? I thought it best to wait. Of course, I would profit from my work, but I had no money for informants. This is the recessional Seventies. The university is pinched. Nobody wants to pay for pure research. People are stagnating in the streets. The food stamp program is in danger. In 1967, sure, there would have been lab money for Cordelia. But when people were starving, paying more than sixty cents a gallon for gas . . .

Since I knew what I wanted—her soul—I was patient.

"Explain," she said demurely.

"That's easy." I was in business not for gain, but for science, employment, tenure, and promotion. Any salary increment was a mere detail. We live in a ladder economy, and academic life is no different from the multinational corporation. It even has its links with other university circles, Cambridge Mass with Cambridge England—did she know that Hebrew University communicates with the University of Cairo?

The eyes of Cordelia were cast down. She was a maiden who wanted to hear whatever I needed to say. She was praying for me, for success in my ventures. She was a true sister and willing to play her part. But she seemed to get lost in the fog. Perhaps she only lost interest. She was worried about legal complications, public outcry, if she led a hookers' strike. Calvina Muir, in her column in the Chronicle, was writing about the degradation of womenkind in massage parlors, topless bars, and open prostitution. She didn't name Cordelia's enterprise. She was merely informing the public. She was prodding the morality sleeping in the Avenues and Districts. When it suited Marietta's campaign for mayor, Calvina would come to the point. Marietta's crew was dangerous.

Luigi Mendoza was supposed to advise Cordelia. She was trying to make an appointment. I was taking her time. Vig was taking her strength.

In the kitchen, naked beneath a wraparound apron that said KISS ME on the front, nothing but strings tied behind, a tucked rose-bud of buttocks rotating slowly as he ignored the machine and rinsed the dishes—yes, Vig. In the afternoon. Helping. I implied he was wearing nothing but an apron, but he also wore a knit tennis shirt with a crocodile above the nipple. A man in a little tennis shirt and a skimpy wraparound apron and nothing else tends to look naked to the bourgeois eye.

"Vig, what're you up to?"

"Like you in scholarly, my friend, I am cover this story for international progressive press. I am live this experience like true combat correspondent." There were red welts along the exposed dorsal regions. His buttocks were nicely inflamed. The Red Army journalist goes right to the front with the troops.

"Is this something your media will want to know about?"

His face fell. "In general, yes."

"Vig. How long are you staying?"

He turned back to the dishes. The spray nozzle with which he showered a cookie tin sizzled under his answer. The stream pried loose a charred raisin. He was mumbling. He said: "Forever, I dream."

"What you say, Vig?"

He turned back to me and shouted: "I cannot think of departure! Never! Never!"

And soaped carefully, piling too much detergent in the sink, a heaving and billowing cloud rising about them both, dishes and Vig, to envelop us in mists of amazement. The mist of amazement is a metaphor, not a description of objective social reality. It describes what I felt.

"This stinkiest kitchen," said Vig, "need honest Soviet worker for stinkiest machinery. Is nice blades of dispose-everything, but is gather to it stinkiest sheet."

His control of English faltered under domestic chores. Like many housewives, he looked dispirited. A male woman's work is never done. As he turned back, flouncing and flopping, the gray tapering uncircumcised diddle under the flap of apron put me in mind (probably incorrectly) of a roll of kopeks somehow melted together and secured with elastic. He was not just any housewife.

Black Barbara brought him a tray of coffee cups, plates with sliced crusts of toast, sticky breakfast things, and clattered them into the sink. "Where'd Cordelia go?" I asked.

She pointed to the back. Unh. Too early in the day for Barbara to speak. I understood.

While her Soviet KGB maid did the dishes, Cordelia curled up in the sunlight near the peace sign in her garden, snuggled into a giant straw and bamboo Huey P. Newton Cost-Plus chair, reading the Journal of Deviance I had lent her and looking disdainfully into the mug which used to contain her yogurt protein shake and was now empty. The sun glinted through healthy dark hair. Teeth, gums, tongue welcomed me. It was early afternoon, shortly after reveille, and she was at peace with most of her organs. "I thought you'd like to do your survey around. I'll have a look at some of these papers you brought me."

"Cordelia, what is that man doing here?"

"Vig?"

"You know what he is?"

"Yeah," she drawled, "the one who forgot to bring my refill of espresso," which she pronounced express: "Viggy! Vig!" a lady-like screech of rage. "The servant problem. These Mexicans and Guatemalans they send you from the agencies. A Russian wetback is more my style, man."

"Okay, can't you imagine what he'll write when he gets back?"

"Al," she said, "I don't think he's leaving."

He appeared silently by her side. He was bearing a tray and a silver coffee pitcher with initials on it which I didn't recognize. He filled her cup. He had brought a cup for me. He poured. He handed it over. "Sugar, sir?" he asked me.

"Vig," she said, correcting him. "One lump or two."

"One-lump-or two," he said.

He retreated in his little shirt and wraparound KISS ME apron. Cordelia shook her head at the miracle of it all. A simple girl from the frontier west with a KGB man for a personal maid. Well, she had been told by her math teacher in ninth grade that she was something special. What they used to say, she informed me, when they were after your cherry.

In this house of the cheerful, one brooding spoilsport, in a pink chenille bathrobe, selected by a couturier of ugliness, came barefoot to stand nearby and utter, "Morning," through clenched, not-yet brushed teeth. Barefoot feet are coltish and sexy. Rachel's were blots upon the sun-dappled grass.

"Hiya there," said Cordelia. "Sleeping late is a sign of depression, dear."

"Tired."

"So is that, honey."

Rachel would not pursue this line of logic. She couldn't best Cordelia in a discussion of cheer, its cause and cure. Her brow was knotted. She resented. Fury slept; fury waked. She said: "I think I'll use the phone." Cordelia shrugged. The long, silky rubber cord had been snaked out through the garden. Rachel dialed the number painted with a felt pen on her wrist. Suddenly she smiled at us. With one uneven tooth, it was a mischievous little girl's smile. When they answered at the other end, she gulped, nodded, and said, "This is the Jewish Observer, a weekly newspaper. We have information that Mr. Avigdor Malchik, a Soviet national, has plans to defect and is currently residing in a brothel at . . ."

Cordelia did not interrupt. Her gaze met Rachel's. Something there enjoyed drama. She was smiling. Her gums showed. She was also angry.

Rachel hung up and stared morosely at her friend and recent landlord. Cordelia said: "Now honey, why you want to make trouble like that? What call you got to go stooling around, even if it's not the Vice Squad?"

The lady expected more than discussion—a snatched phone, a tantrum, or at the least, a cutting perception. "You didn't fuck Vig. I did," said Rachel. "You don't know what he's really like."

"True, too true," said Cordelia, whose life kept her busy with other matters.

"I did," said Rachel, "and I heard about Russia when I was in the Movement. They'll be here in a jiffy, I bet."

Cordelia turned from an irritating factor to continue her conversation with me as if Rachel were not present, as if the person washing dishes inside had nothing to fear. "Al, that quiz, your project. What you're trying to figure out. I've never been in love," she said. "Perhaps I'll never be. But I like to be reminded love exists, and when I make it, when I arrange a case of love, when I plan how it can work for one or two or sometimes three— some funny people around here—I remind myself others want to be tender, not just meat, they want to be close, want to cuddle and trust someone—love," she said. "You know about that?"

"Not yet. I'm listening."

"I dream of a change. A man explodes in me, he splinters and becomes good—I dream he could do it."

"How good?" I asked.

"Better'n all of us!" She stood up and the dry straw of the chair creaked. She swayed back and forth, hawing, tears of laughter flowing in the sunny afternoon. "So much he would love me! That's how good! a good man! that he would discover he loved me!"

Motes of pollen swam in the afternoon light. Rachel stood with her head tilted—what was this strange music out of Cordelia? Cordelia sighed and waved her hand as if it were a fan. She sat back into her wicker throne beside the goldfish pool in which a Peace sign, white pebbles set in fine sand, glistened underwater in the sunlight. Minnows followed instantaneous one-way changes of direction. A bruised rose from last night floated on the water. Later Vig might retrieve it.

On this quiet residential street of Twin Peaks we heard the murmur of well-serviced Buicks. "They're here," Cordelia said.

The doorbell was ringing. Cordelia hated having difficulties, although she liked living among them. She enjoyed solutions, but regretted that problems seem to be paired with them. No time to meditate now. Stately she arose and stately she floated to answer, taking note in passing that Vig had finished the breakfast and lunch dishes and was mopping the kitchen floor. She opened. "Yes?" she asked, blocking the doorway with her body.

"Is Meester Malchik?"

"We're not normally at home to visitors until eight o'clock," said Cordelia, "unless you telephone in advance. Please call. The girls don't work afternoons except by appointment."

"Meester Malchik!"

The voices echoed through the house. Vig was running, apron flaring over his flopping behind, bare buttocks working, and in the garden he was trying to scale the high wooden fence that led to the neighbor's house; if he reached this garden, there would be another fence, and another, and another, till the end of the block, unless he ran through a house; but the thick-thighed consuls and valets bumping through Cordelia's establishment already had him by the legs. He was jerked backwards off the fence. One hand was bleeding. Splinters in the palm. An older man with an especially gloomy face under heavy hornrimmed spectacles took out a syringe that looked as if it serviced Siberian horses. It did its job —a pale, mucousy liquid. Vig made a little cry in Russian. He lay briefly unfolded on the grass, his legs pale and twitching. The pink eyes were naked and childish without their gold-rimmed spectacles. There was the reproachful look in them of a child unjustly punished, overwhelmed by punishment, having forgotten his sin. Since he said nothing, it was up to me to feel his pain, and I didn't. The plump little body in its apron strained like a lost and sleepy child before it suddenly collapsed in a spasm. Narcotized meat. His glasses were broken.

These fellows were speedy and knowledgeable. It looked like a large mail sack into which they slid the sleeping body.

"Do you mind if I call the police?" I asked Cordelia.

"They don't like that," she said.

"This is serious."

"Only for him. But if the police have to notice—"

"You want to do nothing?"

"Looks like they're going to airmail him back to his wife," she said. "That's doing something."

"He's not my best friend or anything."

Cordelia sighed. "Okay. Call Emergency if you think it's right." She handed me the phone. She shrugged because I didn't take it.

"Why don't we try to stop them, Cordelia?"

"No."

"Why don't we call the police?"

"No."

"Why?"

"We already have some investigators."

I hadn't noticed the black Cadillac parked at the curb. Marietta, with her little clan—Benito Renfrew and Calvina Muir, but not Leopold this time—had entered through the front door. "It was open!" Marietta called cheerfully. "I hope you don't mind!"

They were walking through in neighborly fashion to the sun-drenched back lounging space. Somehow, despite their smiles, it looked like a raid. I held the cord of the telephone like a lifeline.

"I gather you just had some excitement here," Marietta said. "I hope it's not the wrong time to chat, Cordelia. I don't want you to think Marietta Kirwin has anything to do with what just happened."

"You know about it already?"

"Oh, dear, I talked with the State Department, but nobody expected the timing to be so coincidental, did we? Calvina wants to do a story about Mr. Malchik."

"You had nothing to do with it," Cordelia said.

"I'm glad you're sure of that," Marietta said.

Cordelia looked at Calvina and wondered if all women leaders have a Rachel in their midst. Though she was sure Rachel was upstairs crying and biting her nails and packing to leave; Calvina would have taken a Valium and a pee and been done with it.

"Cordelia," said Marietta, "perhaps this is a bad time, and perhaps I shouldn't call you by your first name, either—"

"All my friends do, Marietta."

"—since it's obvious I don't approve of your plans and I don't believe you should continue. What I hope is to convince you to cease this activity, and make a public announcement to that effect —Marietta Kirwin will stand by your side as a woman—and perhaps we could work the whole problem out by bringing it to a halt with—"

"Just get out," said Cordelia. "Get that cow Benito out of my sight. Get that hangnail Calvina out of here. Go. Go. Go."

"You're nervous about the recent incident—"

"You're trespassing. *Go!*"

Benito and Calvina voted for departure. They had sensitive feelings about being wanted. They tugged at Marietta. They persuaded her. Cordelia would pay for this; it was what the hooded glance of Calvina said. They practiced the dignity of retreat. "Shut the door behind you," Cordelia called to them.

We were alone. "This is dangerous," I said.

Cordelia smiled in the lengthening shadow of the November afternoon, the strip of sunlight swiftly narrowing; she fluttered her invisible fan. "I believe I know Avigdor better than you do," she said. "He wanted to go home. It's time now. Let that woman use me if she can. Would you do something, Al?"

"What?"

"Please. Be a good boy. Pick up Avigdor's glasses."

9

BENITO HAD CODY ON THE PHONE. Half-sentence tributes to his work, his distinction as one of the painters who . . . his importance to San Francisco . . . And would Cody consent to an interview with Calvina Muir? She was interested in discussing why a person like him would frequent Cordelia, what honest gratification there could be for an artist and man of the world in the company of such women, how he felt about Cordelia's house as a . . .

"Thank you, no," said Cody.

"Perhaps, if you have a show coming up, we could time it to give you some publicity."

Cody hung up on him. He had been waiting at Cordelia's for many months now. She would let him sit there, waiting, till he decided what to do about the second half of his life. Okay: she made him feel welcome. He would not betray her to Marietta and that band of users. How welcome he felt was entirely up to him, but he hadn't yet figured out how to be reborn. "Cordelia, I don't know the meaning of life," he complained one evening as he sat sketching in his pad on her brocaded couch which itched him all the way through his corduroy jeans.

"Then I can't tell you, Buffalo Bill," she said. "You're so much smarter than I am, you're kind of pretty, I like that neat dropout facial hair you grew, you're a terrific artist, really great, you've lived a long time and you still don't know. I only know simple things. When I come, men come, too. When I don't come, they manage pretty good anyway. When we both come, it's like ten billion brain cells all switch into trees, plants, flowers, we sprout into a tree, a plant, a flower, not a computer. That's what I know."

"Ommmmm."

"Something like that. Like an electric train. It's usually louder, especially the Forty-Niners, if it's three organs in one room, those blocking backs we had here last night. Wow. Bruises all over."

"Sorry I missed that," Cody said.

"You missed the basketball team, too. I guess you don't like spectator sports. You missed the trouble with Vig. Bad scene. You missed Marietta Kirwin. She wants to keep me going till she gets her election, and then she wants to kill me."

"I know about her."

"It could get a person upset if she let it, so I just ride with the flow."

"You're a Buddhist, Cordelia?"

"Only when someone asks me to. I lie there and some man presses his explanation on me, he explains everything, he makes it real. I'm rosy. It's nice. I'm happy. Is that a Buddhist? We've done it together. He's sleepy. I do him a little more. We sleep. We don't bother dreaming. We wake up happy, but too early. He goes home to his wife and I never see him again."

"You see me again," Cody said.

"You. You're so sad, though! And were you listening? None of what I said applies to you and me, Cody."

"Your words are almost inspiring."

Cordelia laughed, bent, kissed his forehead, touched his fly. "Someone's got to inspire you pretty soon. You're in worse trouble than Vig was."

"You think I'm queer?"

"It's a thought."

"I guess I better try."

She shook her head. "Find out," she said, "just trying's no good."

"Find out today," Cody said, but so far he was just sitting. He was lonely. He wanted her to tell him something, but he wasn't sure what. He didn't want to talk to the other girls, or to Piero or Jeremy or me, he didn't want to move, he just wanted Cordelia to make magic happen, as she did for everyone else. He just wanted to change everything in his life. Was that too much to ask?

"And now excuse me," Cordelia said, "I got some problems that need my attention."

"*You* got problems," Cody said.

"Well, yes. Though it's hard to imagine other people's problems when your own are kind of heavy, weighing on you like they do. But first there was Avigdor—the FBI. How would I know what kind of agent he was, double, triple, or just a plain omelet, if they don't know? Why don't they tend to their business and let me tend to mine? But no, they want help. And then there's getting the Union off the ground as a tax-exempt foundation in this uptight world of today. Luigi's worried about Marietta Kirwin. I don't worry about politicians, but he says I'm wrong. Okay, never mind. Hooking is my business, not yours. And there's something else running around the house. You take a myacin or a sulfa drug for fungus or whatever and you know what you get? A depopulated colon. They kill the bacteria you need. Itch. And you can't go to Yami or Dannon yoghurt for it, because they're pasteurized, everything's dead as dead shit, only shit should be alive, so you got to ask the health food store for the acidophilus, and even so—oh, problems, Cody, the problems of a madam who takes a sincere interest in the health of her ladies."

"You're excused," he said. "I'll just sit here."

Cordelia kissed her own large, dry, hardworking hand and then touched his forehead with it. "Whatever you're doing, Buffalo Bill," she said, "you're a lovely man and I'll always be happy to look at you. So just say Ommmm till you feel a whole lot better."

However, that wasn't his mantra.

I, I am too young to be the grandfather of an illegitimate Italian kid was the orphan melody that kept running through Cody's head. The ommmm didn't help. The din in his ears drove sleep away, nagging at his melancholy forty-year-old soul. Like an adolescent on a Saturday morning, he had prancing and prowling on his mind, irrelevant to what he hoped to be.

Cody was connected with pretty good galleries on La Cienega and Madison Avenue, living in his warehouse studio, a former ravioli factory on the Kearny steps in North Beach, and his only daughter had written from Florence:

> So this jewelry-maker and I are very much in love. He's into this heavy bambino trip. Too late to do anything about it Dad which is why I cop out to you. Not that he's Catholic or anything, but that's how he was raised. He's a super artisan type of Italian, you'd really love him Dad. If you want to make plans, I suggest you start buying presents for June. Warm nighties, thermal sleepers, and money are always practical.

The idea darting into Cody's mind was that now he was free to find a boy stud and finally have his homosexual experience. He had always been a little curious, ever since he first admired those virile wash paintings by Larry Rivers, hip George Washingtons crossing the Delaware with Frank O'Hara, patriotic old-timey all-male stuff like that, and he felt left out of the normal abnormal San Francisco scene, and he couldn't even recall any adolescent experiments. But becoming an illegitimate grandfather sealed off the last dripping vestiges of duty. He could try, and knowing his famous luck, succeed. A pouting young chap on Turk Street, say, where some hung out, would be a good one. As a painter, he could even tell the vice squad cops he was only looking for a model. And in fact, why not do a Michaelangelo trip, "David in the Tenderloin"?

...a slender boy nude, twanging the harp, shadowed by twilight and strings; pinks, verticals, with a mess of junked stereo equipment piled in the corner and a newspaper with the headline PEACE IS AT HAND—well, it should be both topical and eternal, plus a little whimsical, if it were to live up to Cody's high standards for himself. He would bring the boy back to his studio, which had been drifting into disorder. Last month's socks, an FM radio doing nonstop commute music (he kept it on for company even when he was away), canvases turned to the walls and a stretcher hung with towels. His cork reminder board was pinned with souvenirs whose point he had forgotten and jokes that no longer made him laugh. This meant something, too. He used to be a good cleaner of his own nest. He used to be tidy. He used to make lists.

Today no sketches, no plans. He set the will, his mighty meat computer, in motion. To the moment be true. This was no job for Cordelia, and her advice was all he took: *Find out for yourself.*

As an inexperienced queer, Cody decided to begin his new life in the afternoon. It was less frightening to a timid historical hetero; he disliked darkly shaded things; his reputation was for California Colorism (primary reds and yellows, Matisse, Deibenkorn). He had heard of this potted-fern sodomy hangout called Brucie's Down Under (FFA) on Sixth Street, between Market and Mission. Among motorcycles, leathers, a few chains, and a stuffed bear mounted with its leg in a beartrap, mouth agape expressing agony, Cody might discover a nice selection of thrills. He wore his hard-topped climbing boots.

The light was good. Northern exposure. Greenish amber, antique bottleglass, and a few sturdy chaps in Levi Strauss tuxedos, tall in the saddle at the long old-fashioned bar. The bartender kept a stiff upper lip, saying something in Urdu which turned out to be "Whaddleyahave, Chuckie."

"Bourbon and water."

"A little ice?" Evidently he didn't take kindly to strangers, but Cody decided to stick with it. A man needs courage to be a first-time pederastical grandfather. I got this from him in three interviews.

"Two lumps, Chuckie," said Cody. It was as far as he cared to go. He figured any jokes about chuck and rump steak would send the bartender flying over the bar with his chains and blackjack and his stiff upper lip bared in an uncompassionate howl of revenge. He figured the motorcycle with the zebra skins and nail studs parked back near the men's room, which was strung with colored lights, for it is always Christmas Eve on Sixth Street, belonged to the master of the house. It must mean something. Cody carried his drink away from the bar and sat at a hatch-cover table, naval motif, coated with epoxy for protection, near the yellowish soft drifting light of South-of-Market. Fog. To dream awhile.

He didn't have long to wait. "Hiya, Cowboy," said a young cowboy in blue Levi suit and white vinyl boots.

Everyone had a name for everybody. A specific probing anonymity, with no deep commitment, was that the ticket?

Cody explored the matter with due deliberation, with palpitations. "Okay," he said, as if to answer the question which the cowboy hadn't asked—*May I sit down?*—for the cowboy was already sitting.

"Thanks, Gramps," said the cowboy, and replied to the next unasked question by calling to the bar like a true tough Winchester rider of the range: "Hey, man. A brandy Alexander." His signal echoed through the still, mote-filled air of the afternoon saloon. "Plus a twist, Butchie." He turned back to Cody. "Hey, Gramps, tell me your pleasure. Mine's spanking."

Cody found it hard to summon the words for his pleasure. It seemed so theoretical at the moment. He wondered if he was going too far, too fast, too soon. Lust stood absent from his heart and body, and the cowboy's shiny white boots killed the very possibility of kinkiness, although Cody could appreciate the random chumminess of the bar—amber light, bottleglass, that giant grizzly with its powerful head and paw symbolizing nature, red in tooth and claw, but distressed, and one dollar drinks until five P.M.

Butchie stood there belly-up against epoxy. Unasked, he had brought another bourbon, water, and lumps with the brandy Alexander. He was asking, however, for two more dollars. Cody supplied.

A matronly truck driver watched them in the mirror behind the bar. He was lonely, too.

"Me," said the cowboy, meditating over the retreating form of Butchie, meditating with a lip curling over the dark, fruit-en-riched Alexander part of his drink, stirring with his tongue to bring it all together: "Me, Grampa, I enjoy whatever a fellow has in mind if he's a fellow I kind of take to. But also I have my own ideas."

Cody felt absent of ideas.

The cowboy sighed. He had to do all the work, it seemed. "You're the hunkiest guy around. Of course it's kind of early in the afternoon, but I like hunky guys."

Cody never knew how to take compliments gracefully. Some-times they made him change the subject to his own disadvantage. "You work in the Post Office?" he asked. The cowboy flinched. Cody's reasoning: If this kid's a whore, he ain't too good at it, so he must make his living sorting mail and stealing welfare checks. The reasoning seemed far-fetched.

"Yup, how you know?" Cowboy asked. "You see me on the night shift or something, Gramps?"

Cody felt his feet saying *Move.* He got up, leaving the bourbon for the cats to lick. He ought to say goodbye, so he murmured, with no expectation of sharing a deep interpersonal communica-tion: "I'm missing a money order is all."

He was at the door. Cowboy was smiling. At least he had lassoed a rogue brandy Alexander out on the open range. But pro forma, he tried to make amends: "Whatever I did wrong,

Gramps, I can make it right if you tell me your heart's little cunty desire."

•

Cody was striding up Sixth toward Market. A Woolworth's, a Tad's Steak House, a Macy's all stood nearby, and he had this yearning for real life after a half hour of strange. He stood like a statue of salt in the street near Golden West Savings & Loan. Were those really potted ferns in the amber windows of Brucie's Down Under (FFA)? Did FFA stand for Future Farmers of America? How did they ever find a stuffed, trapped grizzly? Never to know, Cody, he thought; never to know.

I'm the Dvořak of queerdom, Cody decided: may sound popular and convincing and romantic and from the folk, but I'm not really great.

The failed queer hiked up the slope of Kearny which leads toward Chinatown, North Beach, and Telegraph Hill, turf which he understood. Many the times he had taken his daughter, when she was a merest teenie, a virgin like her father, to exciting dinners at Edsel Fong's (teach her to use chopsticks); many the times he had partied at Vesuvio's, and some of his friends were painters of the homosexual persuasion, but personally, he had always preferred girl students from the Art Institute; sometimes a collector invited him for drinks or even dinner, high on Telegraph Hill Boulevard (views, fireplaces, affluent lovers of well-worked things; martinis, grass). Good years he had enjoyed as a young man, as a young middleaged man, giving freely of his wastrel soul, very fortunate that he could splash paint in accord with his temperament; and the tense art-lovers of the world had spent two decades of cold war, followed by southeast Asian imprisonment, buying into this footloose freedom of his. It was terra cognita. Home at last.

"God loveth a cheerful giver." (II Cor. 9:7) "So let us give hilariously." (Luke 6:38)

But where and how to give to whom *now*? asked Cody, his daughter pregnant, himself graying at the chin, his work irrelevant. It wasn't as if there were space in his North Beach pad for a mother with an Italianate child that he imagined in Carrière brown silhouette, very small, faceless, wandering under ruined arches, in an early de Chirico. "Nostalgia for the Infinite?" No, a failure of specific focus. The kid would smell for years (oh, but a delicious little baby splayed nose), and then, like Dora herself, make noise for more years before she became beautiful, with bones in the nose. Etruscan statues are purer. Anyway, it was all a mere sketch in the head. Dora wouldn't consider living with him, any more than she did at age fifteen.

(Dora, recently cute, slender, wispy, distracted, a crafts groupie as her mother had been a fine arts groupie; Dora, now bulged at the middle by some Ponte Vecchio silversmith . . .)

Because of his thirst for experience, and also to take nourishment, Cody decided to stop for coffee and a bagel at one of his familiar stations, Dalton's Kosher Deli on Sansome Street, where he might wash away the taste of Cowboy, Butchie, and Brucie's Down Under (FFA); and then to proceed. He was still young in spirit. He could still do something he had never done before. He could still make it with some loitering Prince Valiant in layered leathers, the sort who would eye Dora in a drive-in, over lolita-burgers, with an order of softie ice cream on the side, but would really prefer her father.

But first, something to wet his dry and anxious mouth. No point in pursuing this enterprise with parched lips. Must be young and juicy for queer fun; a chap needs to relax his organs first.

DALTON'S KOSHER DELI, If Closed, Knock Hard. Dalton, the delicatesser, bought old refrigerators and frozen food display cases. He bought heaps with bad transmissions and parked them in the alley while he tried to sell them to his coffee-drinkers. He collected used paperbacks and paintings and LP's and leftover beatniks here in the ruins of the 1970's. In the great tradition of

Bohemia, he was an honest, upright, enthusiastic decade behind. He kept his hifi, along with representatives of his other collections, in a basement reached through a trap door at the rear of the delicatessen. "An orgy, for me," Dalton explained, "is not like Cordelia, it's good people having good talk. Come to my orgy, Cody."

Cody had never made it to one of Dalton's good-talk orgies. Cordelia was magic and Dalton was nice and Cody liked better to be sad around magic than around nice. But now, uninvited, he found music and laughter vibrating up from Dalton's trap door. He lifted the trap and peeked below.

"Cody! You come down here right away! This is my friend Cody the famous painter, he drops in a lot for a good sandwich" —Dalton was greeting the customer lumbering backwards down the ladder. There was a smiling wisp also waiting below, with long, thin blond hair, a pinched face, shoulder blades, squint, knees knobby, looking about, oh, a very young seventeen.

"Hi," said the wisp. "I sold him my clothes is why I'm here."

"Liar, liar, terrible liar," said Dalton. "I loaned her fifty dollars on the clothes, a bunch of rags, for security, that's all. I don't know this person from the street."

"I can make fifty dollars an hour if it's a weekend," said the person from the street. "I can make a hundred. These are carefully-selected Goodwill funky next-to-new *shmates*, which express my personality more than I. Magnin."

"Who's charging you interest?" Dalton asked. "Who's taking advantage? My fifty is all I want, and you receive my blessing, plus a sandwich. So *I* give the interest."

The wisp, the weekend next-to-new person, perched like a doll in Dalton's lap to be introduced. It happened to be a girl with a crooked smile and Cody was tensing and squinting just like this person and industriously resisting the magic she emitted because it tended to pervert his ideals. He had set out to prove he wasn't too old to be bisexual, like everybody, like the kids. His heart fell. It wasn't fair.

"Are you making goddamn fun of my infirmity?" she asked. She hopped out of the lap of Dalton. "It happens to be my only one. I was practically *born* nearsighted, and I read Sight Without Glasses, by Doctor Bates, and looked at the healing sun a lot, and sat Zazen in the lotus position from age six on, thinking sightly thoughts, but I still need glasses. Hate them. And contacts itch. Once those soft contacts get perfected, no backeteria problems, I'm going to get some of those, man, but till then, me and my tricks are stuck with a squint, no matter how I work it, twisting this way and that, a habit, man—"

It came pouring out.

"I think a squint is cute," Cody said.

She looked angry. The woman thing.

"I mean tough, crazy, vibes, dig."

She looked relieved. She *wanted* to like him, anyway.

Dalton was pouring wine into jelly glasses. It was part of his hideaway dream. Although the restaurant upstairs had shelves lined with filmy, ill-washed glasses, down here he roughed it. Jelly glasses. Jelly glasses once topped with wax sealing when his mother made jam (fourteen years dead now; sadness).

There were others in the room, corner hustlers, Dalton's vision of the beauty and truth people, even Robert Y, the cokesniffing portrait sketcher from the lobby of the Jack Tar Hotel. Cody usually saw Robert at openings, pushing girl students against the wall ("I'm a working artist, like Hans Holbein—you heard of Holbein? you been to the Jack Tar?"). Brain shriveled like a wrinkled almond, Robert retained perfect recall of features through his chalky fingers, and could dirty paper with a likeness in the time it took to say: "Two bags, twenty dollars, meet you in the men's room." He called himself "Y" for White, in honor of Malcolm X, who was Black.

And Bette, pronounced Bet, the laughing girl, hoo hoo hoo, har har har, who made a fellow feel funny until he realized her laugh swept around the horizon every thirty seconds, like the beacon at Alcatraz. She used to make her living as a one-woman studio audience, but was automated onto welfare by electronic laugh tracks. "Hi, Bets," said Cody.

"Hoo hoo hoo, har har har," said Bette. "Heard the one about the Turkish bath?"

Cody would be sure to fall up to her room in the Dante Hotel real soon. She had this new all-electric decorator hot plate.

A few post office mail sorters in their ponytails and jean suits, getting it together. A Napa veteran who still wanted to kill Jack or Bobby Kennedy, and he walked around in a state of funk because someone had gotten there ahead of him. A middleaged beatnik with bad shaving after his recent beard, pale bluish face, the look of an insurance salesman from a defunct Oklahoma company with all its officers now resident in Costa Rica. A few neighborhood hippies-in-training with Quaalude grooviness in their sleepy eyes. They heard it was sexy, but they just wanted to nod. Well, maybe nodding is sexy. A bunch of Cordelia rejects, eighty-sixed by that lady. And now, Cody, the grandfather-to-be.

And that talkative slim wisp who had long since departed Dalton's lap—Dalton smiling; Dalton pleased to swell a progress; Dalton happy his dear friend and coffee-drinker Cody had come uninvited at last to an afternoon rap session; Dalton righteously glad to get one of Cordelia's people, especially after she had said No Dalton since that unfortunate incident with the crybaby hooker (Dalton only doing his thing);—and the wisp was saying, "Carol-Ann, I'll tell you the truth, is what I was born, but everybody calls me Lou-Andreas, I knew Bobby Dylan when I was thirteen, Bleecker Street, and then did anthropology at Chicago, got my degree when I was eighteen, man, and I only been hooking a couple months, since my old man dumped me in Acapulco, just took off, leaving me on the beach and this enormous tab at the hotel, so I picked up my little hook, man, and . . ."

"You're hyperventilating," Cody said.

She smiled. "Testing, aren't you? I'm better on anthropology.

Mead, Fanon, the Metraux family, Rhoda and her mate, extreme studies in native religion—"

"It means you're breathing in short, quick starts, too much, too shallow—"

"Christ," she said. "I didn't say I *didn't* know what it means. It's nature's way of saying hypoglycemia."

"I don't think so," said Cody.

"*I don't think so*," she said, mimicking with a little white-mouth pout.

"My little thing," he said, "is testing," and she slipped into his arms to dance, the way they used to, all ninety-eight skinny pounds of her fitting nicely into his suede and corduroy crevices, as she again whispered wispily, echo-saying, meaning something different:

"Your little thing."

There must have been an existential, that was the word, loneliness in Cody. He wanted to tell this smart little speedfreak hooker everything—about his daughter, about her idiot junior-year-in-Italy pregnancy, about his desire to dump it all by becoming a closet queen, about his effort this afternoon followed by abject failure—

"You're wrong," she said.

"What?"

"I'm not a speedfreak."

"Did I say you were?"

"No, but everybody thinks it, and you were *thinking*, Cody."

"You said my name, I like that."

They were dancing gently together, just moving.

"So I'm not. I sniff a little coke is all, and of course that's another reason I had to pick up my bitty hook and hurry on up to Frisco for a weekend of convention excitement at the Fairmont Hotel. I work tonight, I guess. In the meantime, Dalton over there has lent me a hundred so I can buy my flight insurance."

"Apologies," Cody solemnly stated, "if I looked like you're a speedfreak. It's my age. I have this history from the past which comes out in my eyes and makes people think I'm squinting."

"You're teasing. I like that. Um. Well, to tell the truth, I used to do a few diet pills, just to keep my slim and desirable shape, and it also made me feel good, so I did a little meth, mostly by mouth, but I thought of it only as diet pills. Am I right, Cody? You're only speeding if you get to love the needle. And one thing I hate, it's a needle freak, they'll shoot anything, even Seven-Up. Feh."

"Principles," said Cody.

"It's mostly just esthetics," she said. There was an odd strain of fresh sour in her fragrance, like kosher dill; he found this picklish scent—youthful anxiety, and not washing very much—very touching. He rounded her shoulder in his palm as they danced to Janis Joplin's "Me and Bobbie McGee." Her shoulder was small, smooth, knobby. She said: "I just wouldn't feel right being a needle freak, even if it did help keep me slim and girlish, how you and a few million others like me."

"Thank you."

They were moving and sliding and she was talking and there was the pitter-patter of tiny names dropping: Rod Stewart, Something Dead Morrison (yecch! memories), Ramblin' Jack Somebody, pals of Bobby and Joanie and this really neat dude with a folk store on MacDougal till he got run out by the ripoffs and the cops and the times we live in—

He asked: "You have to tell me everything all at once?"

"I want you to get caught up," she said, "because I really like you a lot and we've only got till probably the after-dinner hour."

"I appreciate that."

They both had hopes, dreams, and a time limitation. Though she was half his age, she too was pursued by demons.

She whispered into his ear—and this took some doing, Lou-Andreas up on tippy-tip-toe, Carol-Ann's chapsticked sweet little East Village mouth pressed against the lobe, sending gently: "I left my hook in Room 1207 at the Fairmont. This is just funsies, Cody, cause I'm an artist in my own way and we're kindred spirits."

"I changed my name, too," Cody said. "It used to be Buffalo Bill."

"Well, we whores all change our names. What's Cordelia's real name? You think she was *born* Cordelia Celtic? You think she's some kind of alliteration lady? Think again, buster. With me, it's more like a pen name. I'm not your standard hooker, man. A standard hooker don't like male persons, they're all yecchy dykes. You ever notice how they clean up with practically Lysol, man, for a fuck? Like it's dirty? Not me with you. I really like you as a person, I'll bet I could even come for real with you—*kum*, man—and this for one reason only: *You listen.*"

Once again he was understanding, kindly, strong, masculine, a failure for his ideals.

She was looking up anxiously, picklishly. "Ride with the flow, man," she said.

"Hey, where you fellas going?" Dalton asked as the wisp and the great white hunter scrambled up the ladder to the trapdoor, pushing, going away.

"Later, man," said the wisp.

"Thanks a lot," said Cody.

"So glad you could make it! What do I do with your wardrobe, kid?"

"Keep it," she called, "till tomorrow, when I'll come back with money and my ticket and we'll have a jelly glass of coffee upstairs, okay, Dalton?"

They were closing the trapdoor on the party, Robert, Dalton, Bets, others. Something of the spirit departed. They would try to have fun, but it wasn't the same without Lou-Andreas, although her suitcases stayed behind. Har har har, hoo hoo hoo. As the trap went thunk over Bette's commentary on anomie and life's confusions, Cody heard Dalton's last correction of people who never, never, never quite got it right: "Upstairs we always use the mugs for coffee."

•

They were walking across Washington and up Montgomery, past the double rows of closed banks and stock brokerage firms, the silent debris of American abstraction drifting in the gutters, memos, papers, carbons, IBM printouts, the forever New Year's Eve of a Saturday in the financial district. The West Coast reminded the wisp of New York and Chicago—business the same all over. Maybe Vegas would be a little more *real*. She explained why she'd never join Cordelia's. Very nice if you like company, but some people are loners. The wisp was a loner. No house for her. No need for Cordelia to interview her takeout callers. You have to be smart to make it on the hotel patrol, but smart was one of her strong points—that, along with slim. "Am I talking too much?"

"I like it."

"Okay, let's just groove."

They were walking in silence, little soft hand in big hard hand, thinking their private thoughts. After the stuffiness of twenty minutes under Dalton's trapdoor, they had hit a moment of time and history, a long, slow Saturday afternoon in San Francisco. Well, it wasn't like other places. There was a warm winter fog, with yellow at its edges like the amber bottleglass of Brucie's Down Under (FFA); there was sun striving at the edges. It may not have been real, but here they were, real people, anyway.

Cody sighed. "You think we're going to bed now?"

"It's strickly up to you, sir."

"You think we're going to your room at the Fairmont? or my pad up the hill about ten minutes?"

"I just came along for the ride, sir."

Maybe they were just going for a stroll. Cody was interested, he was aroused, he was obscurely stirred in both animal and spiritual realms; but he had gone this way before, he knew it too well, and his whole idea for the day had been different. He might feel sad afterwards. How often girls had let him down, including his daughter. He had decided to try something else.

"If you're . . ." she said.

Why, she was blushing. Her face had turned pink. She was embarrassed. The skinny body was contracted within itself; random juts of collarbone and shoulder blades stuck out. The picklish scent came up a notch. She continued, pressing on bravely, a stubborn child who knew Dylan, knew anthropology, had taken up the hook because of circumstances beyond her control.

"—if you're worried about hot, itchy, painful urination," she said, "I can reassure you on that score. I had a test. Also a shot of penicillin to make sure. No clap, sir," she said.

"Call me Cody," he said.

"No clap, Cody," she said.

For some reason he was pleased. "Let's go sit at Enrico's, drink some Irish coffee on the terrace, I like you," he said.

She smiled.

"I want to talk. May I tell you everything?"

She was still smiling, small buds of teeth, the pure smile at the end of the movie, the smile of innocence: "You can tell me everything. Tell me your lies. I'll understand."

They sat on the deserted terrace under crackling heaters. The fog was working well today. Briefly Cody had a glimpse of the whole truth, that Picasso lived to be ninety, but still died before his work was done, and therefore freedom must be practiced with rigorous discipline. Not succeeding with every strong idea doesn't matter. It's more important to goof with a wisp. It was important to share his sadness with her. What sort of bigot thinks unreal is any less real than real? Sadness is there for the sharing.

"Hi there, Massa Cody," said Peter, the waiter, a symphony in suede, "what can I do you for this dewy day? You need a menu, or just something tasty?" He loved to tease. Cody felt at home with Enrico's waiters. Peter's main boyfriend had run off to

Alaska to work a gold claim. He had some theory about the Eskimos would help him get rich. Peter's satellite boyfriend had declared he was into real leather people, not just suede people, and how about a trial separation? In mourning for all his recent losses, Peter was especially nice. "And who is this person with you now? Not one of the ex Missus Codys, I presume?"

"Friend of yours?" she asked.

"We're having a talk, Peter," Cody said. "Irish coffees."

Peter bore no resentment. There was little bitchiness in Peter. There may have been a little in the wisp as she watched his retreating outfit of layered suede, purple on tan, mauve on brown. She may only have admired the stitching. She turned back to Cody with a face sweetly cleared of impatience. She was all there, all to be with him, wherever he chose, till long after sundown— at least until the evening hour of nostalgia, longing, relevance, and identity crisis hit the visiting conventioners at the Fairmont Hotel.

"A splash," said Peter, filling their cups to the top from a silver beaker.

Now the man and the girl huddle together, reviewing the late afternoon marchpast on the sidewalks of Broadway in San Francisco. They seek to know how it is, each with each. Picasso is dead and Bob Dylan married. Some people go with Cordelia and some people go alone. The wisp and Cody hadn't really known which way to turn. It is not yet the end for these two on the open terrace at Enrico's. They dream.

Shapes in the middle distance. Clouds. A city of white towers and pink ruins. The Transamerica pyramid, but they don't see it. It's too huge to see. Far away, in the dream of love, shepherds brood on a hillside; sheep; a crooked staff. Since they are invisible, Cody and his wisp see them and smile. Near foreground, the girl touches the man's hand and his cheeks are pale beneath black and gray trimmed stubble. Perhaps this innocent young creature, fishing into men with her brand new hook, has never before caught a man desperate to cross over into modern unisex, bisexuality—oh, words—and here he was, twice her age, pouring out his soul.

His daughter.

His life.

His work.

"Bobby was like that," she said, "confused, and he was only twenty-four when I met him. And his greatness lay ahead. The electric stuff, Blond on Blond, the Band, all that greatness. Who'd have thought he might ever truck on through a spacy romance with Joanie, plus five kids by another old lady, and go back to calling himself, that's what I heard, Zimmerman?"

"I don't understand," he said.

She covered part of his hand with hers. "*So don't think you'e old*," she said.

He covered all of her soft warm flimsy hand with his big hot hairy muscled painter's middleaged used-up hand. "What if you're sitting here on a Saturday afternoon, just waiting for the romance and glamor of the Frisco evening to rush over you, along with the money you plan to make, and you're talking with a queer?"

She paused a, for her, long second. "You?"

"I think so."

"Um," she said. "They usually make my nose wrinkle. My nose isn't wrinkling today. Are you sure?"

"Well, if I have the idea."

"I understand. Um, well, swell. I don't mind."

"You lack your customary enthusiasm which I have gotten used to in the course of our relationship," he said.

"Absorbing the material of the course," she said. "Are you *certain*, Cody?"

"Well, it's a supposition. No, not certain. But the idea lies there in my head."

"Um, well." She sang: I know a lady lives on a hill, she won't boogie but her brother will. . . . "Um, could you try to think of me as a little boy?"

"No, you strike me as a girl."

"And it turns you off?"

"No, that's the problem. On."

"And you don't like that?"

"Well, I like to live by my principles. And the other was my idea for the day."

"Ah, I see," she said. He was relieved. He hated cross-examination, even by his two wives, his daughter, his critics, Cordelia, himself at midnight as the ceiling stared back into his sleepless eyes. But although he accepted her statement, he wasn't sure she really saw.

"Do you think Cordelia might like me if I promised to give up my diet pills?"

"I'm not scouting for Cordelia."

"Do you think so?"

"Don't know."

She was thinking about what he had said. She needed a talkative space to provide the silence for thinking.

"What to do," she continued, "with this predicament you find yourself in, being carnally attracted to me in violation of all your principles, here as the late afternoon sun pierces the fog an hour or two before I have to begin work for the evening, Cody, to earn back my clothes from Dalton plus a few hundred other dollars?"

"I don't know," he said, but she had snapped her finger at Peter, and the check had arrived, and he was paying, and they were moving toward the steep Kearny steps which led to his place. Another drifting decision made for him. His spirit felt sad, glad, and had.

He glanced back around the corner past Mike's Pool Hall, Sandwiches. Peter was out on the sidewalk, casting languishing looks at him, and maybe Cody felt an answering tug—just a jerk or two, a little nudge—but now it was too late. He wasn't queer, unfortunately, just a little strange—committed to a girl once again.

And tomorrow not to forget Macy's, the post office, and to his daughter in Florence: layette, thermal underwear, money.

10

TENNIS HEAT CLOSES IN after the game is over. During play I run and compete under the sun, swooping after the ball, connecting, slicing, scoring; my shoes are hot and the breezes circulate around my neck. The weather is modified. I dream of defiance. I'm not merely earthbound. I'm both hunter and hawk.

Then that sudden descent. The body's combustion surges upon itself, making stuffy. I am no bird. Okay, ride with it.

Fred Ellis and I loafed after three sets of singles on a sunny afternoon at the Buena Vista courts. What a day. The kids wouldn't come out for awhile. The welfare and foodstamp tennis stars were busy elsewhere; this was a first of the month, federal and state forms to fill out. A few joggers circled the track. We were both seventeen again, playing hooky.

"Say, Fred. That Cordelia's place, you like to see it?"

"Thanks a lot, no—" Like many men, he was afraid. Unclean troubled him, as did sex itself. He liked it, he knew he was supposed to like it, but he avoided whenever possible those sultry female places. Humidity isn't good for tennis, which was his great love. "—no, I'm not up for that."

"Course you're not, pal, hot and sweaty as you be, but we

could just stop by, make it absolutely clear all you require is a drink of cold water, maybe you could take a shower—" Smoothie Al in charge.

"Oh, I can wait till I get home—"

"She got beautiful plumbing in that bathroom, buddy."

It was a challenge. I wanted to drag this timid tennis star into Cordelia's orbit. If he only showered, that was all right. He had beat me 6–3, 5–7, 6–3, not even working hard on our last set. Fred was a scientific tennis player. Generous of him even to volley with a public court duffer. Let him score a shower off me now, too, whether he wanted it or not.

Grumbling, he consented to ride where I was riding him.

"I got to talk with her anyway," I explained, "so if you don't mind too much." Luigi Mendoza, counselor-at-law, would see her tomorrow and tell her if she could lead her girls on a picket line. A strike outside the Fairmont was Cordelia's idea. A strike for what? Higher wages, better conditions, justice in the courts? She had lots of complaints besides the police and the law and arresting the girls but never the johns. The general public failed to appreciate the dignity of selling ass. Other forms of entertainment used massive quantities of petroleum, expensive equipment, and made you nervous. This calmed. It was traditional, like Christmas trees. It kept the forests green. Cordelia intended to strike a blow for what was right and get on prime time.

Fred said, "Haven't you been in touch? Marietta Kirwin is going to get her ass in jail, I'll bet on it. She sincerely wants to be elected. There's nothing more sincere than that."

"Cordelia knows about Marietta."

"You better tell her to watch it. Personally, maybe she should move to Nevada."

"Not her style."

"She better transfer her headquarters *out*, Al."

Luigi would try to tell her what she could do.

Cordelia would make up her own mind.

I parked my VW in front of the peaceful house, very quiet in

the late afternoon, birds twittering, flowers blooming, redolence—
I asked Fred to sniff—of the good herbs of Twin Peaks. Yerba
Buena used to be the name of this place before the goldminers, the
whores, the Sydney ducks, and the rats which followed the
garbage of the covered wagons—like the gulls following the wake
of ships—arrived in El Dorado country. Eureka, we have found
it. Fred was saying: Feel pretty yucchy for socializing, all right
to leave my racket in your car, you lock, kind of dangerous to drive
with loose balls rolling around if you go suddenly for the brake
or clutch or gas or something. . . .

Grumbling.

Here we were in our shorts, our old-fashioned tennis whites,
shambling like school kids up to the door to get our after-school
cookies from the nice neighbor lady. Fred seemed to fear the
cookies might be poisoned. It was the expression he wore to
discuss government bonds.

I activated the electric chimes with my knuckles (blisters,
slippery serve). Inside, feet in pussywillow slippers slapped across
the Spanish Mission mosaic tiles. The peephole slid open and eyes
took us in, followed by doorlatch and open arms. "Al, you've been
exercising again, what a stinky surprise! So glad to see you."

"You see," I said to Fred, "she's glad to see us. Fred would like
a shower, I think. Maybe I should take one, too."

"It's clean sweat," Fred grumbled.

"Tennis," stated Cordelia of the keen logical mind, noting
whites, Swedish court shoes, hair plastered to foreheads, lack of
concupiscence. "Come in, mama doesn't bite, come further in,
boys."

I liked to drop by like this, hoping to find something special, a
cop or a gangster having a snack, a prominent pervert exercising
his specialty, a weak place in Cordelia's armor. Once more she
presented an easy and comfortable house, the tragic conflicts
with her daughter, her mother, Marietta Kirwin's band, with herself, all pressed behind her skull as she tended to business. "Rose
Ann!"

What sweet nothings should be murmured by a passionate, gonorrhea-free nineteen-year-old woman of the world to an innocent young lad of middle years when life and death are both bearing down on him? I'm stuck with the facts. Fred Ellis, my tennis date, high-ranking producer at his branch of Merrill Lynch, was heading for a shower amid the rootlets of fine brass plumbing which A. Garvey, master sculptor from Fairfax, had installed for a fraction of what his labor is worth. Doing well in options and a small mutual fund, Fred could afford whatever his heart desired, if only his heart could be taught to desire something after tennis. He already had a solid backhand.

There were Irish lace curtains over the windows in the parlor, plus drapes, plus the clove and burnt bark smell of love. Sometimes, at night, Cordelia let incense smolder, selected in accord with the astrological signs of whores and johns. She bought it in twelve-packs at Yogaville West, a little boutique in Shantih Town, the hippie shopping mall in Sausalito. Personally, she liked that plain ordinary clove and burnt bark smell.

"Cody framing those sketches of you?"

"Before we get into conversation," Cordelia said, "about me and all,"—stretching and yawning like Atlas holding up the world in his sleep—"let's have a little word with Rose Ann here."

Rose Ann was a thoughtful, intellectual, moon-faced girl with shiny auburn hair and so much integrity she wouldn't wear the contact lenses her parents gave her as a going-to-college present when she went east last year. Now on furlough from Sarah Lawrence, she was wearing her intellectual horn-rims, light in color, the glass shaded a delicate gray. I found this work-study whore quite nice and attractive, although she may have had family problems with her parents in Atherton. Did she need to earn money this way, as a teenage sex consultant therapist? There must have been an element of sulky will. She was strip-mining for quick reward her well-tended female terrain—slim, with flesh, hormones in better repair than her psyche. She had a slightly thickened, pouty face, broader nose than is common down the Peninsula, muscled lips like those of a French girl, and a downcast manner, clotted with intentions of which she was unaware. Personally, I would prefer sex with a lady who looks me in the eye. I don't like her to be thinking about mummy and daddy and what oafs they are, or even about joining Cordelia in a picket line around the Fairmont Hotel.

Cordelia whispered to Rose Ann.

"I already thought of that," said Rose Ann.

"Really?"

"No."

"Why you say it then?"

Rose Ann shrugged her tanned shoulders (halter, middy blouse, a recent past at Sacred Heart Academy). "It's a super idea. I was going out for dinner with my folks, but I got the time."

Her willingness was not the same inclination which makes one person dream on another. It was an inclination to do what Cordelia asked, yes, she would do it. On these early summer days, the long time of the year, folks were barbecuing out in the Peninsula and folks were making love by natural light here on Twin Peaks. Twilight time until she returned to Sarah Lawrence in the fall. There's no Bus Ad or Labor Management major at the fine school out there past Yonkers in Bronxville. The only way to learn is on the job.

"Check," said Rose Ann.

Cordelia turned back to me with the sad little, proud little smile of a woman who has gotten her way in an unimportant matter, probably for the good of her whole family. Rose Ann followed Fred into the bathroom (no locks), and as the door opened—steam from Fred's passionate after-tennis showering and scrubbing—I caught a dull, opulent gleam off the marvelous brass curlicues of custom plumbing. The door closed behind Rose Ann and the distinguished sanitary equipment by A. Garvey.

"Your friend is busy," Cordelia said.

"He only wanted a shower."

"He gonna be busy anyway."

"Okay," I said. "You want me to pick a topic?"

"You always do."

"But we talk about your subject every time. Only we never talk about the real problems in your life."

"That's true, also," she said, smiling that same smile with which she had sent Rose Ann on a mission to surprise the tennis-obsessed stockbroker.

"That makes it hard for me."

"I suppose it does," she said.

When she curled up, I noticed her bare feet were pink and unsmudged. The floors were clean here in word and deed. And she scrubbed with pumice, and ran barefooted on the beach, and kept her feet nice and soft. I could as happily look at her instep as breathe. It might not even bore her for me to do so. But soon I found myself both breathing and gazing at feet. I also wondered with what reality Cordelia was putting me in touch as she picked her way through a fable about a car-parker, aged twenty-three, who made a fortune because he couldn't park cars very good. Instead he found himself a philosopher of power, ending arguments about who crumpled the fender by whispering closely to the car-owner: *"Man, I ain't rational."* So he lost the job at the parking garage and had to make his fortune dealing dope, where irrational doesn't hurt, where it helps to lean close and make a cold whiff in the nose of one's opponent.

"You listening?" Cordelia asked.

"I think I met him here one night," I said. "Smiley kid with a long fur coat, wasn't he?"

"Naturally I don't mention the name," said Cordelia.

We sat in silence. The story was a distraction, which was also its philosophical purpose. A transcendental word, plus a bit of advice. Cordelia knew I needed to meditate and made it easy for me. The false silence of chatter gave way to real silence, and it was painless. Cordelia rocked and lowered her eyes.

A resonant ticking was industriously devouring time while the termites devoured the foundations of this Victorian house. A bronze pendulum swung in a grandfather's clock big enough to hide a grandfather. It was a gift from Piero Grandi, who had taken it from a house he was remodeling by lowering the ceiling and replacing the obsolete-faced clocks with transistors and digits, Pulsars and Telstars and no-time, new time, light-emitting diodes, sensors, read-outs, a computerized off-on seamless slipping through futurity. The old clock did its work here. Cordelia liked furniture into which a small man might crawl, even if no small one ever did. They just don't seem to make men small enough anymore.

The mortality ticking of that relic was like a patient sermon, urging men to sleep close by the bodies of women ere their time be finished. Tick, tock, tick, tock. The century is passing. Centuries have passed. Bodies come to be and move out of being, but during the interval, they require consolation for fate, hard stools, soft peckers. Tick tock, tick tock. Let's do it honey and make so much fucking noise we can't hear that damned tocking.

Just the thought Cordelia needed to keep business moving.

Even I was not immune to sad, erotic thoughts in the sight of a map or a grandfather's clock with its bronze pendulum and those little balls you pull on a chain to wind it up.

Said Cordelia: "It'll get to you sometimes, won't it?"

Yes. I might not get this book done in time for the tenure committee, and then I'd find myself dumped from the university system, forced to find a job in the state college system, the junior college system, the community college system, the cab-driving system—but could they do that to a very popular teacher who once robbed a bank as part of his sociological delvings? I wasn't going to get rich anymore. Food stamps or unemployment would take care of me if they got tired of my intuitive research (we run a statistical department at Berkeley). I lacked a little in Third World or feminist rage. I didn't have Cody's oldtimey, middle-aged, despairing trust in romance. I was a slowed-down cured psychopath who had lost his faith in the treadmill. I liked being with Cordelia too much.

"I'm running this sex module, a little programmed learning feedback system."

"You're running into a little jargon there, Cordelia."

"I like to be understood."

"Despite your errors, I read you clear."

"Haha. You do?"

"No. Everyone knows Marietta is running for mayor and everyone thinks her idea is to use you."

"I *thrive*, Al, on both concord and conflict."

"Do you really want all this trouble?"

She sighed. She proceeded with her efforts while my friend had his bath. "I give them paid active juicy hot love, so good it could pass for fake. But it's really mine and I give it. Maybe Marietta or Fred thinks it's fake because he has to pay for it. Let them. He can whack his tennis balls over that one. This afternoon's wash will confuse him."

Cordelia was pleased to make confusing. Otherwise, if it's all clear, she just gets grossed out with mortal doubt, and her heart is filled with longing, and her ass feels tired. And if so, what's the point of embarking on a life of victimless crime?

I, social scholar, could bear the burden of intellectual fatigue. That's what I hope to be rewarded for.

"Some guys like half-and-half," Cordelia was saying, "but a lot of them make delicate adjustments of what they need. They like three-quarters and one-quarter. Fifteen-sixteenths and one-sixteenth—stockbrokers. Shaving it pretty close sometimes, my friend."

Oh, that amber light of an afternoon on Twin Peaks. The glass might be plastic and single's bar painted Tiffany, those ferns nearby shining like waxed cucumbers, but the colors around Cordelia were warm and deep; the refraction was hers. A woman is especially beautiful suggested and concealed—hair over one shoulder, half a profile at the stoplight, the reflected glass making imagination do its work (sudden apparition in a movie as the lights go down). But then sometimes you see the rest of her, come to know her, and she is still more beautiful! Knowing and giving freely have not yet been thoroughly explored. Cordelia grasped an essential truth—offering to give all is a superb *tactic*. Gratified and fulfilled, a man is grateful and fulfilling. Deep feeling moves product.

My vision runs against my intentions. Now that I'm a cured psychopath, I draw no benefits from my old cunning. I know what I want—to link my stiff wet lonely soul with the welcoming wet soul of someone. I *want* Cordelia. Like Cody, Piero, Jeremy, and so many others, I wish not to depart this life unsatisfied.

Can one legally become a psychopath twice in a lifetime? I mean, once cured, might a fellow reconsider? Cordelia teaches me evil is unnecessary for satisfaction around here. I try to do my research and let the rest pass. I can still hear that grandfather clock swinging and ticking. I wanted her.

"You been to church one or more times, Al? Okay, so the spirit needs to be kindled in men. I kindle. We do it. Otherwise it doesn't get done. Without love, Al, there's only us ladies to do it, the best way we can. Fun and forgetfulness aren't so bad, they're natural. Sing as the birds sing and forget as the birds forget, too. We help the folks through one day at a time, letting them live right now. Marietta doesn't understand that." She turned her face to the light, looking for the sun through curtain, through glass. She didn't mean it was all just fun. There was a sad cold look with pouches of kidney trouble under her eyes, blotches like wine stains. The big teeth, hidden by nonsmiling, made her lips stand out a little. She had something to add. "But sometimes they come in smelling of tobacco, beer, and craziness—that I'm Mad and I Wanna Get Fucked smell—and then we don't try to give them love. We just give them what they want and take their money. Marietta thinks she understands that, but she doesn't, either. I hate trouble, Al. I do hate bad things like trouble and such."

"You should have a man around, Cordelia."

"That kind of man turns into a pimp." She opened a drawer and shut it again. I didn't see what she was showing me inside.

"What's that?"

"My own ways."

"You don't want to explain?"

She gave me a glassy, fishy look. "How much have explanations helped? Do you know anybody who learns from explanations how to tie his shoe?"

"If you never did it before—"

"I'm dealing in things I can't explain. Keeping alive. Striking a blow for womankind. Hustling a few laughs. All I want is the force necessary."

In strong sunlight, lines like the lines in a cake of ice showed the future cracks in her skin. The bluish pouches then looked healthy. The lines worried me.

She has the force necessary.

Personally, I walk in a contained shimmer of no vibes at all. I send, but mean only to receive. I impress with my lack of charm as others impress with charm. Some think I run to deep waters, since I made my way from criminal into criminology. (Bank-robbers don't really exist anymore. Banks are too tough. I robbed the *teller* of a bank.) I suppose people are right to wonder at how there walks a real American with so little, uh, charisma? They wonder who this observant fellow might be.

I am the man who studies Cordelia. I am the man Cordelia chooses for mirror. I am the man who wonders whether Cindy or Marietta can chop her down. I am I because Cordelia knows me.

"Hey, you like me to cut your toenails while we chat? If I bully a person, I have this old-fashioned idea I should pretend to be doing something else, such as servicing the cuticle. Take off your shoes."

"No thanks."

"Try to keep up standards, right, Al?"

I am trying to let myself not be Al Dooley, former teller

robber, graduate student, researcher onto a good thing. I want to float with Cordelia like the orgasm before it is an orgasm, just breaking loose from its vesicle house into a desire for something, a repository of memory, a soul. If I am taking the wrong risks, I can be a lesson for someone. That's all right with me. I'm watching things happen while they happen to Al. I'm a chip off no block. The air out here in California is filled with me.

Back in those days when I was learning I could want the world and yet not get it, they used to say a smart girl figured out how to make a man her slave—good back rub, good blow job.

But does a smart woman really need slaves?

I'm becoming a philosopher. There's no other way. In this sadness I'd like to melt off Al Dooley, me, and become nothing, nobody, nowhere, just a mote of time; give up my American will and just be there; dissolve away from my hopes and float on Cordelia's shimmer. I'd like to be her lover without necessarily being her lover. That's what I am. I get no good back rub, I expect satisfaction anyway. I'm trying that. I'll not monitor my body and soul anymore for signals, desires, energies, flashes. I'll try not having any body or soul. In the stillness of Cordelia's parlor I rise and fall with the sun, the movement of bodies, the displacement of those who still wish something. I watch. Yes, I do want her.

My definitive study of the San Francisco madam is the answer I give to those who ask if I'm doing anything these days.

Here's what I mean about living fully in the moment. When Cordelia sneezed in public, and a bit of it stuck to her nose, she was interested more than embarrassed because she didn't have a Kleenex handy. Crisis *interested* her. The moment is never wasted. In her own slow rhythm, which pleases her, she requested a tissue.

Yet she was not merely perfect. Her daughter and mother made her feel bad in different ways. She thought she could cure the world with the rights of hookers. She had her crusade. She ran her campaign. She seemed to do it with no spreading stain of anxiety, if you don't count warning the girls not to talk to Calvina or Benito, if you don't count consultations with Luigi about Marietta, if you don't count worrying about the police suddenly coming unglued and crashing through all her doors and windows, if you don't count a bit of family hatred and spite.

During Fred's long shower, as I dried off, sticky but at ease in this place, I contentedly filled the space allotted for thought, just as Cordelia's teeth filled the space normally given teeth, her eyes eyes, her nose nose. She was ample in her domain and I was grateful to be allowed to share it. What I felt for Cordelia was more than I can declare, it could redeem me—yet I didn't want trouble.

I wondered about her spaciousness. "Do you always like yourself?"

"Research," she said, and sighed. "I like my daughter. That's fair. Hate my mother. Live with myself. What a crapper of a question."

I would feed her answers—

"Maybe I even love my mother. Maybe I wish I never had a daughter." An extraordinary shadow came over her face—the flesh falling away, the look of a starved woman, of pure longing. "Maybe I don't think too much about such things."

I hadn't seen what I had just seen. I said: "We'll feed your answers into a computer we got in Berkeley. We time-share it with Poly Sci. Once I figure out a program for it, I can make the whole thing sound scientific."

"I bet you will."

"You don't have any confidence? That's the only way I can get it approved."

"Al," she said, "you're a typical john—a dreamer. Cody's found that bony little scarecrow and doesn't come around anymore. Piero dreams he'll be free and easy with a nice wife. I mention his name because you know him. *Piero.* But your secrets are safe with me, unless I decide to break your confidence. Piero *Grandi.* He dreams so, and you also dream you'll be in the clear someday. Piero has fur all over his back, his chest, even his thighs, it's like rubbing a big sweaty alleycat when you nuzzle him—okay, cats don't sweat, but they muck around—and yet he's a sweet fellow about love. He would press a violet in a book if his wife ever gave him a violet."

"Does she raise violets?"

"But she doesn't give him any. I gave him a rose once and he put it in a little Product 19 box for safekeeping. From the kitchen. He thinks he'll never come to see me again. Maybe will and maybe won't."

Sometimes Cordelia's voice came from outer space, where God is dead but a Woman minds the store, her caretaker spirit in constant touch with earth. She was only doing her job.

Ah, no. How was it for Cordelia? Her daughter made her flesh boil off. She was not in outer space at all. She was a gushing lava-flow from the life-hole.

There's my problem again. The computer might take her straight and code the questionnaire. I can't. How to code her blue eyes of no complexity at all?—a laughing girlish blue, and a face around them pouched with pain and excess, sun, health, after-thoughts. (Not.) (Weren't.) (Hidden.) Behind the lack of complexity lay great simplicity. And behind that, mystery.

"I got a question for Piero's wife, or any other wife," Cordelia was saying. "I'll give a first prize, free hysterectomy, to the house-wife who shows me $20,000 in the bank which she has saved out of her pocket money. No pimps, no madams, but no good results in earnings, either. My girls can make it in a man's world with a man's profit if they accept my guidance. I mean to go public and show how this is done."

"Do you have such money, Cordelia?"

Her lips pulled back like a hose nibbling a flower. "Naw. I spend it."

"How?"

"I spend it. I don't count my mother and Cindy. I got to support my causes. Some of it goes to spreading the word. Other women can do like me, and the law needs an education. If I can't teach Marietta, at least I got to give her a lesson. The people can learn. I'm moving with all due speed, Al. I'm going to have me my press conference, make my announcements. Your buddy is sure taking his time in there."

We both turned to the door with interest. Wisps of steam curled beneath. There would be warp in the plywood if it were plywood, if Fred didn't turn off the hot water. I could hear muffled squeaks which didn't come from the plumbing.

My buddy was sure taking a long time in there.

We then took note of his retreat from the campaign of the bathroom. Steamy battle near the soap dish, a struggle with Rose Ann near drains that made a sound of kickle-kickle. Fred came through clean as a whistle. Tennis, hot water, and a busy soft mouth from Bronxville and Atherton had brought peace to his troubled spirit. Rose Ann had the resentful girl's face which nervous young men mistake for profound—especially when she gives nervous young men the value they'd like given.

Cordelia smiled her entrepreneurial smile. Fred was carrying his tennis clothes in a little bag that said Adidas, but still wearing tennis clothes, clean ones now, alligator shirt, shorts, socks, everything new—only his overheated shoes working through the socks to unfreshen him again in the eternal quest for light and free. Rose Ann was in a silk Japanese robe, tied with one silken cord, her girlish bounciness unconfined by being a little held in the flesh here and there. Her cheeks were pink.

"Man," said Fred.

"What happened?"

"Man."

"Well?"

"But not quite what you think."

"Oh, I took a bath with him," Rose Ann said.

"She got in the shower with me."

Pedant. Rose Ann shrugged. Time enough to be precise during the school year in Bronxville.

"She got in the shower with me and she said,"—and he started whispering.

"I can't hear. You're hissing in my bad ear." (Untreated infection while I was held in the county jail on my teller-robbing detail.)

"He's trying to say," Rose Ann said, "I laid it out straight. *This time free; next time pay.*"

Fred's feelings were hurt. He had hoped to whisper his secret, keeping two moments of intimacy, one the magic sexing in the shower, two his fraternal sharing of the news with me. Magic departs when all parties discuss it together. This may be Cordelia's intention: turn the magic on, turn it off, show who is in charge.

"For God's sake," said Fred, "I never expected such a thing."

"For God's sake? Oh, Christ," said Rose Ann.

"How about some tea and apple," Cordelia stated, pressing the heel of her hand down on the gizmo that turned an apple into triangular petals with a narrow meaty barrel of core that contained most of the seeds. "Let's have a couple munchies after all this hard work."

Fred was doing a great deal of careful thinking. Someone had given him a high lob and he was falling back, looking into the sun, discovering resources of strength and patience in himself, need and power in his spine beyond the drains of competition; falling back on Twin Peaks, looking into the sun, arching up, anxious.

Rose Ann was both stern and generous.

An impeccable second serve may be beyond human grasp. Neither Fred nor I could hide behind glass or the swinging pendulum of the grandfather's clock. Its ticking filled the room.

"Let's kiss and hug a lot," he said, "that's what I want to do. Kiss and hug. A lot."

11

"You know what an over-the-hill hooker like me got to do? Go over the *next* hill. I'm gonna just roll right through."

But patchwork legal arrangements aren't enough when a woman is reaching for a new life in the organization of prostitutes field. Cordelia was letting Luigi Mendoza, the brilliant attorney who obtained a copyright on the words "Hangtown Fry," making it available for franchise in the "Hangtown Fry" chain all across California, look into her affairs. She needed to get clear on the problems of an official hookers' union. How can you have a legal local of workers in an illegal trade? How could she threaten to strike a forbidden service? What would be her rights if the hookers picketed hotels, police stations, orthodontists' conventions, demanding better working conditions, equal treatment with other craftspersons, higher payment per production unit? Harassment might well be her lot, it served the purposes of a certain female liberal, so better to prepare for trouble.

L. Mendoza would consider working on it. Cordelia's case was somewhat unorthodox, potentially profitable, very unorthodox, and that was what he liked. Shining with pride and metal (studs in his velvet continental-cut jean suit, fresh from a quarter of a

million dollar decision in a personal injury litigation involving
false pregnancy in a singing transsexual), Luigi agreed to study
her problems. He had added a few pounds since last we met:
hormonal changes of late middle age. Luigi now wore mutton-
chop whiskers, a white aureole around his overweight cheeks.
Splendid with health, glowing and proud, were it not for a little
high blood pressure, hardening of the arteries, varicose veins, memory lapses, and prostatic seepage, he bore up under the burden
of my presence.

"Do you really need this friend? I'm just curious."

"Al came along."

"To spy?"

"Al, are you a spy?"

"Does he sincerely respect what I am trying to do for you, my
dearest Cordelia?"

I shot him a look of sincere respect. It was reflected back in the
speckled gold mirror on the ceiling of his consultation room as a
subdivision of cringing. With a long wet sigh, he assented to my
company. Why would a respected whore demean herself by running around with an academic sociologist? In my corner, I wondered how the IRS dealt with his gifts from clients—the Ferrari,
the condominium in Acapulco. Yet I was in awe of this legal
maverick. He was no mere show-off in the courtroom. He was a
show-off in life. He was a California champion—rich, powerful,
celebrated, entertaining, self-entertaining. He had been married
five times; six, if you count Johnny Jons, the sex-change pro
blocking guard whom he wed in a Universal Church ceremony in
order to get quick visas to Algeria when they visited Eldredge
Cleaver together. The marriage was annulled when Johnny
claimed he still possessed better than 65 percent of his male sexual
organs, due to a drunken Spanish surgeon who left out several
essential cutting, slicing, tucking, and sewing steps in the opera-
tion. At that time marriages between members of the same or
similar sex were still illegal in California. Luigi threatened Johnny
with a civil action under the Consumer Fraud laws. Johnny went

along with the annulment, completed his treatments, but swore never to espouse another male lawyer in lieu of legal fees.

"Please make yourself comfortable. There's a chaise over there. Here's a lovely watercouch for you, Cordelia."

Luigi went all the way.

Bidding me keep my place—pimp, companion, researcher, whatever I claimed I was—Luigi turned the setting on his ice-blue eyes to Maximum Intensity. It would burn him out if he kept this up too long. In the meantime, we would become Very Close under the welding, melding laser of his gaze. I reviewed the moment, without finding evidence of genuine closeness between us, but felt his power. He was great before juries. He was also formidable among all the accumulated things of his office. These too—souvenir plates, silver forensic cups, electronic calculators, framed citations from the South Korean Bar Association, Native California gold rush relics represented a rage for magnitude. And they succeeded. He was large and fearsome, despite his panty hose. I wanted to snuggle for protection in Cordelia's strong arms, and therefore slid my chair closer in possessive masculine fashion, hoping that the difference between what I felt and what I did would be misperceived. Instead it went unperceived. Luigi's secretary, a pink blond with a series of face-lifts that gave her the look of a tragic burn victim, poked her head in and strained to open the stretched mouth. "No," said Luigi, "no calls, no visitors, no interruptions."

She was gone. This was probably a choreographed interruption. No calls: it doesn't hurt to make people feel good until you need to make them off balance. Style works in depth for Luigi, content is only another form of style for him. He has given up the effort to rescue the past through words, acts, loyalty, memory. Despite the memorial museum in his office, he has abandoned the past, as has Cordelia, and they recognized a sharing in this. They know their longing, that emptiness, that rich presence of a lack: and therefore, through surface and flash, they might reach profundity someday. Through suffering, failure, and loss. Which they earn.

But not yet. Just now, these premonitions were only the shadow passing over their victories. "Excellent," said Luigi in a mood for English, "very well, what can I do for you? I don't fit I.U.D.'s or shoot penicillin, so it must be something else."

She stared. "Try again. More polite this time."

"My dear, am I in a position where I must worry about hurting your feelings?"

"You're more likely to catch something in your sauna than from me."

He shook off this unusual touchiness with a wet doggy gesture of the shoulders.

"I'd like to help you with your legal problems, Cordelia. I'm probably the man to do it."

"Not funny, but polite. Nicer that way," she insisted.

He sighed. He studied his Ferry Building Landmark cuff links. "Life is so short."

"It doesn't need to be fitted with a laugh track. Luigi. I'll make it with you if you prefer, but now I have my problems. I'd like to deal with them first—"

His high-intensity gaze was creating a field of force which attempted to make me say: Uh, ah, got a class to meet, see you later.

"—in Al's presence. He's my good friend and researcher. It's okay."

"Okay. Okay."

Discipline time was over. Cordelia had made her point. Luigi's turn.

"Let me outline what Marietta Kirwin got you doing," said Luigi. "She got you working for her. She doesn't want to stop you till she starts running hard, she's running hard already, till she starts running *really* hard for mayor. Then she'll smash you with a big loud noise." He brought his hand down hard on her knee. Cordelia jumped.

"Don't do that," she said. "I ain't working for her."

"You don't know you're working for her. She's got you on a long leash, but she'll shorten it. Listen to what I tell you."

"I'll fight her in the courts."

"Oh, nice, nice. Of course. That's what she'd like. She uses the courts and you pay. And she gets to be the clean-up lady, and you get to go to jail."

Cordelia considered this. "You rattle like the muffler on a Chinese kid's Buick. So what are you suggesting?"

Luigi's face folded up into a Chinese mask. "I can't tell you not to do what you are bound and determined to do. But it would help if you know the plan. Get your own plan. I too can make a bigoted metaphor, Cordelia. Just don't take a fall like a teenie at the bus station in the hands of some spade pimp."

"What about Calvina and Benito?"

Luigi frowned. "Usually you think about what's important, Cordelia. They're the troops. Think about the main thing— Marietta is employing you to get her elected, and she can get you in a lot of trouble by so doing. Try to consider that."

Cordelia hummed impatiently. She had her own life to worry about. She didn't enjoy Marietta, and therefore didn't enjoy thinking about her. "Are we having that coffee?"

In the presence of Al, in the presence of plaques, Christmas cards, antique furniture, watercouch, and joke pillows, Barbary Coast chandeliers and exposed brick, decorator decorations and electronic aids, records and scrapbooks of battles past, in the presence of sunlight through tastefully parted slats so that pass-ersby on the street could see the Maestro at work, Luigi and Cordelia sat down at a silver tea service to discuss her problems. It would be their problems together as soon as she explained. Luigi would let her explain as soon as the Filipino boy in shorts finished setting out the napkins with the coffee, pitcher of hot milk, buttered croissants and long-sliced tartines of French bread. Luigi enjoyed this fine old tradition in the middle of the morn-ing, when a Barbary Coast gentleman takes his second breakfast.

Cordelia's mouth was huge and magenta over tartine in the distorting silver curves of the pot. Luigi was hilarious. I was furtive and broken into cubist planes. Cordelia said:

"My first problem is this. I received this envelope from Internal Revenue, plus a card from Lucas Hastings, Junior, of the Feds. Like he wants to come *calling*. They want something called Net Worth Study. I think he said something about—"

"You telephoned him?"

"I called him back. He came to see me already."

Luigi was shaking his head. Pity was one of his resources, cross-filed under contempt. So sad. So often his clients came to see him only after they had done everything wrong first. If only everyone would remember to consult with Luigi before they do anything.

"So he came to the house?"

"He came to my home. He asked to see Business Tax Forms, he wanted to know if I was registered as a union organizer for the union, all kinds of questions, he thought there should be a treasurer—well, there *is*—I think it's me. He thought . . ." Cordelia lifted her arms and a negative whiff of Right Guard sifted across the hot milk. How to express her annoyance with all this bureaucracy? She lowered her arms and poured hot coffee over hot milk. "My question is this: How do I declare financing on an illegal organization? How do I register dues? How can I pay taxes on a business such as hooking?"

"Have you thought of opening a laundry?"

"What?"

"Cleaning, pressing, and alteration of money?"

"You say?"

"I'm only kidding. As your attorney, member of the bar of the State of California, I cannot counsel an illegality. Anyway, you're too well-known for normal illicit activities. You're in the public eye. Your only chance might be very thoughtful, Cordelia, *thoughtful* illegal activities—"

"I want—"

Luigi raised a hand. Stone cuff links gleamed green. Genuine Navajo handiwork. Somehow, sleight of hand, he had gotten rid of the Ferry Building Memorials on his wrists.

"Your wont is only to do what's right, Cordelia," he said soothingly. "I know what is your wont. You can't call your union a Union because you can't have a union to perform an illegal act. You can't pay taxes on a felony organization or business. Therefore..." He put his Italian Afro head in his hands and peeked roguishly through the fingers at Cordelia. "Therefore, call it an Affinity Group?" he asked, earning his money.

She looked puzzled.

"It's better than a Gypsy Band or Caravan."

"Sounds more stable," I said to nobody listening. A little anxious headache of not being wanted suddenly appeared over my left eye, ice-cube shaped, but hot, radiating slivers of hot. I tried to slip it under a bone where I wouldn't notice it, but it pushed and nagged at my eye, my forehead, my need to be friendly.

"Not a legal entity makes it hard to tax legally," said Luigi. He squeaked in his wicker Huey P. Newton throne with its dangling straws (low humidity) that tended to pick holes in his panty hose. Not many saw him in his undergarments, but once Cordelia mentioned it, I couldn't get it out of my mind. Maybe thinking would help the headache.

"Free All Twats (FAT) Association?" Cordelia suggested.

"Not on my beautiful engraved stationery," said Luigi. "Nothing of that sort of disgusting ilk goes down in a class barrister's office like mine," declared finicky Luigi. "I spent a lifetime or two building up this business and you ain't gonna spend ten speedfreak minutes tearing it down, over my plump living body."

"You're beautiful," said Cordelia.

He smiled. This consoled him. Oldfashioned and dignified as he was, he kept most of his gold teeth, capping only the front ones with tooth-like plastic. He was a beautiful old man who thought *responsibly* young. "I'm fond of Cindy and want to help take care of her, you know. How old is the child now—fifteen?"

His mouth was wet. He salivated like a youngster. Perhaps he had saliva implantations at that clinic on his last trip to his numbered bank account in Switzerland. *Where were you, where were you where were you, when I needed you to see me through? Darling darling darling I need you.* The FM radio cube on Luigi's desk was turned on. Rock music makes me sad sometimes.

"Keep your hands off," Cordelia said.

Luigi beamed. He was slipping into old age, but could wait till Cindy was sixteen. It had to be less than a year. "For proof of guardianship, deductions, that's important, get me her birth certificate." He stared affectionately at the young onion plant in a pot on his desk near the radio—yellowish shoots, like some of the hairs in his ears. He sniffed. The onion in the air so delicate a fellow had to be really sensitive to smell it. Luigi still could. He smiled. He folded his hands over the double-breasted vest, the watch fob, the UCLA frat key, the navel. He listened. Like me, he treasured how Cordelia began many of her explanations with very basic inquiry. She had a metaphysical rather than a practical temperament, though her life was more practice than philosophy. Such may be true of many of us. I was already used to my headache; understood it.

Luigi's spiritual needs were satisfied for the moment by the idea of having Cindy within the year. Yet he had to live with Cordelia's asking: "Who made me like this?"

"God," snapped Luigi crisply.

"*Who?*"

"Okay, Mary then. Or Adam."

"I've not heard from any of them in a long time. Okay, let's call it Affinity Group, I kind of like that."

"Now I remember, she'll be sixteen on March ninth, a Pisces," said Luigi. "Didn't I make out some school transfer forms for you?"

Cordelia patted her purse. That pistol she never needed to use. "What will be won't be," she said.

Since Luigi mostly wanted to laugh, eat pasta, drink wine, stay rich, and have lots of young girls, once in awhile a boy, while also making legal history with his brilliant jury-tampering, and also enjoying creamy Italian desserts despite his cholesterol count, he took note of the gentle touch on Cordelia's purse. No sense in imperiling all his pleasures for the sake of one evanescent teenie-kink. Fate had other plans for him. Cindy could be kept safe for some other mature man. Luigi, snug in his panty hose, could find puppylove elsewhere, if puppylove he must, and now back to legal business. He took on something of that shrunken look I noticed in men whom Cordelia chose to discipline—a skeletal peakedness despite the flesh, like the bony, crispy remains of a bug in a plate of raspberries. Surrounded by her opulence, men sometimes gave up. It was a choice she made for them. Yet I once opened a drawer in her bedroom, and it was filled with pieces of paper, drawings of flowers, houses, little girls, and each one said I love you, or I love you Mommy, I love you; stars, skies, farmers, fences, drawings by Cindy when she was a child, all marked in crayon or pencil or chalk: *I love you.*

Perhaps saving these drawings, but keeping them hidden, Cordelia had helped make herself formidable. Secrets can do this. She dealt with her pains, but did not let them victimize her. She treated her responsibilities as pains. Ah, is that what she's like? She doesn't brood, except when she is brooding? I would give up the little knowledge I have of myself to know this woman. Now Luigi and Cordelia sat at law practice together; me watching, filling up my life with her life.

"There are several matters they could get you on," Luigi said, "and if not these several matters, they can look for others. As a business venture, the city business tax. Fire laws, access laws, are you up to code? The inspectors find what they want to find, as a general rule. That's the norm. If you had a 501 C.3 certificate from Internal Revenue, you could accept donations for charity. I don't suppose you're eligible. You could call yourself Emotional Therapy Research Center, though. It might could be worth a try. Then there are—"

"That's a righteous idea for our affinity group. We do Emotional Therapy. We lick toes and things. We make old men see the Buddha."

"A legal case on entrapment, on favoritism. The men are never charged. Judge Avakian in Alameda got a case thrown out because the johns—"

"Clients."

"—the poor scared johns with their skivies around their ankles were let go. So equality before the law could become an issue, but it would require a fight. Is your house zoned R2, for secondary educational facility? Are you registered with the State Board of Equalization? If your girls—"

"Women."

"—are paid as independent contractors and no withholding was taken from their salary, it might be okay if you say they are part-time independent contractors."

"Oh then they are, they *are*," said Cordelia. "Hey, they are part-time independent contractors in oldfashioned micro-minis, unless they got lumpy thighs. Then hostess gowns until they slim down."

Luigi licked his lips. Sometimes the saliva glands cut off in time of worry. A certain number of persons are taken out of the market by lumpy thighs. The total population is therefore a poor indication of sexual riches. Luigi had had to face that problem all his life. Even in the sex business you found unqualified performers, although Cordelia knew enough to keep people getting what they want—perhaps sometimes they might need to close their eyes while they were getting it and use a bit of imagination. Lots of fellows like that usher at the wedding who languished in Cordelia's arms for love of the bride. Not everyone can have Greta Garbo licking his toes. . . . Oh, back to business. Only a few years more till the vacation of senility, and then Luigi could spend all his time on pleasure.

"Let me bring up some other elements on your side, Cordelia. Search warrant. Discriminatory harassment unless the male criminals of the masculine sex are also booked. The changing mores of the time. Sex therapy as a science and the art of love. We got lots on our side, just to organize it a little."

"If you don't have someone to love," I said, "you can't have love. I mean you lose a dream if you don't share it. If you're all alone, you lose what's yours alone. I mean—"

Cordelia touched my arm. No sense irritating Luigi with this foolishness. Even if he wasn't charging full price, his time was measured by the hour. Her eyes passed over mine for a moment, like a cloud, cooling me. Okay, I could just sit. Luigi was modestly looking at the floor, his heart constricted by the desire to kill or be rude.

"I understand my good johns," Cordelia said. "Some of them fear themselves more than women. They fear the noises in their heads. It's a terrible racket in there. They fear the night because they have nothing good to dream. No good dreams. How can you sleep when you know your dreams are bad?"

"How do you understand this?" I asked her.

"I barely made it over to sleeping," she said. "I discovered this energy, that I can be more than a hooker, more than a madam, I can be the meaning and salvation of the hooking profession. So I dream. I remember my struggle. I dream of victory."

"I think I see."

"Of course you see, Al," she said very patiently. "I'm helping johns sleep who have nothing but nightmares otherwise, because their days are daymares. Of course you understand, Al. The noises are heavy for you too, and you want some life out here to carry back into your dreams."

Luigi was thrumming the desk with his plump, surprisingly noisy fingers. "Very interesting. Forty years ago, when I was in school, we didn't have to take philosophy. Maybe we didn't need it then, hah? We didn't have Valiums, either. Now maybe you like to talk serious, Cordelia?"

"We're sorry," she said sweetly, with lowered eyes. But again she had granted me a whiff of need, her own need, through the need of men. How she demanded power. How she required it. How she only survived by becoming more than others. How the leader does it.

Luigi's plump fingers thrummed.

"This thing is so complicated," Cordelia said. "It's not just hooking, it's not just law. I also want to *understand*. That's what Al is remarking about."

"I can help you with the law. I can't help you understand."

"I know that."

"Well, maybe I can help them understand you," Luigi said.

"I doubt that."

"But none of what I say can help you if you're Marietta's way to viability. Plus I think she really means it, she thinks what you're doing is really evil and bad. Which makes her a difficult opponent, Cordelia. A sincere enemy means sincere trouble."

"I'm sincere, too."

Luigi was counting off the possibilities on an unlimited supply of fingers. "Marietta could go for the law first, or get Calvina and Benito to start a grassroots morals campaign, or do them both together. She might try to use the Federal Crime Task Force. You got lots of Italian friends besides me, honey. She'd like pictures of herself at the airport flying to Washington."

"She'd look lovely if she'd only lighten up."

"Okay." Luigi smiled—large wide rosy face, dappled with wetness due to his heavy couturier habits—"use me as I'm designed to be used, please." His weary eyes swept over us both. "Be careful, please stop the dreaming."

Cordelia would not be stopped. On such occasions she was pregnant with philosophy, and expelled her offspring in the field where she stood. "You see those brides sitting in bride pictures with the white roses in their laps? Like hiding their laps with white roses? What are they hiding it for? They're selling it, too, everyone knows that."

Luigi fussed and hummed. "Yes, spousal support. Spending

money. Community property. I can stipulate to such." This was boring him, and boredom is death.

"To do it is legal, but to suggest it is not. To receive a gift is legal. To ask for money is not. Marietta makes divisions among women and calls me whore. It's cruel, Luigi. Al. I don't mind, but it's cruel. I used to think so. Now I think: Okay, I'm a whore." She patted herself comfortably. "Listen, my johns send me flowers, but I don't sit around with them in my lap for pictures. I press them between the pages of my bible, I suppose—you believe that?"

She grinned. Would I like to examine the flat, browned, juice-squeezed parchments from satisfied customers?

"I think I understand what you're saying," I said.

"No you don't, Al. When a john says I think I can, it means he can't."

Luigi gazed at me with all his intense hatred of bullshit other than his own. He would blame me not only for what I said but for what Cordelia said. Adversary was his style with men unless they were clients, queens, or suppliants. He didn't want Cordelia for his very own, but I was his rival anyway. Sumptuous, untranquil, he quivered, warning me off or—I wasn't sure which—suppressing a fart. He would wear out his panty house with all this twisting and turning. "I was at Selma, baby," he said. "I love the music of Miles. Satchmo played at my first wedding."

"I'm not black," I said.

He looked at me in some surprise. That's right, I wasn't her pimp. He was making an unconscious syllogism. I was *like* a pimp to her. Old creep, I'll express critical insight against him in my thesis.

Cordelia had gotten her good humor back. She loved this kind of dispute over Cordelia. "Men," she said to Luigi, "have been ripping women off for centuries. But it happens that Al here is *mah frien'*...." She loved it. It was her joke, like the ten dollar gold piece glued to the floor in her parlor. No one touches it; it's hers. Study it, tickle the idea, flirt sideways with it, but it's stuck tight. However, it wasn't glued at all. Her authority kept it there. Once in a while someone ran off with the coin, and she replaced it, nothing said. She also liked this proof of man's fallibility and her own. "I don't want to interfere with the friendship of you two boys," she said, "it's not a woman's place, but I notice you hate his guts."

Who *his*? I only hated Luigi a little bit.

So she was noticing he hated me.

I was only sore at him for not letting me fill my space silently, as is my desire.

"It's okay," I said.

"I don't mind this kid," said Luigi.

"Nothing bothers you men but your personal relationships. You make money, you get laid, you get along. Somewhere along the line you have a wife or two, a kid or three. Try to focus on *my* problem. I'm running a whore house with a lot of fucked-up women in it. Wake in the morning. Headache. There's a mess on the floor. The ashtrays are supposed to be emptied right away, but they get put under the bed, around the couches, or spilled. Mess. Girl is crying. Some other girl is sick. Call the doctor. Worry. It's not so simple. Love would be a lot easier, one on one, me and mine. Whoring is complicated. A hooker is a machine callibrated to do work it doesn't really want to. And the girl inside is crying. So how did I get into it? Because love is too complicated?"

"You're saying this is worse?" I asked.

"You're starting to listen, Al."

Luigi stated: "Well, I'm here because you're trying to make it work—"

"Something that can't work. I'd like to find somebody for the morning who would..."

Hold me in his arms.

Not so easy.

"I don't know about Al here, Al Dooley, isn't that his name?"

Luigi said, "but what I'm good at is courtroom problems, Cordelia. So if you want my help to rustle up the papers that might help you in court when Marietta taxes you there, I'm here. Otherwise, you want to give me a good time, I know you give a good time, you give good time"—he cleared his throat of the repetitiously croaking frog—"well, Luigi Mendoza, obediently, at your service."

"Me too," said Cordelia. "For a hundred dollars I'm an all-night woman. You're an all-day man—"

He was smiling sleepily. His rates were negotiable. He looked at me and stopped smiling. Lord, he wished I would go away or have a painless heart attack or just *depart*. No matter how rich and clever and friendly and well-dressed a man is, epaulets on his shirts and velvet epaulets on his jackets, epaulets even on his panties if he wants them, it seems he can't get everything he wants. A little secret Cordelia was also on to.

"My idea, once we get started and you say we're clear, is call a strike and lay a picket line around the Fairmont Hotel. The ladies. We'll get our demands up before the public."

"There was a girl named Lysistrata who did that."

"She better get a catchier name."

"She got a good name. She did it to stop war."

"Did the war stop? She ought to do it for herself, man, and her other ladies."

"The cops'll hassle you, friend. You start talking about arresting johns. You start demanding things."

"That's why I want you. I want you to protect me—"

"Legally? Or public relations, is that what you're after? Marietta can afford to be after that, but you got to stay out of jail first, Cordelia. Do you hear me? You're headed for bad trouble."

She fought it out with bosom, ass, deep warm looks, and a laugh.

Luigi fought the good fight with thin charm, quickly degenerating to a Western adversary brawl. He was wearing tooled boots. It all added up, boots, panty hose, velvet, epaulets, ruffles, folds of flesh and whorls of hair, ears and nose gone wild with cartilage, but I had difficulty making the sum. He was a real presence, and his aura penetrated our electromagnetic field. I didn't have to like him to know that his soupy aura had more nourishing substance in it than my lean one, mere California dream and hope as it was. He sighed. He was radiating, trying to take over. "I think we're all just hanging out here together, Cordelia," he said with evident compassion for the stupidity of others. "It's a nice time and place for that, but I got a lot of overhead in this office, you wouldn't believe the utilities, and you got a lot of problems. So it seems. And I'm very very happy to meet your escort Albert or Allan or whatever his name is here, he's a delightful little fellow I'm sure, but naturally in your and my business we definitely got to finally get down to it or there's no action at all. You understand?" His voice was rising. His panty hose was sticky. He wanted something better to happen.

"Can we incorporate, non-profit, medical, some way?"

"There are several possible options to take. And I'm going to, regretfully, pass you along to a younger and therefore more patient member of the firm,"—finger on button. "Would have liked to handle the case myself, Cordelia." Glacial whiteness on finger pressing button. "Would have done good for you, Cordelia."

Cordelia took my arm. It tingled like a hit of niacin where she touched me.

Luigi lay a paternal hand on my shoulder. It also tingled.

He was too old not to speak his mind. "If you want free legal aid and counsel, don't bring your social life in to see me!"

Cordelia was young enough to speak her mind. "If you want to give me bargain legal aid and counsel, for your own reasons, plus because I ask you, don't tell me how to get the rest of my thing together. This man is studying. I need his help and counsel, too. He's a friend aren't you, Al?"

I nodded.

"You don't have to like him. Just give me a little respect,

Luigi." And she touched his freckled hand with its dime-sized liver spots.

Luigi's lower lip trembled. I received a hint of extreme age, how he would end in his perishing melancholia with nothing to say and saying it with his gums in front of a poorly tuned teevee, mumbling the weather report like a prayer to the Mother Mary.

"Okay," he said briskly, "I've made my point. Perhaps at some moment in the future—"

Tingling gently, we were given the redwood door. Luigi beamed. Cordelia may have been very famous in San Francisco, accomplishing a great deal for the women of the streets, as well known on the local level as Sammy Davis Junior or Richard Nixon on the national scene, but Luigi Mendoza would take no shit from her. Like the thirteen states, his motto was Don't Tread on Me.

We were moving by impulsion down the brick hallway filled with potted plants. The secretary with the tragic burn excess of facelifts had me by the hand. Her smile and hair were those of a Singles Bar survivor. Cordelia floated a half-step behind, riding the waves on her invisible surfboard.

Dan Bronika's office looked like Luigi's, only shrunken, made of wool and washed in hot water, and with a lot fewer trophies. He had a speaker-phone, however. He had a cube with pictures of loved ones. He had his diplomas in carved wooden frames, plus a big wooden golden *D*. Someday he too might be a celebrity on the local level.

"I'm Dan Bronika," said the younger member. "Luigi says we should explore some options together. I'll study the file this afternoon. But first, sit and tell, my dear friends."

It was a pleasure to be with someone who was not yet authentic. He was going to smooth school. He was practicing on non-network talk shows. He was still willing to work.

12

THIS WAS CLOSING DAY for Piero Grandi—one last visit to Cordelia's. He was not worried about her taking the Union public. He was not terminally ill, not suicidal. Piero was merely returning to his wife.

How did he know it was for the last time that he had come to pay his respects to Cordelia, her staff, their memories together?

He didn't. He just felt it so, and the feeling of knowledge made Piero heavy in the belly in his time of crisis. No offense meant to his slightly withered, occasionally stale-smelling wife. Of course he loved her, as one loves history, obligations, and fate. No need to dwell on those matters; they had the rest of their lives for philosophy.

It was midafternoon and an aquarium glow filled the front parlor at Cordelia's, a sunny deepsea greenness. Invisible bubbles arose through the air. You could almost hear the pop at the nonexistent surface of some grave cranial liquid. I too, heading home from Berkeley, swam more slowly here. Piero swam in regret, desire, and hope that henceforward he and his wife would live in conjugal peace, as his wife's God intended. He assented. His present condition of spirit: need for consolation.

"Foo, foo, foo," said Cordelia, gracefully loping about to open the French windows. "This place smells like an expensive funeral. Aren't you going to say that isn't what it smells like?"

"That isn't what it smells like."

"It smells like a lot of juicy screwing, and also somebody spilled the apple juice last night."

Piero liked Cordelia and her girls. They liked him. He could afford them. Barbara and Rose Ann were napping upstairs, but even in their sleep, if they knew he had come for a visit, they would like him thoroughly. If they had been out shopping, they would like him even more to go shopping with them. Frequently it was their birthday. Sometimes they gave him Specials without charging for it. What began in the commerce of need had reached the point of friendship; Cordelia pulled Piero's earlobes sometimes. "Good dog."

Sad dog.

The dried flowers and last night's incense, the punk of desire, the faulty dispose-all in the kitchen, they all smelled like regret and goodbye. It was a house of drowsy women and hasty men who wished to be less hasty. There were few traffic noises. The twin peaks were a nice part of a nice city. Piero remembered his grandfather telling him about Genoa, another hilly city by the sea with obliging girls to console a man. Grandad was dead now, but Piero was still mostly alive. He had no particular hopes for the future, so he wasn't going to worry. He and happiness moved together through time, like a timid child on the carousel, comfortably seated in a car, enticed by the music, watching the painted horses rise and fall, wondering why he didn't climb on. Others were having fun. One day the ride would be over. It was already another goodbye—goodbye to tearful erection, grateful detumescence, whispered confidence about marital misunderstanding, confession of love of kiddies; goodbye. Piero performed all those old tricks, and yet he was a discreet, polite, and worthy client, for he never asked, *How did a nice girl like you*—?

His proper place was to brood and complain for himself. He

paid for the service. He offered a reasonable sum for what the girls gave—a partial, temporary equilibrium. Cordelia was fond of him. The girls respected him. It was a deal. They each took their share of the responsibility.

And soon, reconciled, he would head home to his wife, that sour magistrate.

"Come now," Cordelia said.

She invited him into the kitchen for a cup of rose hips tea before his valedictory screwing. He took the offer, chockful of Vitamin C, for the compliment it was. An honored guest might be given a drink or a pot of Lipton's in the parlor, but the atmosphere of formality would be preserved. Cordelia meant an opening of more than her fully-employed labia—of the frontiers of reserve which protected her integrity. For the same reason she wanted to go public with the demand for justice, she sought to unprotect herself. In the business of magic, she wanted to demystify. In the business of dispensing demystification, she made her domestic service magical once again. There was a fly circling under the light globe. There was an open can of Sunrise Clover Honey (now the fly found it). There were black smudges where porcelain had been scrubbed, and shiny places where formica was very recently wiped. The decorator who had done the rest of the House had not done the kitchen. It was a place for friends, for the crossing of boundaries. She would take the chance with Piero.

Cordelia celebrated by releasing a trade secret. "A whore's honor means," she said, "she acts the part of a lover. And the john, he shouldn't act as if he loves. But the john wants love, and the whore does, too. The trick is to become what she seems."

"You're a philosopher," Piero said, "it's too deep for me."

"I wake up early. Long afternoons. I'm learning to read."

"Is it fun?"

She grinned. "Better'n daytime television, man. Reading tells me I want to be better. Lovemaking tells it, too, but reading lasts longer. I can remember the book I read. I remember something in the book. I have a hook for my sadness when I think how people were sad in stories. Another hook for a hooker. I see I'm like something else."

"You're like nobody else," he said.

"I'm like lots of people. I wish Cindy were with me. I hate my mother. I don't know if I need a man, but I miss one. I get depressed when I think of so many things. I'm your typical whore with heart of lead."

"You have so many friends. I'm the type notices, Cordelia. That's another reason it's time to bend. I can't help it. It must be time to go home. My wife and I might as well. I'm getting jealous about you, Cordelia, just like a wife."

"Shush, baby."

"No. I got to tell you the truth. It's my only chance."

"Me?"

"I might get jealous, but I can still tell you the truth. I want you for my very own, sometimes. Especially when I'm all alone."

"I'm glad you said that."

"The sometimes?"

"No. The very own want you."

He sighed. She sighed. This is a child's primer about loving. To become jealous meant he was losing the very thing she could give him—ease, consolation, no jealousy. Another failure. A difficult trade she practiced. Now they might kiss, but didn't. It was rare to talk so much when a fellow is Piero. Yet now he talked. It was a moment he thought to remember, even if he wouldn't. It was a kind of turning for Piero. Today was to be a happy moment and it deserved a full quota of pre-nostalgia, even though it would soon be over and then lost forever. But exactly because he had already dreamed it into the past he needed to make it full and present this afternoon. It was only fair to the memories he would have. Such complications made Piero a little dizzy from incorrect breathing—mild hyperventilation. Being a Latin, he would be better off to breathe in the here and now.

"Being a Latin," Piero said, panting a little, "I don't always like being a Latin. I'd like to find some poise."

"What? Peace?" She was used to the idea from her old johns.
"Poise. Balance. Equilibrium."

"Librium I've heard of."

"I'd like to be in key, in synch. Look, when I make it with you, do I want to scream and kick? Make a big deal like the movies? No. I'd rather sigh, Cordelia."

"That's the truth."

"It's not bad. People think you have to yell a lot. You have to be a hero. Well, I like to feel soft and warm again. Maybe I liked that when I was a baby, too." There was an oldfashioned razor fire across his cheeks, a blush of rash. Confession. He felt the tight snapping, like a festive flag in the wind, of his heart in his chest. "That's all right. I don't have to be a man all the time, when only one person is looking."

"Me."

"My wife doesn't want to see that. She has some kind of idea she wants for a husband. Ah well. Let's cuddle now, Cordelia, I need some attention."

Cordelia knew how to use her time with Piero. She could cuddle in her sleep. Normally she paid close attention to the work, but sometimes she did better work if she just let her mind roll on. And this was what she decided to do while she cuddled Piero, a little meditation without emptying the mind.

The times change. That's true. My body changes. That's true. Men change. Even that is true. Love remains the same. That's an illusion. The juice flows, it dries, we wash it off, we bathe, it flows again. Nothing changes. I grow more clever as I grow older. But there's nothing to be done for it. I grow older. I sell a moment of privacy to end loneliness. I sell it on order, just like a wife. But I'm the secret night depository of loneliness. I give no interest; they say some wives give interest. They can't draw on their account with me. They can come back, I'll remember them with a friendly pat, a friendly lick, but nothing changes although everything is changing. They keep coming back because they think something must shift for the better in their hearts when they gasp and cry, and in mine. They think it doesn't. So they are sad, too. But it does.

And it doesn't help.

She woke up as Piero repeated the question he was asking her:

"Who was the best customer you ever had?"

It was easy to answer that one.

"A Jewish lawyer who married this really terrific rich girl from Atherton. She was slim, clever, a good quick fuck. They made it twice a week at night, plus Sunday morning if she was feeling friendly. But he also wanted something special which his wife couldn't give him. She didn't know how. A special, but easy. When he told her, 'I love you,' she used to answer, 'That's nice.' So it was my job to answer: '*I love you, too.*'"

"That was such a good job because it was easy?"

"No. Because I really wanted someone to love him."

She had thought about this many times. The answer flowed easily because it was frequent on her mind—not as frequent as Cindy, her daughter, but part of her brooding anyway. She would have liked to explain it to her lawyers, to the other girls. She told Cody once. He understood. She told me. I tried to understand.

Cordelia sighed.

"What's the matter?" Piero asked.

"The times are changing."

"I know. How?"

"I'm getting older. You're getting older. Nothing is as it used to be."

"Is that bad, Cordelia?"

"It's good for my business. It's what makes men come to the house. You get to do specials like that. But it makes me sad, anyway."

"I'm sad, too," he said.

Cordelia smiled. She knew her men. "I like you different from that lawyer, Piero. I could tell you apart in the dark."

"I suppose he's circumcised."

"Bitter, bitter. Yes, I suppose he is. But you have a kind of . . . sweetness, Piero. A kind of yearning."

"Doesn't he? the legal Hebal beagle?"

He was driving her to the wall. "Yes, sure, but a different kind of. Everybody's special."

"Oh, God."

They both knew it was very complicated. It was not just a matter of putting Cordelia (clitoral shaft, clitoral hood, clitoral glans, urethral opening, outer lips, inner lips, vaginal opening, hymen ring perineum, anus, reading from north to south) appropriately near Piero (urethral opening, head of penis or glans, foreskin, coronal ridge, shaft, raphé midline, scrotum, testicles, root of penis, perineum, anus), so that animal warmth, friction, and an electro-magnetic axis could generate a predictable convulsion. That was the fairly simple part of it. The vocabulary could be reinvented, corrections made in the seismographs. But the feelings had to be discovered anew, and Piero wanted to join the common ranks, the world of others, with something unique from Cordelia; and Cordelia wanted to give him what every man thought he had, and give it to him different, and give herself something no other whore ever had. And something every whore knows she has—the power to give.

Ah, difficult.

Satan, Cordelia had read once in a Hilton bible while she waited out a man who thought he should shower first, since he had had a hard day at the AMA convention, listening to hematology and socialized medicine discussions—Satan went to and fro in the world; he went up and down in it. And she put her finger in the book, closed it, and considered: Just like me. Only I go to and fro, up and down on men. She removed her finger.

She stood in a corner and adjusted the cowl she wore for occasional special jobs with Catholic doctors categorically opposed to abortion. When the doctor came out of his shower he just let his towel drop and fell to his knees.

"To and fro," Cordelia said, "up and down."

"You want *me* to do it?"

"No, no, I was just reading this Book here. You tell me what you want."

"I want to say your beads first, Sister."

"As the elevator says the floors, so shall ye say my beads."

The doctor looked stern. "Please, no kidding. Not on my money, Sister. This isn't your Medicare situation. It's my own funds."

Cordelia looked obedient and contrite. She told Piero about that doctor and she told him about others. She wanted him to know he was in the company of genuine human beings, melancholy brutes like himself, when he came with her.

"I get all kinds," she said. "I got this yoga hood runs the Cow Hollow Health Spa. He reduces women. Get rid of those unwanted dollars! A cobra."

"What you do for him?" Piero asked.

A mosquito drunk with rich San Francisco blood staggered onto Cordelia's wrist. She observed it compassionately. "I didn't know there were mosquitos around here. The salt air, I thought."

"You see them on Potrero Hill."

"News to me."

Compassionately she smeared it, and continued the recitation. "Man, that Zen gangster doesn't trouble himself to rip people off—he swallows them whole. Promising those women he can make them beautiful, man. That's evil."

"Judge not," said Piero.

"Listen. I'm not evil, but coveting thy neighbor's wife is *wrong*. Personally, I try to prevent that eventuality. I'm the lesser sin, Piero. So much lesser is not a sin, just a little appetite. If only Marietta could understand that. Nobody need know who doesn't want to tell, if you understand what I mean. Also, I take my own chances. I do the risky things myself. I eat cops. I make it with pro football players who tend to get a little cruel, or they're babies, and sometimes I think S & M is better than baby, it's cleaner. I yell at the landlord. I read a lot of paperbacks when I get the chance."

"You're gonna get evicted if you yell."

"I pay the rent. I do what's expected. I just run this little employment agency for out-of-work pricks. I give them compensation while they're waiting for a steady job. Oh, some of them only want temporary help. Some of them just want a husky hello. Poor Marietta. People like that Benito Renfrew who have to make it with Marietta or Calvina. You should be grateful, Piero."

"Why me?"

"Everybody should be grateful."

"You know I am."

"I have to deal with Marietta. I have to educate the public."

"Okay, thanks," he said. "But now I'm sad because I'm sorry, I can't see you anymore. I promised my wife. She's taking me back."

"Correct, and I'm happy for you. So we'll make love one more time. I believe that's the program for today."

"Let's," said Piero. "Let's, oh let's, let's, oh Cordelia, yes, please, one more time!"

"Shush. You want to be good for your wife? Calm, friend. Just one more time, but shush, quietly, okay?"

Piero blushed under the dark stubble. "Cordelia, you're right again. I promised I would never see you anymore, so a peaceful goodbye."

He was hoping somebody would find something to do about this.

She began to pull off his pants.

This is a sadness which has been little analyzed by social psychologists. Maybe there's no grant money available. The tristesse of the man who is closing down with the whore who consoled him as he stood absent from his spouse. Farewell, adieu, till we never meet again. A departure through uncharted seas, a heaving pain of chagrin in the lower regions. Fondness brings grief, too. Destiny and need make fondness unavoidable. Oh, even in California, even in a San Francisco brothel, even with Cordelia and Piero, feeling cannot be eliminated.

Cordelia made the decisions around here. She knew what to do about sadness.

Levis on sturdy fellows like Piero make people smile because they're so tight at the hips. Unzipped, tugged, it's comical. Cordelia was laughing. She was pulling his pants off goodbye. After today, he would just let himself grow fat.

13

I SAT WITH CORDELIA in the house on Yerba Buena Terrace, drinking Yerba Mate tea, which calms, stimulates, befriends sexual appetite, and puts the emotions in order. It does whatever she needs it to do. An honorary consul from a Central American country recommended Yerba Mate as a faithful associate, never inflicting the ups and downs of coffee, dope, or Luigi Mendoza. It encourages the kidneys, the ovaries, the prostate. I hoped it would help my concentration. I doubted it would help Cordelia's organizational tasks. Her big press conference for the Union was coming up next week. She was squeezing away at the fret in her heart. The sun poured through an amber plastic baffle skylight. High wicker creaked. We rocked and conversed. "If you rock in that chair it'll break, but go ahead and rock, they break on you anyway, they get brittle."

I took the hint and stopped rocking.

"I said rock," she said, "I'm sorry I interrupted myself."

"You were telling me about your family."

"I know what I was telling. Didn't interrupt anything but my train of thought. Cindy. My stupid mother. Train keep on a-rolling."

Whenever Cordelia heard from her mother in Seattle it was about her daughter who lived with her mother in Seattle, and this made Cordelia sad because she disliked her mother (dislike is not the best word for fear, hatred, scorn, spite, and in family, neither are those words the best), she loved her daughter (what is love?), and she missed her daddy. Missing her father was an act all by itself which hardly included the actual person, many years gone in the grave. But Cordelia knew what it was to long for him. It hurts. Today she was nervous beyond the competence of Yerba Mate.

"My father had good luck, like me. No medication when he died. He wouldn't take the medication for the pain. So he got to say a few last words."

I asked what they were.

Cordelia closed her eyes to remember her father in the same way she closed her eyes when she heard her mother and her daughter were coming to visit, but this shutting of the eyes meant something different. Remembering. Pain. Yerba Mate. This is not medication. She had read that some people closed their eyes, slept, felt other emotions besides grief for their fathers. Then she opened her eyes and smiled her horsy smile. "*Well, here I was.* He was just like me," she said. "I liked him, too." Forget Dad! "I wish I could see them separately, so I could bitch Mom and have fun with Cindy, but for that I'd have to keep Cindy with me."

"Why don't you?"

"Too selfish for that."

"She's not a baby anymore. She can take care of herself."

"Here? In a *house?* Reconsider the point, Al. I'm grateful because the old bitch takes care of my daughter. That old bag is good to her. I'm pretty sure, when I think about it, I'm personally very selfish. Um. Only doing what I want to do, which is all I can do."

"You're okay, Cordelia."

"I'm your run-of-the-mill modern woman, I do fear. But how I look at it is this way: living in a house wouldn't be too good for a sweet young thing like Cindy anyway, not till she reaches the age of consentation. And if she stayed in my little home away from home on Turk Street, that would be worse—"

What place on Turk Street?

"Never mind. Not everything is your business, Al. Anyway, I don't know why seeing her makes my stomach go sideways. I'm a woman who doesn't like her own mother, I'm afraid. But I think I'm missing something about my daughter which I wish I weren't. I don't know how to make it up to her."

"And to you?"

"And to me."

It was true. Cordelia's judgment was often correct—this helped make her a great whoremaster, master of herself. Sometimes she didn't know what to do with it. And sometimes her judgment was wrong, which is a trivial matter, because she worked her way through events anyway. Judgment was not crucial; it was crucial to get along with cops and lawyers, not to underestimate Marietta Kirwin. She found reality one way or the other, coming, going, topsy, turvy, her mane of hair shaking and that equine smile working across her muzzle. Confused pleasure and feeling also helped keep her in touch with others. I could imagine her picking up her father's last words forever, but I couldn't see her dealing with a fourteen-year-old girl's first guitar, the smelly body stockings left all over the room, the zitsy boyfriends, the girlish mopes. Oh, sympathy, and a lot of it, for the troubles of her staff in the house on Alpine Terrace. But for a growing daughter? Difficult for Cordelia. Her luck and judgment, and perhaps her good nature, too, stopped there.

I liked to think I knew about her. I was learning. I didn't know about her place on Turk Street and why she needed it. I didn't know what she was doing in the Tenderloin.

We stopped talking because the telephone was ringing. Cordelia counted the rings until the service picked up. Seven. She sighed. Another day and she would phone back, saying, Pick up at four goddammit, I told you to pick up at four, my callers get nervous.

She didn't want to talk about Luigi's warnings, Marietta's threats. She didn't want to talk about the press conference, the strike she had in mind. She didn't want to talk about yeast infections. She absolutely didn't want to talk about filling my emptiness. Cordelia's face had a rare look of undone, lines pulling against each other, teeth showing without smile or snarl, an edge to composure which was not composed. Her mother. Cindy. I was happy. She could fill my need of her by living out her sadness. She wanted to tell about her mother and her daughter because here they were.

The girl and Cordelia's mother were paying their visit just when the press conference for the Union was coming to a head. Her plans were ready and here was the goddamn mother, here was Cindy. She had so much in mind; she was inventing her life; and there they were, those reminders, those stone anchors. It seemed to bring back Cordelia's father's good fortune. "No medication. He got to say the last words."

"I bet that's hard for you."

"Naw, naw, he's dead a long spell now. My mother was actually his wife!" She smiled her horsy smile and said, for herself this time: "*Well, here I was.*"

"You're glad to see your daughter?"

"Cindy? Shit yes. But my mother, man, even on the phone when I hear that person, I think: why did he even stay around long enough to say where he was? He admitted to a location! He was persistent. He had a lot of sterling qualities for a man. I have sterling qualities, too, just like dad. I'm spiritually fulfilling sometimes. I always try to smell moist and sweet. But unlike dad, I have no scales on my eyes. I see my mom clear and true. I forget her telephone and social security, but I got her number. She takes care of Cindy good. She don't ask for much more money'n it takes. Course I support the old bag and my nice kid. She complains too much. I talk—*tawk* like—*lak* her when I think about her. Oh, I hate the bitch."

"That's a pretty common result in families."

She just bugged her eyes out. She wanted it to be self-explana-tory. It was *her* mother she was talking about. Now she was not talking about her very own *mother*.

"Oh," said the deep-thinking sociologist who didn't catch on quickly enough. I wished she had noticed my new haircut.

"You'll help me drive them from the airport? You don't have to wear a uniform. You can dress up like Friend. I'll give you some flesh anytime you say the word. I think you know the word. Al, I don't trust myself to drive when I haven't seen Cindy in so long."

•

Cordelia believed she was growing up. Usually when her mother announced a family visit, her first thought was: I'll think about that later. What were doormats for, if not to shove telegrams under? Later the thought could be thought about.

This time she promptly remembered, sorting it all out: I've missed that girl, oh good, she'll be here, oh lousy, I've got to see Mom too.

Cindy was Cordelia's daughter by the high school senior prom. Brucie Throwback might be the father, she believed, it could be, though Cindy was blond, like the other Brucie, What's-his-name, whom she would prefer to list in her memory book as father of her daughter. But she accepted the fact that it was probably Bruce T., the first kid of that festive springtime evening; Japanese paper lanterns hanging from the gymnasium ceiling, golden lights, smell of lilacs and tennis shoes; somehow a mother knows which stupid creep sires her first child. It was that dumb Brucie all right, and she still remembered the radiators hissing near the boiler room as they sneaked through the janitor's door, the ricky-tick of the band overhead, Brucie happy as an ape because he had finally gotten to be first in some line. Cordelia had only taken on a couple others that night, but it must have been the worst, her dumb luck, that Brucie, who had done Cindy the honor of becoming her father, riding one-handed with a bottle of Coors in the other. Cordelia never mentioned it to him.

The arrangement suited Cordelia's mom. As a lady with one of the best collections of mads in the Pacific Northwest, raising Cordelia's bastard daughter provided a rare opportunity, putting her well ahead of all those other angry victims of husbands, children, and menopause. Her friends owed her a lot of coffee and doughnuts, plus trips to the laundromat. Poor Mrs. Gilchrist, her daughter got herself knocked up and dumb thing *had* the kid and took off.... Say, she's in Frisco, ain't she?

Cordelia's mama just loved it.

For Mama's birthday Cordelia sent her a catalogue from Adult Eros Industries, including the full-length Super 8 mm. film, "Open Beaver," illustrated pages of Novelties, featuring VIBRATORS: Cordless Portable Marital Aids ("She'll blast into orbit with this one, $12.95"), Mr. Humanoid, the artificial doll, Johnny Stud, the *real* doll ("Life-size, erectable penis, built-in anus, complete with all essential male organs"), and jars and tubes of Vice Spice, Peter Power, Passion Plus, Emotion Lotion, and Finger Extensions "for sanitary sensuality."

Mama wrote back:

Thank you very much for the thoughtful gift. I am sure I will enjoy perusing it very much again and again, as it explains how you turned out as you did, and now I am taking the responsibility for your mistakes. Just wait till your birthday, Cordelia.

Mom

Cordelia said: "I respect her for that one. She's not always a total loss."

"You shouldn't have done it," I told her.

"For the woman who has everything, including my daughter."

"You shouldn't."

Cordelia looked at me with superior wonderment—probably the look the Bruces had earned during their boilerroom throbs at the high school prom. "Hey, before we drive out to pick them up, you want to make love. Al? We've never done that yet."

"I realize."

"You wanna?"

"Well, thanks."

"Right now? I'm nice and clean."

There is an argument according to which a frank offer by a clean lady should never be postponed. And it wasn't that I treasured my abstinence from Cordelia's favors as a mark of special distinction. And to be held in her strong arms appealed to some deep need for female strength. I was sure it would be tender, not wild; it would be sweet, friendly, and grateful for my long listening to her. Now she was appreciative of transportation, too. I wanted her more than she could imagine.

"No thanks," I said.

"Well, I didn't think you're the type."

"I'll drive you to the airport."

She laughed and laughed. "An assumption," she said. "You're always making assumptions. They're coming by bus."

"To the *bus* station?"

"You don't have to fuck me," Cordelia said, "even though I'm nervous waiting around for my really awful mother to bring my kid, but you do have to believe me when I tell you something about which I have accurate information and no reason to lie. It's at Seventh and Market. Greyhound, not tacky Trailways. Is that precise?"

"Check," I said.

I felt like the man on the Beefeater Gin bottle. At your service, sir or madam. All dressed in swollen red.

•

The kid was fifteen going on twenty-seven. Luigi Mendoza had a point about her. She stood tapping her foot at the door of the bus while a load of sailors, soldiers, blinking oldfolk tourists, and working gawkers pushed her to get off. This is Frisco, where the action is, and they wanted some right now. They wanted to pick up the baggage and find a shower. And this kid was surveying her new scene.

Cindy condescended to dismount. Her grandmother carried the shopping bags with the leftover sandwiches and the screen magazines, plus a copy of Foxylady as a house present for Cordelia. Cindy was turning pretty, with the temporary hardness of a child who has just discovered makeup, and you could see from the sailor helping Grandma that Cindy got what Cindy wanted. Cindy understood the needs of the all-volunteer armed services. The interstate highway is a menace when such kids are on the march. Afraid of airplanes was no excuse. Afraid of pursuing soldiers and sailors, Brucies, should have taken precedence, but didn't. She was a girl hero of fifteen, and the armed services felt in her presence a stringent need to be liked. While Grandma dozed, Cindy could have cemented a half-dozen Greyhound relationships.

The sailor had lost her attention. And Cindy was down below as the sailor realized there was no hope, he might as well proceed to his aircraft carrier. And on the poured concrete path, near the pellmell dumped baggage, the belly of the bus ripped open, the guardrails telling her where to go next, gazing at Cordelia, Cindy was blushing like a shy lover.

"Mother."

Cordelia put her arms around her daughter.

They were both crying.

The one who did all the work around here was left out; there is no justice in the world. The child's guardian and grandmother said, "What about me?"

Cordelia looked up, tears streaking through her nice clean worn whore's face. The tears were making muzzy tracks through the mascara on the nice clean fresh sexy child's face. It was an old child. These were two old children. I was moved, moved by them, by others, and I'm slow to give way to anything but California emotions; moved by myself. We were paying the price of leaving out family. Even in California, we still can't leave it out. The rest of us, the bus station, the smells of oil drip and dirt, of scheduled aimlessness on wheels, of popcorn and 25¢ TV chairs which had been slept in, of fried grease and people waiting till they got there, wherever *there* was, for the shower—Cordelia and Cindy were in an unfurnished place. Cordelia and Cindy Gilchrist were alone. With all the noise Cordelia makes, she is the person who stands silently at the edge of the bottomless pit, looking down and listening for the sounds of that essential part of herself which has broken off and is bouncing forever toward the astral center of the earth. Now I knew which part had broken off. It was her daughter.

The bottomless pit was a smoking, very quiet volcano.

And she had been standing there long ago, before anyone recognized her, when Cindy broke off, so it wasn't just Cindy and I didn't know what I thought I knew.

Her arms were around the bony, pretty, hard-faced child and they were both crying.

Grandma repeated: *"What about me?"*

"Hey, Al," said Cordelia, dabbing with a paper napkin from my pocket at her cheeks, "hey, do me a favor, will you? Will you hug my mother for me?"

"Hi, Mom," she said at last, since I wasn't hugging the old lady and it was incumbent on Cordelia to pay her back for housing and caring for the child.

It wasn't enough and Cordelia's mother said nothing.

"Hi, Mom," echoed Cindy.

"You making light of me?" Cordelia asked, "brat? Honey, I been looking for you."

The kid was chewing gum. "Then you knew where to find me," said the breath of spearmint which filled the non-silence, pinball, pay television chairs, announcements of departures for Modesto and Bakersfield.

"Honey."

"Hi, Mom."

And they stood there in the bus station, near a soft drink machine flashing like a Wurlitzer, kissing and hugging as if this were wartime (it was) and they were off to combat in vehicles with blackout-masked headlights. There was bellicose struggle and love in the air, along with motes of peanut and illegal indoor dogshit and a whiff of Inverness grass off somebody's backpack. They should be gentle with each other. A superfly dude, your basic black bus terminal stud, stood shaking his head at three weird generations of fay madness in action. Man, none of this shit made any sense to him, though he could sure use the teenie in several of his little dealies. And then he did a take—*why, that there is Cordelia!* He had locked thumbs with her at Malvina's Coffee House; everyone knows Cordelia; I should have recognized him, but he had given up his Afro for a Tomahawk and it changes the familiar contours of a head.

"Go away," said Cordelia to the Tomahawk, so he bopped off to try his luck meeting the Vallejo bus. Cordelia was busy judging Cindy and remembering what her soul had dreamed of at that age: money, love, secrecy, revenge, no pregnancy, and more than anything else, getting away from Ma. And now she was a Ma who had stuck her daughter with the Ma she got away from.

She felt pains and pins of longing, around the eyes and heart, a pinched nerve of nostalgia for what she never could be—wife, mother. Instead, she had this job, a leader of women, that's all; a mere great lady of San Francisco; Madame Cordelia. Cindy thrived without her, she supposed. Did that make the pains useless? No. Pains are painful anyway; they prickle.

Cordelia and Al could do things together. We could find remedies. I thought of a Mexican movie we saw one night at the Granada on Mission Street, Cordelia and Al at the movies, the Yankee spy tied to an antheap, honey spilled over him, and his screams, and fadeout, fadein, and the bones wiped clean, and the next morning the fat bandit licking his mustache and chortling.... "It tickles to be eaten by ants, don't it?" Cordelia had remarked in the dark.

Ah, what had Brucie done to her.

We must have stood for minutes near the parked bus.

I should have gone straight to unpark the car and load in the shopping bags Cordelia's mother traveled with. Unmanageable life made us manage the moment badly. Oh, it hurts me, too, and if there is anything I hate, it is to be hurt. What do we know about life, what do we know, what do we know. That's not a question. We have such trouble telling north from south, the sinister from the magical, desire from love, children from burden, hope from death, filth from fertility. Oh, but what do we know, my dearest?

I wish I could end this meeting. There are feelings spilling under the chassis, like the radiator in a ten-year-old Buick Roadmaster. The thing overheats, it won't work. It could be the distributor, sir, or the voltage indicator, or do you have any gas? Put it up on the rack. I know it wants to start. This model'll overflow on you sometimes. So there was Cindy yelling at her mother; and the mighty whorelady, the madam of San Francisco, stood abashed by a child who looked like any runaway in the Greyhound bus station. Only she was a run-toward, and it was her mother she was fleeing to.

"I want to stay with you, Mom!"

"We'll see about that."

"You always say that! It means *no*!"

"Let's have fun and talk about it later."

"If you don't say yes right now I'll throw up! I'll put my finger in my throat, I know how, I learned at school."

"So happy you're learning things at school."

"Ma!"

"I said later."

"Oh, Ma!" A wail from a child, the merest pale skinny child.

"Oh, Cindy."

But they were hugging each other. But there was no answer for these two.

III

14

ESPECIALLY PLANTED BY CORDELIA, who liked to make vegetable puns, pussywillows were swaying on the little patch of city earth in front of San Francisco and world headquarters of WOO, the official, unaffiliated, and non-accredited union of American working whores, in a Victorian house on Ellis Street in the Tenderloin district, which is near the traditional center of the relevant labor force. The house glowed in patriotic colors, red trim, white board, blue shutters, with little additional mounds of pulverized bicentennial gray at the foundations, where the termites continued a ceaseless labor of making their own cellulose pun on the nature of man's fate. I watched Cordelia come out in the early evening to pack fresh loam near the roots of her pussywillows, embattled in sour soil, abused by welfare spitters and dogs. She stood there, Tenderloin farmer, thinking calm thoughts, bucket and trowel in her hands, nostrils flaring for a scent of baked downtown garden at the end of the day. This too was important. Not enough of the green and feathery, of silky catkins, in her life. Dust, dust, dust be our destiny. She liked ferns a bit less— that oily green. Sometimes ferns made her angry. She knew they were what others liked.

"Hi, Cordelia."

She went inside to prepare for her press conference. She nodded at me without speaking. It was better not to interrupt her thoughts. When she gardened, better not to speak. When she prepared for her public, better let her do the speaking.

Evening; night. She had given her mother and Cindy money and told them to have fun someplace. Maybe she had sent them back to Seattle. She didn't want me hanging about, either. I drove across the Bay Bridge to Berkeley and prepared a class, poorly. I listened to KSAN and its Paul Harvey of the Left, a nasal assault on multinational corporations and top-forty radio. I was nervous for Cordelia. What would he and the others do with Cordelia's plan? She was convinced that women and the world needed the hookers' union. Luigi was certain Marietta and her clan would be attracted like steel filings to the electromagnetic field of a press conference. Marietta thought she could be elected mayor by standing up for another sort of woman, and surely there were more of her.

I slept as I had listened to KSAN and prepared my class— fretted by fears.

And now it was morning and the pussywillows had enjoyed a night of good loam and Cordelia had taken her rest and retreat.

Up the steps of the house on Ellis trudged the carriers of teevee cameras, the toters of pads and pencils, the bearers of refreshments. Once this was a dwelling, and a part of it remained a crash pad for women in refuge from evil employers, hyperkinetic pimps with razors and carbolic acid and hats too large for their heads, but mostly it served the serious business of organizing the lady toilers. The stairs creaked under back and forth trudging. The door was propped open by an old Zenith radio on which had been written: PLEASE SHUT THE DOOR.

At the curb, in a red no-parking zone, a black Cadillac with tinted windows stopped. The driver, an elderly man, switched off the motor. The two women inside, with their red-haired male companion, waited for the press to gather. They were often early for appointments.

Inside the building, in the front office, volunteers were doing their best on a row of surplus Army typewriters beneath a poster asking the question, MEN'S VASECTOMY CLINICS—WHY NOT WOMEN'S? There was an enlarged Christmas card depicting Cordelia in her nun's habit, kissing a priest, their tongues fluttering together; cork boards with various notices and souvenirs, including a letter to Cordelia from the President's wife: "I appreciate any and all patriotic communications from concerned citizens...", straw bags filled with beauty aids, beanbag chairs, a popcorn machine, a rope ladder leading to a balcony from which sounds of kissing could be heard, cuddly animals.... Several of the typists were white. "You like my bear to sleep with?" a typist with her hair in a suburban fifties blond flip asked me. She brought it to work every day and she noticed I was looking for something. I wasn't tired and did not accept the offer. I smelled good coffee brewing someplace.

An electric trout stream on a treadmill, bearing its rippling green burden which was not real water, ripped off from some tavern by an acquisitive electronic whore, had been reconnected and advertised, in deep neon pastels, Olympia Beer. ("It's the Plastic.") There were Chinese paper tigers, bumped and worn after the Year of the Tiger, and a Mexican bread sculpture of Mary Magdalene, out of which someone had taken a bite. There were women in flowered hats. A slim girl who looked like a crisp horsewoman—steeplechase, I. Magnin—put her phone down and called out, "Hey! Anybody want to make an ultra-core film? Need some people down the street in ten minutes."

A girl stopped typing, picked up her straw bag and asked, "What's the address? Shit, I know the outfit. Okay, okay. I'll be back at six and finish the mailing."

"What's ultra-core?" I asked her.

"They don't just flash on fucking," she said. "It's *ultra* core."

She had stuck the teddybear on top of the other wiggling loose things in her straw bag.

Cordelia, student of behavior, organizer of the Union temporarily called WOO, was just like folks, she still sought her reality. Being a whore and madam was real, but not really real. Being a celebrity was a little better. And where does a celebrity find reality? In a press conference. And where does the press find reality? In celebrities. And where would Marietta Kirwin also find reality? There, along with those other folks.

Thus, obeying a fine symmetry, we found ourselves passing through the small stand of pussywillows to gather one morning at ten, in time to make the late afternoon news, in the crowded offices of WOO. The staff was busy typing through flow charts, filling In and Out boxes, spreading information about the current virulence levels of gonorrhea, explanations for the absence of credit card availability for servicing businessmen unless it could be prescribed as Medical Massage—still another proof of how the Mafia controls the AMA and the massage parlor business. There was much to do. Cordelia had put cardamom in the coffee, and a spicy tang filled the air. The cardamom smelled like cinnamon with wings, like chocolate with many articulated insect legs, and the steaming, thrumming urn sent it clean into the room. Good for nose, good for sinus, good for temperament. Joe Kearney, the Examiner's expert on subversion, student rebellion, and the counterculture, wrote in his notebook: "Patchouli."

Two smiling, slender men were going over some accounts. They were just helping out. One of them, FitzHugh Gross, was both a lawyer and a C.P.A., plus a voyeur. He was very successful in his three major fields of endeavor. He also had a small piece of an organic cosmetics factory (silent partner). He knew that we've come a long way in America, but perversion still sets a man up for extra expense. He was ready for blackmail with Swiss mad money. The other male volunteer, Jeremy Jensen IV, a gentle bank officer and attorney, was your normal insatiable idealist about Oriental girls. He was FitzHugh's equal in accounting, taxation, limited partnerships, nonprofit corporations, and hopeless nostalgia for the perfect oceanic and unearthly soaring unified field sexual congress.

Cordelia, sitting on a desk in her busy nest, murmured to me, smiling, "Hi. This is proof positive, isn't it?"

There came the dainty half-heel footsteps of Marietta. The candidate dangled between plump Benito in his sunglasses and round little blue blazer—shirt tussling with belt—and neat, concise, murderous Calvina, who would be Minister of Information of the Sovereign State of San Francisco if Marietta led a revolution of the Richmond and Sunset districts, firing the banana plantations and silver mines. Some must burn when Justice raises her steel scales to strike the forehead of Corruption. Hi there, Cordelia, we'll crush you.

Cordelia had checked things out with Luigi Mendoza's office. Her lawyers said: Fulfill yourself if you have to, follow your star, we'll defend you to the limit, just be sure to put up the retainer. We follow our star, too. Courtesy cashflow here should be fifty dollars per lawyer hour minimum.

Passion asks to be hassled. Luigi's office overhead made Luigi impatient with Cordelia. Cordelia touched my arm and smiled her huge horse smile at Marietta's little cluster.

"I'm here for the Chronicle," said Calvina Muir.

"Do come in. I'm not throwing you out. You can fly around like Peter Pan, never touch the floor," said Cordelia.

She had expected Calvina. Benito also had credentials. Marietta had none; she wasn't press; she was just there. Good. Cordelia was sure it was okay.

Leopold, dozing, waited outside in the black automobile. He liked this retirement job—lots of excitement, plus occasional moments of honest repose.

Probably it was the baby blue collar of Calvina's white blouse that reminded Cordelia of Peter Pan.

"They came out," Cordelia was saying. "My associates in the media are beginning to see the issues. I'll fill them in."

"Not too much philosophy, my friend, as I understand them."

"They're here. They want to learn."

"Every single one of your visitors is wearing a watch, Cordelia. Please better begin."

"Ah!" she said. It was a little bark of comprehension. She clapped her hands. "Fellow persons!" she cried. "I notice you are all wearing watches. Perhaps we had better end the foreplay!"

Good woman. A graceful way to flatter me so I would hardly notice the glow of pride and warmth in my chest, just a little fine feeling for advice taken, nothing serious.

"You will follow me, please, from these offices to the grand ballroom, where wine will be served."

The men and women of the media trooped through a corridor into what had once been a ballroom, just after the earthquake on Ellis Street, and was now a conference room when it wasn't a ballroom again. The New York Times, West Coast editor, was there, suffering exile (well, it beats Toronto). A Chronicle feature writer, hearty and pink-cheeked, was there in his racetrack-checked leisure suit; he had covered Offbeat Frisco for twenty-two years now, and the pink of enjoyment remained fixed to his cheeks like a decal while his eyes went a little sad. He had never fully resolved a gnawing doubt in his mind: *Is this a Harvard man's work?* The electronic teams from radio and teevee struggled with their equipment, but their pains were worth it to Cordelia, who loved equipment and the good things equipment can do for a girl. Counterculture and subculture filled in the gaps between major media. The Bay Guardian's maleperson, serioso, asked no one in particular as the electronics set themselves up, "Looks to me like the sex business is getting reconnected with the ripoff culture" (he was thinking through to a politically-aware lead); an aware himbeing, he was on the watch for a Mafia-Bell Telephone-Drug Company-Sexist-CIA-Hearst conspiracy. The three-woman committee news team from Nouveau Lesbos, a monthly review, stood ready to check on each other for doctrinal error. There was also a pale young man from Heliotrope ("I'm covering the Growth Movement—it's credit for my Project at Lowell High, so I don't have to take the final in Civics"), and Sam Silver, bearded and stout, with peeling prewar Leica: "I am shooting for Jewish Observer. I observe."

Benito and Calvina made a walking Wonder Bread sandwich, with Marietta the tunafish in between.

Lester Jones peeked through the door, the only bisexual brown bartender and goldminer the natives trust—particularly popular this year among Eskimos, in his opinion. Someday they would show him the gold-mining areas near abandoned Hemstein Camp, a thousand howling miles due northeast of Fairbanks, as the snowgoose flies. He had the pans and sluices ready, and 6-12 Lotion for the mosquitos, and credit with a polymorphously perverse bush pilot, and could rent at Avis whatever else he required to get rich. He came here today, before going on duty at the Feroce Bar, to show solidarity with Cordelia. He made a Raza clenched-fist salute which is also appropriate to Eskimo get-togethers in the igloo. "Hi there, Cordelia! Solidarity, you hunky chunky honey!"

Avigdor Malchik strove to be unobtrusive. He happened to be back in town for reasons as yet unknown. Allegedly he was covering this event for Tass; his goldrimmed glasses sparkled, as did the flecks of dried saliva in the corners of his mouth. He moved away from Sam Silver, and shot him rapidfire Third World hate looks. When he changed corners, his two tails also changed corners, a middleaged FBI man in a porkpie hat, with press credentials from the Aggie, the school newspaper of the University of California at Davis, and, in the blue uniform, a two-hundred pound Postal Telegraph delivery boy who spoke only Russian, plus a little German and Ukrainian.

Cordelia speaks!

Cordelia rapped sharply with her pink toy dildo, or maybe it was a real one, stamped from genuine Avid-Pink rubber, on the Goodwill breakfast room table which served as a podium. "First, let's get this whole deal straight. I don't sell my body to anyone, never did. I rent it." She showed her porcelain caps, she grinned shamelessly—no gum anxiety—she also showed her business vocabulary. "Not even on a leaseback arrangement. I'm against any such thing. Anyone thinks I sell my body can't buy from me. I'll go down the line on that. What we do is high volume retail work."

She paused after each sentence to make sure it was properly recorded. She knew that logical order was not her task. The Chronicle needed a punchy remark or two, and so did television. Everyone in the world requires ambiance; she would give them some. She was now in the business of feeding lines, not constructing an argument or telling a story. Perhaps she saw a media advisor when she wasn't seeing me, some cunning dude like Sam Bowers, who knew the record business, how to promote singles in such a way that the longplay would get the business, too. Bowers made me jittery. He seemed to know what he was doing, like Cordelia. She was providing the basic silly-putty for a five-minute segment or a news section feature. She round-eyed the room to confide an item of her credo: "I told the Chief of Police the other day, *Chief!* I said. We're into the same field. I want to make the streets safe for walking."

Laughter. That was good for a thirty second spot on national television. Along the way, she might construct her argument for herself, for those she loved, for those she sought to love, tell her true life for Cindy and history as she invented it. She too required a context. She discovered reality by making it up. She would see how it all came out.

"Of course, my house is *everybody's* castle. There's minimum security. It's a place of peace, not vice or crime or noisy ruction —oh, maybe a noisy erection now and then. The police feel differently about their headquarters. Heck, they need heavy artillery to protect the district stations. Every passing kid wants to grow up to be an urban guerrilla. Their parents teach them to shoot up the establishment in the morning on their way to pick up their food stamps...."

Someone was tapping a pencil on a notebook. Benito was humming softly, cranking himself up. I felt my mouth twitching. I was embarrassed for Cordelia, not when she did dirty things to a whole basketball team, but now, when she tried to entertain these journalists. Her canned jokes weren't working and Cordelia knew it; they were unworthy of her; and so she fell back on depth, which often works. She reserved her sincerity for emergencies. She used it as she used the secretions of her body, summoning them against invasion by foreign objects. Her sense of privacy was different from mine. Nevertheless, she knew what privacy is. Like a miser, she saved and saved her own soul. She could receive into her body the avid projectiles of greater San Francisco, including Sausalito and Daly City, and still remain secure behind her own strict needs.

Cordelia took a breath and said: "Get away from the normal miseries into the abnormal pleasures, so you can return to the miseries of everyday life and make them seem restful after your joyment—that's the long version of my task. The short one? Get stoned, get drawn out socially, and no diseases or hacking coughs. I lead my girls in exercises to strengthen the diddle muscles, I teach them the uterine pack, I take books out of the library and buy worthwhile paperbacks, I don't neglect Vitamin C, either. Your average whore, batching it out on the street, does none of this. Constantly she is fighting a runny nose. But in Union they will learn to do all."

"You have a welfare program?" Joe Kearney asked.

"I prefer to call it educational. With good grooming plus care of the mind, the lowliest streetwalker can aspire to callgirl, to mistress, to favored hostess of a Chinese owner of a chain of discount stores—this is an actual case from our files. Naturally, most of our work is still classified. The Chink is dead, so it can be released to the public."

One of the team from Nouveau Lesbos whispered, "She's so smart and never gauche," which the teamplayer pronounced *gauchay*. "I love her jive, man, even if she makes it with the pigs."

Joe Kearney, the veteran Anti-Communist and Student Protest Editor of the San Francisco Examiner, said, "Hey, Cordelia, you got us here to tell about the Prossies' Union. But you're still talking about streetwalking."

"The thigh bone is connected to the hip bone, Fred."

"Yuh."

"But I'm glad you asked that question. Someday, I suppose soon, the whole game will be charted in computers. I can look at myself with a speculum, and that's where love is, and the color and shape and neurons and protons and whatons and hardons will be predictable. They'll trace it everywhere. I can be programmed, you can be programmed. We could be on dry punchcards. Tape. Little bits of wire. Know what, Fred? When that day comes, I'll still know I'm really me, the lady hustler Cordelia."

Amazingly, the anti-communist was writing it down. Maybe he would offer it to the Science Editor.

"Any other questions from you boys?" she asked.

Marietta was folded like a poison flower between Calvina and Benito. In hatred and spite, she too was sincere; in the desire to kill, she was pure. She also needed an election gimmick.

"Pavlov invent science of operant conditioning," Avigdor Malchik whispered to me. "However, is neat groovy gimmick. Tell please, how to spell spec-u-lum and what is?"

"S-p-e-c-u-l-a-t-e," I said. "It's a way of looking inside."

Cordelia rapped sharply with her pink good luck charm. "Please, if there are points to be made, let us all share." Avigdor looked ashamed. Cordelia winked at him. "Well, I have another point to share. I work with men in trouble, too, husbands—husbands of wives, fathers of kids, men like that. Even some visitors to our wonderful country from faraway places. Denver. Beverly Hills." Another wink for Avigdor, which he intercepted before it ricocheted off him and was trapped in the pudgy hands of the Postal Telegraph messenger. "I've heard it said the first six months of a marriage are the most difficult. That's not true. It's the last six months."

"Would you repeat that, Cordelia?" said the man from KRON-TV. "Lemme make sure I got the audio clear."

"I'm hip. Okay, ready?" She touched the flower on her hat in a little salute. "In my house the girls are all clean, guaranteed dainty, everything shines and nothing drips. The doctor comes on Monday, four times a month. My girls never give the gift that goes on giving."

"Hey, Cordelia, you didn't repeat that."

She shook her head. She repeated enough in life; she liked to show independence; she was sure the audio was okay the first time; she hated to repeat anything but those crucial physical acts of which the soul needed regular reminiscence. She held up a finger: *Wait.* She slipped behind a screen and reappeared in her nun's habit. It was a familiar trademark. She adjusted the cowl. She smiled demurely in its shadow. Suddenly her lashes looked longer. She was at peace in the non-silence of explication. "Folks, I sincerely thank you. Thank you for coming, as the john said to the hooker. I now take up the main burden of my message, in a form which teevee can splice and use according to your needs. Notice, please. You see, of course, that I am already somewhat ugly and, any day now, will soon be old. This is the fate of hookers and others alike. Nevertheless, there is an answer to old and ugly. I am a woman, I am strong, I am here. Negativity remains far from my thoughts. And furthermore, because of me, *you* are here, friends. And that makes me happier than wise, lovelier than beautiful. I make no other claim for myself. You can find beautiful women out on the street, you can find clever ones, too, in the highways and byways, you can even find good women. But to make things move, people move, what Cordelia does is to make things happen, my fellow persons!"

A spatter of applause. Avigdor and I helped. None from Marietta, Benito, and Calvina. Cordelia turned from side to side, swaying in the black and white costume, giving each camera a full front shot. She saw this as a segment. Avigdor was whispering to one of the persons from Nouveau Lesbos, discovering that Speculate and Speculum are not the same. I had lied to a man who came back for another go at Détente. From across the room he sent straight into my face the ocular version of halitosis, deep and penetrating. He would write me down as Bourgeois Wrecker.

Now Cordelia thought she might do something further for Educational Television, for Cable, for the countercultural media, and even if the networks couldn't use it, they might like to talk about it. She was feeling herself inside the habit. She was looking for something, buttons, zippers, snaps, or catches; probably no zippers in there where it was warm.

"I do my work and I am just smart enough for what I want to do. There is no excess. My brain is trimmed down to fighting size. I am performing my appointed task and I know what it means. Tell me, if you can, what more I should know. Tell me, if you can, what more I should do. Tell me if you know something, friends. I'm famous, but I'm not proud. Shine a light on me. Take my picture. Notice the stretchmarks, but the muscle tone is good, pectoral tension, Pap test okay, cleanliness squeaky-clean—"

She was naked. The nun's costume dropped in a black and white cascade to the floor. That was no nun, that equine figure with overtanned shoulders, mane of healthy hair, smilelines, muscular puffed mound of Venus, buttocks for gripping and riding hard. "Sisters!" The teevee lights remained on, the cameras strapped to the shoulders of stocky bearded young men in short-sleeved shirts with vents at the sleeves. This would not be shown on the Six O'Clock News, but it could be used somehow. The Postal Delivery messenger was blushing. He had been chosen for KGB work because he was made of stern stuff, but this went too far for even a tri-lingual (Russian, Ukrainian, a little German) security person. The FBI man, a sophisticated graduate of John Carroll University, didn't flinch; he only bit off the rest of his cuticles. There was nothing in his training to prepare him for a bare-assed nun delivering a lecture on love with a lot of big words and subordinate clauses.

"Sisters! Fellow brothers! I'm fit. There's not an ounce of waste on me. As my brain, so my body. A little fat here and there, but it's not really fat, it just looks that way. It's for warmth and comfort." She looked deep into the eye of the KRON camera. "Enough?"

And now she was consecrating herself again. She picked up the habit and inserted herself with a horsy wiggle of adjustment. She was a woman bound by solemn vows. "I'll take questions from the floor, but first, I've got to tell you about the Hookers' Ball."

"Just a moment, please!" It was a hoarse croak from Benito Renfrew, and his face was mottled and red, and he was crying with the jagged griefs of his outrage: "I don't care what you do with yourself! What about those movies you show?"

Cordelia was puzzled. "Well, once or twice I entertain the people with loops sometimes. Whatever gets a person off is nice."

"Snuff movies! I hear you showed a snuff movie!" Benito shouted. "I saw one myself!" Calvina was touching his arm consolingly. Marietta seemed to be dreaming, her mind in Brazil or Ghana or elsewhere. "First they did it and then the girl got killed right after she, she, they—for real—they cut her throat—I think it came from Brazil—the poor child didn't even—"

Cordelia moved forward swiftly and, as she touched Benito's arm, both Calvina's hand and Benito's arm leapt away. Cordelia ignored the refusal of consolation. "Shush, shush," she said softly. "I never showed such a movie." She looked into his eyes and said, "Whoever told you that . . . you saw it elsewhere." Benito turned to Marietta. Cordelia said: "Which is not a threat. What I mean, Benny, is *no*. What I mean, Benny, is fight fair, okay?"

"May I say something, please?" Marietta called. She had come to life and she was rapping the class to order. She had not been dreaming; she had been preparing. Benito fell back, his eyes filled with a pale liquid of impassioned exhaustion. He was veiled, and it was impossible to see inside. The interior lights had been burned out. Cordelia turned her back on him. By her silence, moved by Benito's rage and passion, she gave permission to listen to Marietta. "Sexual exploitation," stated Marietta quietly at first, "sexism, sexual exhibitionism, sex, sex, sex, selling bodies for money and the degradation of Our City! I'm not a prude. All of you here know me. I do not represent downtown interests, except the constructive ones. I am open to new experience. I have been married twice, I admit it!"

"I've never been married, I admit it," Cordelia said. "I could be married in white."

Marietta went from quiet calm explanation, with the subterranean force of an express subway, to a sob of fury: "You see what this woman does? She mocks innocence." Benito, recovered, whispered something to her. "She mocks and degrades all the lovers,"—Benito still whispering, Marietta nodding: "—their arms round the griefs of the ages, as Brendan Behan—" Whisper, whisper. "As Dylan Thomas wrote. I am not against joy and tenderness. I am opposed to their materialization, the commercial imitation of love." She turned her earnest, pretty, doll's face to the red lights of a camera. "Should we sell?" she asked it, "should we sell, should we encourage our daughters to sell what was given freely by nature for pleasure, in the bonds of friendship and affection? That's a very simple question which I ask the people of the City and County of San Francisco. That's all I ask."

Cordelia seemed to be enjoying meeting another woman of feeling, and she said enthusiastically, "Not everyone can find those bonds of affection, dear. Some can't find the bondage. Are they to be left out in the cold, Marietta?"

"And I answer," said Marietta, giving her passion to a different camera this time, "that the people of the City and County of San Francisco cannot and will not permit this fraud and farce to be continued. If elected in the coming scrutiny of the voters, I propose to instruct the new Chief of Police, the City Attorney, the Sheriff—" Whisper, whisper, this time from Calvina. "—in accordance with the advisory powers of the Mayor, to enforce the existing laws, and if necessary, with a cooperative and responsible Board of Supervisors, to pass supplementary legislation which will protect not only business, the convention and tourist businesses which are one of the glories of this City—two—but also the very peace and tranquillity of those who make San Francisco their home, their schools, where families of all cultures and persuasions—" Whisper, whisper, agitated whispers from both Calvina and Benito. "More I shall say when the proper time comes."

The proper time to depart had come. Marietta's little group departed.

Cordelia turned to watch the dainty footsteps of the candidate for mayor. "And now," she said calmly, "while we are all waiting, I must tell you about the Hookers' Ball."

What the world really needed was a dance sponsored on Halloween by the Union. To organize an illegal activity, such as prostitution, is not legal, but to have a party sponsored by the illegal union might make fun, money, and conversions to the cause. Cordelia's lawyers thought a little special account would be an excellent idea. The ballroom would be open to all hookers—black, white, gay, Nazi, semi-professional, transsexual, without proof required. A five-dollar admission charge was a way to make sure that only serious people applied. Those who might perchance happen not to be whores or whoremasters could also buy their way in. It was for the cause. Sparechangers could sparechange their way in by hustling tourists and softhearted pimps. Cordelia said: "The Hyatt Regency, Grand Ballroom, October thirty-first, eight o'clock, see you all, won't I? Optional dress required."

If you have trouble making a revolution, a union, or a political party, make a coffeehouse: this was the lesson of the Sixties. For the Seventies, Cordelia believed in throwing a dance, free to everyone who could pay five dollars. I thought I heard the gentle purr of the Cadillac's motor.

"There's a depression," said the man from the Bay Guardian.

"Everybody can," she said, "and if they can't—" She shrugged. "Somebody else can. Some good friend. We'll call it 'Who's Woo,' where all the really vital people meet to spend Halloween."

"*All?*" inquired the finicky Maoist from the Bay Guardian.

"Well, the Cockettes and the Angels of Light have their own thing. You know how it is, that ancient festival when they wear their voodoo flash. Some of them will honor us. And maybe the Mayor and the President won't come, but we'll send invitations. Five dollars for them, Marietta too, and my dear good friend the sheriff and everybody. We're not fucking around. There will be special tickets for bona-fide charity cases. . . . And now, will you please pick up your press kits as you file neatly out so we can get back to work around here? It gives full details, and just one last thing"—she smiled, she smiled, Cordelia smiled—"I'd like to emphasize, may I see you all there on the appointed day?"

Spontaneous applause by the three-person team from Nouveau Lesbos. Avigdor Malchik helped, putting his pen in his mouth like a bit as he stood as tall as short could stand. He clapped, indignantly staring at the non-clappers. The FBI corresponent from the Aggie and the Postal Telegraph KGB husky moved their flippers symbolically. The electronics unplugged; the newspaper reporters were already out. Leopold Kirwin and his cargo had gone. Cordelia, active celebrity for another few seconds, stood smiling over the dwindling attendance. She was still an amateur. She had not yet learned the secret of quick departure. I watched the happy glitter in her eyes. Now it was gone. The smile remained.

FitzHugh Gross said to her, "Good job, kid. You'll get lots of exposure. That woman's crazy."

Jeremy Jensen IV, waiting in the doorway, also contributed what the performer needs after the performance: "Nice. An almost Japanese elegance about it, Cordelia. It was very nice. They won't use Marietta."

Was she confident of victory in the self-display field? Was she just jazzing the empty air? Did she prove something? Did she hope to get rich? Win through for the whores of the world, just as she said? (Yes, my thesis will credit her good motives in the cause of lost women.) And was she also another person who needed attention and praise, who needed to touch others, greedy for true love as she swung her purse down the slopes of Twin Peaks, North Beach, and the Tenderloin?

Well, perhaps I should just stick to the facts.

"Avigdor," I asked, "how did you—?"

"I am not Avigdor. I am now Victor."

"Did Cordelia know you're back?"

"What she knew, I do not know. As U. S. of A. expert in filth field, I am here on mission for my papers."

"Thanks for the information."

"I am in profession of truth. You will tell Mrs. Celtic I hope to gain interview shortly." His Postal Telegraph escort had moved toward his elbow. He handed Avigdor a glass of water and a blue wafer. "And now, I file my report. I take my capsule. I go."

His FBI and KGB détente advisors went with him. I was alone with the spirit of Cordelia.

And I remembered what she told to me many years ago, on a Sunday evening at the Coffee Gallery on Upper Grant, when she was just a new young whore on the street and I was a kid gathering my thoughts about robbing a bank and I said, "Business bad? Buy you a coffee," and we sat in silence over glasses of half-coffee, half-milk, grateful for the rush of caffeine and sugar on a foggy, chilly, sad, long North Beach evening, feeling good fellow-ship, a shared regret for psychopathy, a shared regret for the dangers we were both running in living with our isolated bad characters, our satisfaction in twitches, our ability to forget the past and ignore the future; and we looked out over a path once trodden by goats and goldminers, and then paved over for sailors and salesmen, Portuguese fishermen in their cottages and Italians in wooden tenements, a hillside now devoted to street people, flower children, and tourists; a light rain was falling inside the fog, a drizzle in a sack, one of those San Francisco miracles of mete-orology; and she said:

I offer a stranger my hand. He wants to take it, but he's scared. He dives for my hairy latitudes. So instead of giving him my hand, I take his money. He goes away thinking he's had a good deal. And he has. He hasn't taken the chance he would take in taking my hand.

She was running other risks with Marietta Kirwin.

15

BACK FROM HER PRESS CONFERENCE, Cordelia found a visitor waiting for her. I had driven her home to Twin Peaks, listening to the
slow deceleration of media thrills, the thrumming down of a
revved-up motor. Almost any other time would have been a better
time for this visitor.

"Don't you want to come in?" Cordelia asked me at the door,
very politely, not meaning it. She had not yet seen what waited
for her.

"I've got to type up some notes."

I turned to go, I was into first, I was going, when Cordelia ran
out the door. "Al! Come back!"

I left the car, wheels turned out, a yard or two from the curb,
and ran up the walk again. "Al, help me," she was saying in a pale
hushed exhaustion.

If it had been rape or murder, violent crime, police crackdown,
berserk berserkers, she would have been cool and precise. It was a
gum-chewing and angry child, feet on the furniture, straw bags
overflowing. Cindy was back. She had run away from home.

"Can't run away from home to come here," Cindy explained

with teenage logic, lovely arrogant soft lips. "This is my mother, this is my mother's house, see? So this is my home."

"Why didn't you let me know?"

"So I ran away *to* my home, Ma."

"You didn't let me know."

"Now wouldn't that be stupid, I mean really *stoo*-pid, Ma? If I'd of said, Ma, I wanna come stay with you, I can't stand that old dishmop, you'd of said blah-blah-blah, wouldn't you?"

"Blah-blah-blah," said Cordelia. "Sounds just like me."

Cindy was wearing boots and a cartridge belt and a whole lot of black Maoist shit, and she had her hip flung to one side, and she smelled of Patchouli—she was wearing ten-years-gone nostalgia drag. However, she wasn't here just to model for period photography. "Mrs. Kirwin called Gram up home. She also wanted to gas off with me."

"Did you?"

"Not zackly."

"About me?"

"Not zackly."

Cordelia asked me please to stop all that fidgeting. There was nothing to fidget about. Yes there was. "Where'd you get them vinyl boots?" she asked.

"Leather," Cindy said.

"Man, lots of people be fooled by you. Think you're fifteen and a half and you're only a ruffian of fifteen. Someone call you up longdistance, day rates, and you think you're a big person, wear leathers, got lots to impart. Come off it, will you, child?"

"Very good. Okay. I'm going now," I said.

"Wait!" said Cordelia. "Because she's a funny broad, someday she'll be—"

"*Broad*," Cindy repeated with wonderment at the ancient languages her mother spoke.

"Because I laugh at her don't mean everything is all okay settled. It ain't."

Black Barbara poked her head in, poked it out again. I heard the neat scurry up the stairs, like a chased cat. She was whispering to another girl, maybe Rose Ann, how really, really, really glad she was that Cordelia finally got home from her media hustle to handle this dumb thing. Rose Ann was whispering back, probably, yes. And then suggesting, if I knew Rose Ann, they take a bubble bath together so as not to waste the bubbles. Ecologically the bubble bath salts are bad for the water drainage systems. So two friendly persons should always seek to use them together.

Cindy was sitting there chewing her gum at her mother, her feet on her straw bags, her boots pointing, her cartridge belt undone, her mascara smeared, her eyes like those of Black Barbara, darting, shrewd, alert, ferocious. Cordelia shuddered. She didn't want her in the house. No use pretending Cindy thought it was a boardinghouse for lonely Dial-a-Secretaries. But she didn't want, couldn't have, needed her away from here. *Out* she wanted her.

"Tell you what," Cordelia began.

"I'll listen," Cindy said, drawling, "if it's what I want to hear." She covered her ears with her mitts, parting a couple of fingers to leave room for something to which she might pay attention.

"How the heck do you know—?"

"Cause when you say, *Tell you what*." And Cindy dramatically closed the aperture between fingers. But she could lipread. She could hear what was said and what was not said.

Cordelia decided to stall for an opening. "I'm talking to Al now. You don't have to lock up on me. Al, you're Doctor Gloom around here. Tell you what—why don't you ever smile? You're always working. This is a totally incomplete way of life."

"You want to make me happy?"

"You and me have a special deal, my friend. I make others happy. You, I leave to your own devices. Just throw some water at yourself and you'll wake up, maybe."

"I only look that way."

"Tell you what.

"I've got something for you, Al. Something you can really do. You like to babysit for Cindy this weekend?"

"Him!" Cindy shrieked. I didn't have a chance to complain. "Me babysit that old professor?"

I whistled. Cindy whistled. We whistled in unison. She stuck out her paw, ceasing to cover her ear, with a put-her-there grin of fellowship. I couldn't decide whether to take her hand for a millisecond, did the joke need to go so far; and she thought fast, she removed it. She picked up a copy of TV guide, probably Barbara's. She left her ears uncovered. She read. She chewed her gum. The noise she made would drown out her mother's noise. Everything in her slouch, her lean, her sprawl, her graceful gawky girlish presence made one short statement: *I'm trouble.*

I heard myself taking an initiative, something I have hated to do since 1967. Since then, I like just to pick my way with care. "Are you pregnant?" I asked.

She looked up, chewed her minty sugarless gum, stared, said, "Not yet. In about nine months, you ain't careful."

"Listen, kid. I'll be careful. You couldn't get pregnant from me if pregnant you got from breathing the same air."

She popped her gum. Cordelia peeked into my face. Al angry? Pissed-off Al? I would like to say: New Respect; but I think it was only amazement at the odd twitches of the mild former teller-robber, weary of it all. "Temper temper," said Cindy.

"Well, it's not just up to you," Cordelia said. "Those are facts."

"Mrs. Kirwin would help me. She's a funny broad, too."

"Bullshit."

"Right, Ma. I don't need that noise."

"But?"

"But I know a lot already. I know if a man blows on my titties it makes me giggle, and if I do the same to him, it makes him crazy."

"Some girl. I can't stop your education. I bet you seen a lot of Bruce Lee movies, too, but you don't know any karate."

A sly carelessness in that smallboned slouch. Cindy's body trembled with desire to make her mother acknowledge real danger, feel real fright. "I also know," she said. And didn't say.

"What?"

"Luigi Mendoza would help me if I need to get pregnant."

"How you know about that?"

"About *him*?"

"About that and him."

"I can write. I can read. I can telephone. I can smell and taste and lick, too, Mama."

The mother leapt like a nimble flabby lion on her cub. She wasn't cuffing, she was slapping. *Ow, ow, ouch!* shrieked the kid. This cub's mane was flying from side to side. Cordelia was cuffing her face with her open hand, slapping, slapping, but it must have hurt. I'm sure it hurt. It made me feel better for a moment, but then I disliked it.

"Stop!" I said.

She didn't stop. The kid's face had welts already. Cordelia was working her over. She had gone limp. She flopped around like a rag doll. But if I tried to interfere, both of them would jump up with their nails out. I didn't need two generations united to scratch my eyes. Any violence from me would ruin my clothes, my complexion, plus something serious, my little deal with Cordelia to tell her story. For once I thought fast.

"If you don't stop, Cordelia, I'm leaving."

Her hand paused in midair. The hotline telephone had rung. Call off the missiles and the attack B-51s. She was panting. Her face was boiling scarlet. Tears were running out of her eyes. I suppose they were tears of exertion, but Cindy was dry-eyed despite her bruises and her mother was crying. Some girl. Some mother.

"Don't go," said Cordelia, "can't you see we need you?"

Cindy echoed her mother's words: "Can't you see?"

Cindy tucked her head into her mother's shoulder. Suddenly the great sobs heaved up, nearly choking her. "Oh God," said the kid. Cordelia parted and stroked her hair as she must have stroked a thousand johns' turbulent heads after stock market, wife, or night fright reverses. Teenage turbulence is just as real to teenager. True mother's turbulence, needing to touch and stroke after cuffing and punching, is just as real to Cordelia. I had nobody.

"I still have this terrific idea," said Cordelia.

My heart was sinking. I knew. I may have had nobody, but not this. "What?"

"Oh *no*," said Cindy.

"If you saw how I live, Cordelia," I said, "if you saw my pad, I still think it's the Summer of Love, how I live, I've never gotten organized in my living space, Cordelia, I don't think that way, Cordelia, I—"

She raised her hand to stop the flow. "Shush, baby," she said, "don't fret. Listen. I have my own little place where I keep cats, too. I go there sometimes to be by myself with the cats."

"Who takes care of them when you're not there?"

"Somebody comes in. The janitor."

"Where is it?"

"If I wanted people to know," she said, "I wouldn't need it. I could just go to my room right here in the House. But I want this little place all by myself."

"It's in the country?"

"I didn't say." She paused. "I'm not teasing. It's not."

I thought: How can a whore be faithless? She can't.

So perhaps she can only be faithful.

"I can't have my daughter living alone by herself in that place."

"The kitties could keep her company."

"And I can't have her living here with me, either."

"She's your daughter."

Cordelia's eyebrows pushed together. Caterpillars humping along. Men have doubts about whether their sons and daughters are really their children. Women know. This awful certainty makes difficulties. To *know* Cindy was legitimate gave Cordelia no out, even in imagination. Little bitch was all hers.

"Now's your chance," Cordelia said, "to find out all about my second life, my secret life, my third or fourth life, my daughter, my place someplace else—okay, it's downtown, I'll tell you that much already—Al, do you want to take care of her? Can you use a boarder, Al?"

"Luigi Mendoza can," Cindy said, grinning. Now she was where she needed to be, at the center of all attention.

Luigi, Florin, maybe even Cody, who had experience with crazed teenies, would have delighted to take charge of this fifteen-year-old anarchist with the congealed mascara peel on her cheek. "Cordelia, can we talk seriously and sensibly?" I asked.

Cindy rolled her eyes. "I dig squeezing orange juice in your machine," she said. "I think I'll go squeeze awhile."

"You do that."

So we were alone. Cordelia decided to answer my questions as a way to set me up for what *she* wanted, which was not only to provide me with answers. In the kitchen Cindy was playing with the electric juicer. Whirr, whirr, and a bowling ball thump and roll of equipment. Cordelia sighed. She wasn't going to say unless I said, and so I said: "She's your daughter, Cordelia. I think you've got to figure out something."

"I know. I've given it careful consideration."

"I can't. I'm not the one."

"You'll wish you were."

"I'm letting you down, Cordelia?"

She hadn't asked very much of me. I was letting her down. But I also believed this mother should do something with her child besides passing her to the nearest semi-kindly man. If I were a mother, I'd not hand her over, I like to think, to a psychopath emeritus. I wouldn't give her to Luigi Mendoza, either. So although I was letting her down, I believed she was letting her daughter down. A new stage in our friendship. The woman who could do anything was not doing all she could do. Quarrel and disappointment. There was a problem in my adoration of Cordelia. Friendship had become a cult. Its mysteries had sustained me. But now I could no longer tell myself I would do anything for Cordelia when I refused the first difficult thing she asked. Even adoration is complicated; I thought it would be less tricky than love or lust. It doesn't get around the troubles of obligation, either.

I cleared my throat for a little lecture. It was time I told Cordelia about how she was a parent, how she would not forgive herself, how Cindy, then in the kitchen whispering curses to herself and mopping up orange juice, needed a real mother; and I was clearing my throat because it all came rushing out for one self-serving bad reason: Cordelia had asked some babysitting of me and I didn't want to do it.

"Love. You're so bashful, Al."

"This time that's not it."

Cordelia wouldn't stop, though. I had a whiff of how she used her gift to avoid her responsibilities, her talents to shore up against her fears. It was so easy for her to get to primary matters; it was what men enjoyed about her, this coasting affability about dark desires. She engaged what other women evaded. She was special for that. And she evaded what other women simply accepted or went crazy not accepting. She dodged, teased, and went to the heart. She said: "All my clients, almost everyone, they were conceived in an illusion of love. Perhaps the game only lasted a moment, but there it was. And so they spend a lifetime trying to repay the debt, looking for that illusion which made them."

"Sad, okay. Everyone suffers—"

"It makes for soul. It makes something soulful. If God existed, he would be grateful."

"It's a hard life, Cordelia. I agree. I don't think anyone can get through it without love. And with a child—"

"Some do. A lot do. And look at the world they gave us."

This pain I feel. I'm not sure if it's an intuition of the truth or a touch of arthritis. I'll lose Cordelia. I never had her. I failed her. She had no right. And yet I had no right to fail her. Perhaps love is a diversion from the necessary, like personality—the index of inefficiency, as my coffee-drinking pal puts it. Russ has tenure already. He has a wife and kids and a house on Tamalpais Road. We used to hang out together at the Mediterraneum.

Me now. Just a second. I've displayed a stiffness and coolness which makes some people envy me. Within this, I throbbed with tidal angers. When I was jealous, all the horrors tilted against my liver, my spleen, my pancreas, my belly. If I called a girl late and she wasn't there, and called again later and got no answer, I threw up to relieve my anguish. It didn't work. I was left with anguish plus sour mouth. I imagined someone with someone else. I tried not caring, but only seemed to succeed at caring wrongly.

With Cordelia, my imagination went inactive at last. What luck. She had done everything with everyone, and it didn't matter. She was only Cordelia, herself, communing with her powers, no matter what she did. If she chose me, her history only fortified us together. Of course she wouldn't choose me, would she? But I could imagine it with joy and, a thing almost as important in someone as dangerously awash as I am, I could predict it without pain.

Oh, the belief in God is so precious! Without it, look at me. I worship the strongest being I know, Cordelia, a flesh-stuffed madam with evidence of incipient kidney trouble around the eyes. Wide pores. Teeth growing bigger. Convinced of one thing, her charm, and right about that; and charm fails to move those who are in real need of their ambitions, Marietta and Cindy, for example; and Cordelia was failing her daughter while giving me lectures and an education. It would be good sometimes just to be together and not talk, just to sit and look or lie together, body to body. Instead we talk. And that's how it is. That's how we both take it. That's how it isn't. There were silent sand dune flies in the air above us; this neighborhood had been built on shifting sand dunes, shaped by the wind. The Pacific lay a few minutes to the west, and it led to the east. We couldn't hear the flies because we talked so much. Their wings were invisible, too, as they hovered like air worms. I would have liked to lie quietly, silently, with Cordelia. I needed this. I needed her. Yet I couldn't run her errand to be seduced by her daughter. She was saying:

"My problem, which you can't answer for, is I'm getting this power I want and therefore I can't have this love I want. For love is secret, simple and sweet, and power is public, complex, and brutal. But can I have the love? I've been waiting. I look at men, which I like a lot, and think I should settle for what I can get."

"Anyone can fall in love."

"I'm getting the special things. Maybe I'd prefer what anyone can get."

"Would you like some fresh orange juice?"

"Fresh-squeezed? I'd like that."

"It's fresh-opened Bird's Eye," I said. "I hear Cindy doing the can, she drank all the fresh, she's starting on the frozen."

She nodded at me as if we had just agreed about something. Her face was flushed with discourse. Her skin broke out with all the unspoken words which appeared dimly, like internal tattoos, in a pattern over the capillaries. She had a look of furious irrational composure, as if she had lived these indelible words which were almost, almost, not quite visible to me. There was so much to spare in Cordelia. There was so much beyond. I knew why I treasured her. It was easy to see why Marietta was preparing to mug her. It was hard to see why she was not mobbed by jealous hordes, starving for vitality as others have starved for potatoes or wheat. She was terrific, I decided once again.

And yet I saw the shadow over Cordelia of a plump and angry mother; and the shriveling, lumping woman, Cordelia herself, who would watch critically over her grandchildren; and these other rejected faces, never was and to be, who were folded inside Cordelia's over-tanned wary one, waiting for their chance. Cindy awakened the demons in Cordelia. She wanted to be merely herself, Cordelia, madam, inventor of the Union. But she was also mother and grandmother to be, and daughter, and someone's only true love. Her sharp little ears were those of a baby fox. Could Cordelia also have been her awful mom's cute little dumpling? So many souls jam together in every soul's instant. If I grasp them all, I can be one, a specific something.

"I know you pretty well," Cordelia said. "You think I like certain things about you, that you do my work for me, don't you?"

"Yes."

"So you're patient. You watch over me. You think that pleases me more than anything."

"I don't know."

She said: "Maybe it should." And she looked at me a long time. That look: penetrating and sweet, with large sad pouched eyes. I didn't know just what it was telling me. I should have known. I learned in due course.

Through the swinging kitchen door Cindy came with three glasses of orange juice on a tin Canada Dry tray. She was smiling. When the door swung open, I saw the debris of her efforts, a teenage orange juice caterer gone berserk while her mother and I discussed love once again. Cans on the floor, rinds, seeds, puddles of juice, a broken squeezer, citrus-soaked paper bags, Bird's Eye blue scattered under the sink. But she brought tall glasses with little hairs of orange floating in them, and paper napkins, and the kid smiling with her mustache of orange.

"Thank you, that's good, honey," said Cordelia. "You can't stay here. I haven't figured out where you can stay."

"You gonna have trouble with me, Ma."

"No, I'm not."

"I'm gonna stay here."

"No, you're not."

I thanked her for the orange juice. She barely glanced at me, because her mother said: "I'm ready for you."

"You know how to raise a girl right, Ma?"

"I been doing my best."

Mother and daughter began to smile at each other, then laughed, then I decided I should have left earlier. Tomorrow I'd see. Cindy was winning her war: "You gonna do better," she said.

16

CORDELIA HAD NO MORE ORANGES LEFT for the visitor that evening, so she offered her a Tab. She kind of knew the visitor coming alone on her important duty wouldn't care, this time and this time only, if it was or was not a low-cal beverage. The heat coming off both their bodies would burn up the energies, and any liquids they drank would only feed the fire.

The visitor lined up her little boxy red jacket on a drycleaner's metal hanger so that it didn't look too unhappy. She was finicky. She was thinking. Surprisingly, there was a soft spill of breast rising and falling under her blouse, harried by her thoughts. In her tailored jackets, this had not been evident.

"You are my sister, like all women," said the visitor. "I would like to save you from yourself."

"I would prefer to save me from you," said Cordelia.

"If I grow disturbed, I won't be calm and rational," said the visitor.

"Be my guest. I'm not rational," said Cordelia.

"Do you want nothing but trouble? Yes, perhaps you do. But will you consider what this does to the cause of women, the future of women in this city, the dignity of women?"

"I think about this more than you know."

"Please. I beg of you. I am not used to pleading, I am used to getting my own way." Cordelia smiled at knowledge; she bowed her head at self-knowledge. The words were spoken without pride. Cordelia was touched, and the equine smile faded. "I came here alone. There were certain risks. I took a taxi. I wore pants." Cordelia reinstated the smile. She smiled at histrionic vanity. "I took a Valium. I want not to lose my temper. I programmed myself a little, Cordelia. I want to help you almost as much as to help myself. I want to help all women as much as I help us. I seek to do the good and the right even if I don't always succeed."

"I understand that," Cordelia said sadly.

"I can only do what I do if I remember it is for others. Sometimes I forget. Sometimes I must crush my opponents. I do not want you to be an opponent. I do not even want to use your body in my campaign. They say it would be better for me to do so. I know this is true. But that is another sort of prostitution, I think. Others would not think it so. But I do."

"Prostitution is not unfeminine, history shows this," Cordelia said.

"You are teasing. History is irrelevant. These are new times. I could lie and tell you I hate you."

"It takes a clever person to lie. Your strength is the truth— your truth. It's not mine."

"I have friends who hate you."

"They don't lie either. They have their reasons. But they're not smart, either."

"Sometimes I think I deceive myself when I talk to others. This is part of the profession. Some say Cordelia, your profession and mine are similar."

"Because we both have to flatter the public? Because we cause them to feel need and then to satisfy it with us? Because we take their need, love, contempt, and money? No. And give them back refreshed desire? No. No. The differences are far more important.

The pleasure I give is simpler, and lasts longer, and causes quicker heartbreak, too. Do you want me to explain it to you?"

"I didn't come here for that. I came to tell the truth and try to help you. I came to warn you away from the trouble you are making for yourself."

Cordelia gazed into the lady's eyes. "Good. Then all I ask is not to make more trouble for me. I make enough for myself. You said it. Don't interfere in the natural process. You already mentioned some of my troubles. Let me speak for women in my own way. You speak in yours."

"My way says yours is the enemy. If I let you, I destroy my way."

Cordelia shrugged.

"You won't be moved, will you, Cordelia? Then I've done my duty. I can proceed with a clear conscience. I followed my feeling even though I knew it would do no good. So I'll leave now."

"Thank you for the visit. I do appreciate that always. You did expend a bit of energy for me. Thank you. And to relieve yourself a little, also. Thank you for that, too."

"I didn't even ask the cab to wait," she said mournfully. "I trusted you to keep me awhile."

"You want some food? I don't keep anything in the house. If Cindy lived with me, I'd have to have food. I send out. There are prunes in the window of the Lebanese grocer down the street and I meant to pick up a pound. You want a drink, another beverage?"

"Can I get a cab in this neighborhood? It's not safe."

"I'll walk out with you, if that's the problem," Cordelia said. "But probably it's safer for you to take a chance looking for a cab than to be seen with me, right?"

"Oh I'm not worried about that."

"So you want me to go to the corner with you? They cruise up Taylor to the airline terminal."

"No. No. I'll go myself. I know the way."

Cheerfully Cordelia gave her a bit of advice: "You'll be okay. Just watch out for the all-night dude in the doorway of the Adult

Variety Store. Walk sideways, maybe, but fast, and use the licensed weapon I'm sure you carry in your purse."

"How did you know?"

"Mine isn't licensed. I know you advise women to take Women's Defense Training at the Y or the Metropolitan Club. So I imagine you take care of yourself. Those windows in your car."

"In the public eye, with all the crazies. I have to protect myself."

"I know. I know, sister."

"I am speaking simply but from the heart. Cordelia. I beg you. You have a child. I plead with you. You have a daughter. Cindy. I get down on my knees to you. I kiss your hand."

She did it. Cordelia pulled her to her feet. Her knees were dusty.

"Ah, that's silly. I should have taken another Valium. Cordelia, listen to me: I am dangerous. My friend, *I am dangerous*. Do not organize this union. Do not have this strike. Do not cause the police, the public, the people, and me to strike you down. As a woman I plead. As a mother. As a sister."

Cordelia leaned forward. The woman was swaying drunkenly. A sour smell came from her breath. No Binaca. Sincerity. So are they all sincere. Cordelia was overwhelmed with love of the creature. She was convinced of the justice of the woman's mission. She put her lips on the plump, girlish, dry, slightly chapped lips of her visitor. They kissed.

"What's your answer?"

"I like you."

"What's your answer?"

"I like you very much."

"What's your answer?"

"No."

Cordelia held her in her arms a moment and then let her go. Marietta ran, the little heels clacking.

17

CORDELIA USED TO TELL ME someday we would have more fun than a busload of Japanese tourists with an unlimited supply of Super-X film. She said she was not used to the ideal man and therefore I would qualify. As a true friend, I might be eligible for true lover.

I wondered if I was making a few more mistakes in my life. I had tried to graduate from 1967. I was trying caution. I told her to watch out for Marietta. She already knew that. I had even recently cut my hair, which was perhaps going too far. I was working at my thesis. I was feeling these drawing pains in my chest—desire for another. Perhaps I should have done it differently.

I imagined pulling her toes, bent from shoes, tanned from running on the beach; making them crack out like the prehensile claws they were meant to be, with little iguana mugs of blackened nails. She was no daisy in the field. I collected her style, a bundle of odd deals and manners, but these were also her substance (what's so superficial about flash? it explodes the depths), the evidence of her longing, the smells, liquefactions, sighs, tricks, generosities, cupidities, cunnings, power explorations and expeditions. I looked for her in that hip-sprung greedy Cindy with her

Patchouli, her cartridge belt, her get-a-little-kick cinnamon Chiclets, her Seattle Maoist leather drag, especially in her gimmes and I wanna, her defiance. Within the over-sunned envelope of Cordelia's flesh, soft and discolored as an old wallet, too much sat-upon—no beauty, my love Cordelia—lies that familiar newborn innocent. A blank longing, like Cindy, like me; yet she is not Al, she is only like Al. Nobody's perfect.

Then Cordelia said she would not go to the Danny Doomsday's benefit with me. She said she would also not go without me. That is, she would go to the party and I could go to the party if I chose to and maybe we would meet and greet at the party to-gether. Or maybe not.

We were riding with the flow, weren't we? Doing what we felt like doing and not doing what we didn't feel like not doing?

I was lost in a swarm of double negatives, San Francisco fleas nipping and biting at my pride, raising little rows of welts. Maybe, preparing for her strike in front of the Fairmont, she just needed to be alone. Preparing to face the new use for her which Marietta had in mind. But alone was not Danny's party.

"Would you like to talk about why you don't want to go with me?" I asked.

"No."

"I see."

"No more'n I'd like to talk about why I don't want to *not* go with you."

"I don't see anymore."

"Well, we ain't dating, Al. I believe we're not lovers."

"If you try to mix friendly feeling and work and . . . you might get into trouble, is that it?" I asked.

Her face was horsy, Egyptian, bronzed by sun, closed to me.

"Then what's the answer?"

No admission. I adored that noble equine person. But she was no longer with me.

"You remember my definition of the perfect lover?"

I remembered: one who can push a felt tip pen up the Crookedest Street in the World with his tongue. "Yes," I said, starting to smile.

"Yes," she said, "you remember. A man who would take off a couple days from his thesis to keep my daughter out of trouble. But it's all right. Luigi lent me his housekeeper, Lester—you know Lester? Used to be a goldminer?"

I remembered. I had all the correct data noted down.

"Hey, man," said Sam Bowers to the tough thing with long black lashes and a navel she didn't bother to manage, who stood singeing a fern frond with her cigaret, "don't you realize plants have feelings?"

"That's why I'm doing it," she said. A prickle of fern curled, browned, shriveled.

Sam shrugged. He was on the northern side of thirty, too old to save the vegetable world. He could barely even think about the dolphins. He had his own problems with closer relatives and this castrating plant sadist wasn't his type, anyway. Nevertheless, on a warm evening in San Francisco, as the Holy Kazoo reverberated inside the mansion, he tilted his gray-flecked, slit-eyed head. "Why?" he asked the lady. She was wearing an exposed belly-button above low-riding cut-off velvet pants.

She moved her current weapon from fern to lips. She drew. She exhaled. "Fuckers," she said. "Bored, I'm so bored, man."

"Then why'd you come?"

"Cause I like to watch the assholes perform," she said.

Something was troubling this lady. He had seen her before. Their unpromising personal meeting was taking place on the steps of the Victorian wooden mansion of Danny Doomsday, distinguished dope lawyer, a house which was precariously balanced on the back of skinny, speedy, tirelessly-crunching San Francisco termites, a law practice which was supported by the devoted and profitable defense of underprivileged former collegiate and Third World narcotics millionaires. A party was in progress on a Saturday evening. The counterculture never sleeps, never rests. It was a benefit for the FCC, Free Cocaine Conspiracy, a non-Red Feather Agency.

Among the many red and runny noses present was that of Cordelia Celtic, who happened to be standing with can of Bud in one hand, cigaret in the other, her belly in black velvet pushing out a little (she was swollen with annoyance), grabbing a toke of evening air, when Sam Bowers, record producer, shambled up at midnight. He had been working late on a mix at the studio. He was a little depressed. He had recently gotten a divorce from the three girl singers called The Epitomes. They weren't legally married. Due to backward California bigamy laws, they had never been able to take out a license, which only made the divorce more painful.

Sam was tired and sad, although rich.

Cordelia was morose and irascible, although poor.

They met under this hanging spider plant as Cordelia tried to burn the frond of an adjacent male fern with her lighted cigaret. She might have napalmed the spider plant, too, but she believed spider plants have got their shit together, they're not pigs, they reproduce by planting their own roots. She was not a botanist.

And if she lifted her arms, some creep was going to cop a feel—tits, ass, exposed bellybutton—at least that was her experience and judgment of matters.

"No, they're cool," said Sam.

"What do you know about it? When were you last a woman?"

"Okay, okay," said Sam. "Let's agree about one thing right away. You got a mad on your mind. So you want to wipe all over me."

"I can smell assholes," she said.

"And I know these people," he explained patiently, "and they're not into grabbing a female whilst she's busy incinerating the flowers. But personally, maybe because my age and experience, I'm interested in the background of the crime."

"You mean you're horny?"

"No."

"You think I'm an easy fuck, some kind of life's reject?"

"Not at this point in time," he said, doing his famous H. R. Haldeman imitation.

"You sound just like Johnny Carson," she said. "Oink, oink."

"You'd like me to leave you in peace here on the firing range?"

And suddenly, at the crucial moment, just at the point in time of no return, she flashed a perfect country-girl smile at him—clean, friendly, brilliant, with a couple of honest, slightly crooked teeth at each corner. "No, you're nice, I heard of you, let's converse," she said. "Only thing is, I might as well tell all. I hate small-talk."

"You do all right. I'm tired of crooners anyway."

"You been hanging out with *Rudy Vallee*, man?"

"No, two sopranos and an alto."

"College girls?"

He nodded. No need to go into it now. Orthodontists had put retainers on The Epitomes, their smiles were even and capped, they looked like sisters and even performed like siblings, but their smiles all together didn't add up to one storm-clearing jagged grin like this crazy lady's. Await developments, he thought, unused to dealing with a single.

"College girls. Not me, I was nigger-poor, man, grew up in Elko on a cactus ranch, cooked up that cactus and tried to say it was mescaline, it wasn't, came late to the Fillmore, didn't even go to Vassar like your friends—"

"You're smart. Somehow you got educated. Many people can't express themselves."

Slit-eyed gaze of scorn. "You interrupted, Mister." Sometimes, when Cordelia went into one of her full-fledged whore acts, she believed the stories she told. "Mister, you can interrupt with questions, but don't *you* tell *me* about *my*self. I'm just a shy child of the desert. I learned to talk from faggots and spooks, the beautiful people, man, the old Haight, but I'm also a feminist, and I don't like being interrupted. Can you imagine how it was to tell my story to that tall, indifferent Nevada sky? Contrary to what people think, there was no Gregory Peckery or Kirk Douglas riding the range. It was some slobbery sheep farmer, that was the *best*, he drove a Toyota pickup, whose big thrill was turning the lambs upside down and pinching off their oysters. And all I got was dry skin, peeling nose, empty squeeze-bottles of Jergens Lotion filling the backyard behind the trailer where the goats bunged each other and my half-brothers chased me around the Bendix—hey, what are *you*?"

A short, bull-headed, bearded old man was stumping up the steps of the Victorian mansion. Two men with parted lips accompanied him. They were eager; he was important. "Hey, what are you, man?"

"This is Judge Crater, Cordelia," said one of the parted-lips escorts, "Superior Court of San Diego District."

"Hey, Judge, what do you think of victimless crimes? You convict? I'm going up before one of you. I'm a victimless criminal, Judge, I'm a whore, I suck, wanna meet me later?"

The Judge looked happy, and spoke the truth. "Pleased to meet you, Miss Cordelia. Call me J. C. I'm off the bench at the moment." The two lawyers, like sucker fish, were tugging him up the stairs. They didn't want to lose him in the stream. They nibbled at his elbows, his shoulders, they pushed and tickled. He followed obediently. He was a wounded elder, burdened by too much flesh. But he had always known Frisco would be like this, just the ticket to pull him out of the post-prostatectomy slump.

"Hey, Judge! Every dude should do something bad once a month. I'll be here if you need me, Judge."

Wistfully she watched him into the crowd. "Shitass old fart," she said sweetly, and as he looked back, she waved to him. "First he wants to see if there's anything better'n me inside. Fine. Let him," she said with deep inner peace. "There ain't."

"Maybe he thinks we're together," Sam said. Her repertory of deep inner peace riffs reminded him of something between Berkeley before a riot and the Haight after the Tac Squad has rendered its comment on social dissent and sidewalk penny-tossing with the aid of Mace, cattle prods, firehoses, and dogs bred for savagery. "Who's that fellow knew your name?"

"Used to be Sergeant Boger of the Vice Squad. Busted me a long time ago for giving him—"

"Ah, that must have been a long time ago," Bowers interrupted her.

"Yeah, lawyer now. Defends black pussy by pleading them guilty, it's like a G.I. line in court Monday mornings, one after another, takes the hundred dollars from each and every one, sentence suspended, they go out on the street to earn his hundred for him."

"He's helping out that judge who wants a good time."

"Um," she said, but there was something wolf-like, tooth-sharpened, and dissonant in these alpha waves of hers, although she remarked: "He's a Type B. Can make do without me. Not one of those determineds who suicides himself out of love, just because I'm very exceptional." She diddled a singed fern with her little finger. It crumbled. She didn't bother burning the stump.

"You know where I been working?" she asked. "San Rafael! Where I made up this hit tune, since you're a record producer, big man in your own estimation, here's my hit tune:

> O where the hell
> Is San Rafael?

Unless you're aiming for top-forty, AM, car-driving music, man, in which case we can make it: *San Rafeck can go to Heck.* But I'll tell you this, Mister Music Man: It won't even get to the charts if you cut it down that way—"

"What you taking? Speed?"

She slowed down around the curve. "Shit no. Beer. A little coke, but it's wearing off already."

"You got a healthy metabolism."

"It was my desert-country, clean-air uprearing. I tuned in,

turned on, and dropped around, which is how I'm able to survive life as a fallen woman.

> Gluppy mouth and ass awaits,
> How can this boy resist me?
>
> Hairy bush and piggy snout,
> Ooh look! my lover kissed me.

She singsonged this little ditty. "You like it?" she asked. "Is it professional? How about the fifteen-year-olds, they like it?"

What's to like about this hyperactive motorcycle freak Hell's Angel bulldyke style? What, if anything, to like about a woman playing out her anguish, if any, through these dumb games?

"I like you," he said.

"A dude who smoked a pipe said that to me once," she remarked. "He was my freshman advisor, Nevada State at Reno. He just crinkled up his friendly little eyes like you do, nice smile, sweet face, smoked a pipe, said he liked me and also liked me to go down on him after conference."

Haha, haha, said Sam.

She singsonged again: *Around me the world turns, under me the bed burns.*

The midsummer, midnight trees were flowering, pollinating, in the close musky heat of the Tenderloin. Rarely does a San Francisco evening shudder with this humid warmth of an eastern summer, but this was one of those rare nights. Mites arose in a swarm from the alley nearby, where sunflowers scraped against a gutter; a cat stood watch, and then scurried before the lurch of a wino; the mansion, which had stood here since the earthquake of 1906, might not survive the good vibes of the rock band industriously at work within. A redwood sign, LAW OFFICES, D. Doomsday, Esq., Associates: Brenda Quintilla, Bud Williams, Booker T. Washington IV, swayed along with the stomping of the celebrationists within. Benefits for a worthy cause usually develop like that. A skinny little tycoon, who had driven up in a Bentley, swept out of his carriage in a floorlength ermine cape to greet Sam. "Hey, man, remember me? I used to park your car in the righteous autopark next to Enrico's."

"I remember, I remember. How'd you get all . . . all this?"

"This? Oh, I was a lousy parker, got fired for fender violations. So I took up dealing."

"Doing okay?"

"Okay. Two arrests, out on thirty thousand bail—diplomatic pouch off a Peruvian, man. Shit, they got no respeck for diplomatic immunity in this country. Doing okay."

"What's your goal?"

"Listen, I ain't greedy, man. Two hundred thousand *or* my next birthday."

???

"I mean, when you turn eighteen it gets serious. So even if I ain't fulfilled my game plan, man, I quit on October 29. Cold fucking turkey on the international trade scene, Mr. Bowers. I can do it. I'm a Scorpio."

"You don't seem worried."

"Why worry? I got the house, the wheels, the friends, the lawyer. Plus about four hundred thousand. Plus a little dealie in blank airline tickets. Who, me worry? A seventeen-and-a-half-year-old Scorpio in a world of tired old straightarrow narcs with sludge in their arteries? Man, don't you remember how I put that dent in your, what was it, that Alfa-Romeo, and I just said, Who, me? So that's what I say now I'm a coke tycoon: Who, me? My style ain't changed that much, man. Scorpios are like that."

Shrill little tycoon on high cork heels. The heels were no higher than the soles, however. The kid had style.

"So next time you need your car parked," said the tycoon as he entered the party, "whyn't you call on me, for old time's sake, man?"

Sentimental strutting little cork-lifted, coke-lifted seventeen-and-a-half-year-old tycoon disappeared into busy clasp of benefit celebration. Cordelia watched and said, "It's tums for the tummy to see a real man like that, paid his dues."

"So there are some people you like," Sam said.

She shrugged. "Didn't say I like him. Said I dig him. Maybe admire a little. He's a creep, though. I'm a *woman*, man. Smart or ignorant, take no shit, I'm just like that little creep, I'm not going to type hundred words a minute for no asshole. An I.Q. of 164— we should park cars? So I'm not going to be an executive *or* a fucking executive assistant. I'm going to run round the whole deal. I'm a whore, only I forgot to kiss the guy on the lips before I took his money. The cardinal rule Margo taught me. So I got entrapped by a goddamn vice squad pervert who gave me the public's money to blow him and then busted me. You are looking, man, at a victimless criminal."

"I'll tell you the truth. You looked more like a wife who ran off to Mexico once with a spade drummer and thinks she can talk dirty."

"Haha. I can also talk clean. I got plenty of good straight friends like Professor Dooley watching me so close over there. That fellow really cares"—she waved—"do anything for me, that's what he says." She kissed her fingertips at the man she was waving at. She caught a new glimpse of the car-parker emeritus unsteaming the window with his ermine sleeve. She transferred the wave and the kissed fingertips from Al Dooley to the former car-parker. Sam realized it was polyethylene ermine, because the tycoon wasn't the sort who killed any animals except two-legged or four-wheeled narcs. The tycoon gestured to the music thundering within. Cordelia wet-kissed her fingers again and made a lip motion which stated, *Later, man*. The tycoon vanished within. "Clean," she said. She curled a little finger, pulled in her belly, and remarked mincingly, "Oh dear, don't you think it's too gauchay of that silly thing over there to wear her bikini and show those stretchmarks? She's only had three fiantzes, you know, which doesn't even add up to one husband."

"I guess you've had your fill of life experiences."

"I'm going for a Veteran's pension. I been in and out of the Life. Hi, Arthur."

Arthur Pesche.

Arthur Pesche chatting with Al Dooley, asking why he's not with Cordelia. Al failing to explain.

Cordelia was saying to Sam Bowers: "Trouble is, the Life is an attractive nuisance—the money, the loving, the snare and the delusion. For example, when I was nineteen, dropout that first time, up in Oregon that first time, my first john said he was a director, get me into the business, I believed him. He told me the truth, man, that's the sad part! But he was a *funeral* director. When I found that out, I wanted to snuff him. Oh he apologized, he was in love, he wasn't really the type, it was a family business. Only thing wasn't stiff around him was his little dingie, man. So I decided to depart from Oregon."

And she hummed the theme from her hit song.

"Funny thing is, you're nice," he said.

"Funny thing is, you're sinister," she said. "You say you're a record producer—FBI records? CIA records? *Po*-lice records? And you say you're divorced—from a group? Cause if you were married to a group, less it was the Supremes or those Pointer Sisters in there, I don't dig it, I don't want to play my part in your crazy fantasies. I got my own, man. I dream I'm a pretty young thing, say fifteen, stead of a thirty-three-year-old old old old *old* whore." She moved closer and brushed shoulders with him. "But I'm nice. I can do you good. I am not too old to smell sweet, not too young to smell ignorant. I'm *jussssst* right." She pronounced right *raht*, nearly *rot*, and she tried to say *iggorent*, but her accent was no more consistent than her story. Her intentions were confusing. There was a turbulence in her.

Judge Crater popped gasping out of the throng. His mouth was open. His teeth were startling—bright, even, and true. He looked ten years younger than a half hour ago, but his thighs, jowls, and boobies still flapped worn and heavy. He had examined the crowd, ducked his sucker-fish escorts, and returned to the front stoop with its injured fern. He said to Cordelia: "I feel I'd like to discuss your case a bit further, Miss. I'm not sitting in my district till next week."

"I feel an appeal coming on," she said.

"In hallucinogenics, illegal search and seizure does the trick. In, uh, your line, entrapment usually can handle it. Now, did the vice squad officer present himself as enticing, seductive, uh, *anxious* to make, uh, out?"

"He entrapped my little seizure in his search, Judge."

"Just call me Your Honor, haha. I made a joke, like Dr. Kissinger did once. Henry. Miss, if you want me to handle your case a little, I think we might could meet privately—"

"Right now?" He nodded. "I thought so. So you might could get me to seize your little searcher, ooh, ah, that sort of scam, Judge?"

"Uh," he said, gulping like a fish. His teeth gleamed a little less with inner radiance. The patrol car, red Cyclops eye turning— noise control, abate the nuisance, Buster—doubleparked in front of them. He stumped down the wooden steps. "I'm Judge Crater, Superior Court, San Diego District," he opened up on the officers. "I believe the relevant neighbors have been invited to the, uh, religious and legal celebration. . . ."

The cop car slithered away. He stumped back up.

"They'd rather deal with noise and whores like me,"—the judge was wincing as she explained—"because it's not dangerous, noise and cunt don't pull guns, and they can shake us down. You heard of my organization?"

"I think so."

"I gave a press conference. Six o'clock news, plus Mike Wallace was going to do me again, plus NEA Syndicate, plus all the papers—"

"Ah yes, of course. I have lots of briefs and reading matter to wade through, Miss, you wouldn't believe how much they're trying to tinker with the Constitution. Had a case of a young man, civil employee, refused to sign the oath of allegiance to the State of California because of the bear on the flag. Said his religion forbids animalism worship. And that bear stands for a wonderful tradition of frontiersmen, Miss. That California state flag bear, he had the weirdness to say, was animalistic."

"I get lots of them animals, too. The crazies. The cops, the pimps, the lawyers, the conventioners, the enticers. Snakes. But you know who they arrest? Me. My girls."

"I know, I know, you have many legitimate, justifiable complaints against our legal system as she is constituted," the judge purred, rotating his rump in clockwise fashion, slowly, in such a fashion as to put his warm, soft buttocks between Cordelia and Sam and thereby to sweep Sam away. Sam knew enough to ride with the flow. In many ways he was smarter than Al Dooley. Mumm, mummm, the judge was humming. "We should speak of this in chambers, my child. You are perhaps an orphan?"

The poor child rolled her eyes. "One mother and about seven fathers, the latter a veritable bull of a man—a machinist. My legal father, who says he conceived me, is Professor of Poultry at Cal State, Hayward. I see him now and then. He hears about my life and, man, he *clucks*."

"Tch-tch," said the judge, and cleared his throat. He was slitching between his teeth a little, not clucking like Dad, and his rump was working hard on the subtext—*get away, Sam, abate, move.*

"Dere went de judge," said Cordelia. "I was stolen from the gypsies and raised by my parents in the great northwest. My mother still hasn't learned anything. She's like our legal system."

"Do we have to be antagonists?" Judge Crater inquired. "Won't you let me help you, my dear?"

She rolled her eyes at Sam, asking if he was going to let this greedy senior citizen help her. Because if he let him, she would. She was just a defenseless innocent female, free on bond on occasional soliciting charges, plus aiding, abetting, and renting a house, lost in our troubled society of today, ready to make a move that could get her in some trouble. *Man*, said her eyes, her downturned lips, *you gonna just stand there like Al Dooley?*

"Well, now I go along," Sam said. "Give my heartfelt greetings to Danny, spent a heap of time out here with you folks."

"Sam," she called, "ooh, Sam, before you leave. Where'd you say I could apply for that shot of penicillin?"

Sam stopped dead at the doorway. The judge's buttocks took a rotational rest. Sam started to laugh and said, "Okay, okay, Cordelia, you win, I'll listen to the dregs of your sad story."

She turned sweetly to the judge. "Sir, would you mind waiting just three to five days? I believe the contagious part may be over by then. Unless you think you haven't got that much time till your stroke."

Judge Crater was exhausted. He had always known San Francisco was like this—infected, degenerate, and leftwing. Back to the surfer boys of La Jolla. Sam and Cordelia watched him stumping down the street toward Van Ness, looking for a cab to the Jack Tar Hotel, where surely he could find something to give him a moment of repose.

•

There was this unaccustomed silence between Cordelia and Sam as the judge retreated. The music within the house swelled to meet the warm and humid silence without. "I think he liked you," Sam said.

Cordelia touched the fern. She sighed. It would grow back. She had only singed the extended tips; it was a fern treatment, a veritable singe job. "Naw, not so much he liked me," she said, "so much as nothing inside he could get it on with—I always find these specialty johns... Sam?" she said tenderly. "Know how you tell a vice squad cop bent on entrapment?"

"The shoes?" Sam asked.

She shook her head sadly. Oh, sleaze. Here was this distinguished record producer, so smart, rich, and slim, and he thought cops still give themselves away by wearing black brogans. Oh, man, the morbidity of it all. Next he'd say shoulder holster. Well, every celebrity has feet of clay. Time to pour a little water on his feet. "Kiss him," Cordelia commanded.

"I never kissed a cop," Sam said.

"He goes stiff, back like a board. Ooh, don't want it on the lips. Just Doing My Job kind of stiffness. Lemme show you."

An electrocuted death spasm of body hurtled against his mouth and ricocheted away.

"I see. Could break a front tooth. But I thought most guys don't really like to kiss," he said, "you know, just pay their money for . . ."

"Haw! Believe that, believe anything. You believe in Executive Privilege. You believe in Sinister Forces. Shit no, man, they're all boys like you, sad lonely shot-up kids, loving they want, they want to get honeyed, licked, loved, kissed, man! You think they just want to get their rocks off? Man, you're *sick*!"

Sam wished to defend himself. "Perhaps I only lack understanding," he said.

"Let's hope so. Me too, I should of kissed that cop before I took the money from him. One thing I hate, it's a hard dingie with no insight at all. Wow, that's so oldfashioned, man. How old are you?"

He decided to play this cagey. "Bob Dylan's generation. Over thirty, I guess."

She shook her head at the additional wonderment of it all. More fun to torture this overage record producer than to singe a fern or a superior court judge. She watched the quiver run through him. She thought it desire; he believed it to be masochism. This Hell's Angel madam would know the meaning of the word and the deed. The sanity of his grief for the close-harmony trio, O lost for all but a final recording date, was slipping away. The Epitomes had sometimes scared him, but essentially they were normal kids who happened to like tricycle behavior. Like good little troupers they would meet the contract for one more LP. No more reptilian backbending juicy inventions; just music, plus a long moment with lawyers about the royalties. But this single lady was *dangerous*. He had better strike back fast.

"What do you like best, men or women?" he asked.

"Depends on what I'm with. Sometimes it depends. What are you?"

"You're bisexual? Groovy."

"Shit, I don't know. Have to take a test, I guess. Far as I know myself, my opinion don't matter."

Sam considered departing within for dope, food, music, conversation, a less complicated antagonist. Al Dooley was watching. Sam could have a merry exchange with the professor. She would let him go, he knew that. She knew he was considering ending their struggle. It was only words, anyway, words, words, plus dear life. He could end this lifetime on the stoop by merely saying, Well, see you. He could depart. If he didn't need The Epitomes, who needed this brinky creature? He knew who he was. He was the best producer, including sound mixing, in San Francisco. He was somebody's man, his own, thirty-two-track. He didn't need single trouble when he had barely escaped triple trouble. He was intact. He was not going to have his back broken again by a yoga-crazed madam hooked on doing good for the sacred cause of strolling and stationary women. She tipped the empty beer can slowly into the fern box.

"Say, Mister Record Producer, you know the test'll tell me what I am?"

He stared. They were belligerents again. Maybe this was the crisis. He knew better than to talk, since she always won the conversation Olympics, Put Down, Outdoor Standing. He hoped for divine intervention instead. Here it was. A girl in a greenish, yeasty, fermenting fur jacket, over little else up top except wild eyes, asked: "Which way he go? that judge? where he go?"

"Jack Tar Hotel, Room eight six four," Cordelia said.

"I thought I was going with him," the girl whined, and shrugged, shedding mites into the air—her fur dated from the time it was okay to kill, eat, and wear animals. The girl from olden times went inside to drown her sorrow in brownies.

Sam smiled. A barefoot albino queen with a pink Reggae fright-locks hairdo, pink eyes, mashed features, was leading by the hand a small iodine-tanned record p.r. director whose leather needed oiling. He creaked hello at Sam Bowers.

Sam shook his head. He had standards and, tonight, was not going to say hiya to a man who chose to get himself up like that. "The Harder They Fall" was okay in its day, but off this act. At the window a cat, speeded up by the music, leaping at the sill, was raping the curtains. He would omit hellos to this intact pussy in its false rutting season. Lots of people—Henry Garrett, Fred Ellis, Luigi Mendoza, Piero Grandi, What's-his-name Flavin—he would not meet and greet tonight. He was less fretful now. The world was full of delights, so why hang around on a Victorian front stoop with this champion nag? Inside there were skinny chicklets with confused eyes, stately Black Panther newspaper vendors, tense but knowledgeable lady lawyers, the Pointer Sisters in their Depression flash, undone acidic pretenders to the crown of Janis Joplin, even Ms. Grace Slick herself, now thirty-five, still in cartridge belt and Maoist drag—well, in his present state, better confine himself to bringing a momentary glazed blue clarity to one of the corn-yellow-haired groupies who were waiting for fame to strike. She could be his magic, he could be her lightning; let's go, tasty morsel.

Cordelia wins the Standing Outdoor Insight Title, too. She watched the reel unwind among the wounds of Sam's cortex, a confusion of ganglia and electrical impulses, memories and dreams, expectations and undischarged primal screams. She held a finger to one nostril and blew. Hiss. Sam thought it must be a gesture of contempt learned from some visiting john. For a moment he feared she was going to blow her nose, actually snot him out, but it was just a hiss. He felt relieved and grateful.

"You're jumpy," she said.

"Always thinking."

"I have a friend like that. Al Dooley."

"The Professor over there?"

"Wants to be. I think he's writing a book."

"Do we have to talk about him?"

She laid a finger on the other nostril. Hiss. This time he feared nothing. So she was into primal nose-clear. He was beginning to see how much space she needed around her. She sighed. "I got to go home, there's something I got to attend to."

"Uh. Want to see my place?"

"I'm sure your place is nicer'n my place. But I said I got to go *home*."

He shrugged.

"I have this place in the Tenderloin, place I was going to use for a friend, take these people there, but I never did—like to see it?"

Sam Bowers was urging her elbow to move.

"I might as well show it to you as these other people."

Sam was nipping lightly at the elbow joint with his closed fist. He didn't like the sad face. Who else will ever know why she looked sad? Cindy and I might discuss it someday, but we still won't know.

Cordelia had decided. "Okay. Okay. You could take a look at my place, only a short walk through unsafe streets from here, down Eddy two blocks, across Ellis and we're there—"

They were walking. Judge Crater, who might have aided her legal entanglements, given her good advice on union activities, had disappeared the other way. They were strolling through the Tenderloin on a summer's evening, just a guy in leathers and a gal in logorrhea, no song there, a woman who liked to explain and thereby had kept Sam Bowers from getting any further into the benefit than the front stoop. He'd send a check on Tuesday, when his secretary came in. The streets were rather quiet except for eight motorcycles starting at once in front of Brucie's Down Under. Too much metal for racing cycles, too many studs, too much hype. She was watching the cycles thrum-thrum-*blawww*! and murmuring, if he caught it correctly, "There is neither Jew nor Greek, slave nor free, there is neither male nor female? *Paul*. Galatians 3:28. I sincerely doubt that statement. Even if it was Paul McCartney said it. No goddamn peyote in the cactus out back in Elko, so sometimes I read the Bible to get high. We are all one in Christ Jesus? Not true. There is attorney and defendant, cop and victim, hooker and john, mother and daughter, me and Marietta. It's never just what you think it is. All men are sisters."

"No one's listening, Cordelia."

"I reach when I'm nervous, Sam."

Silence. Humid. Warm. Distant cry of ambulance siren, dying fall of Honda. She had taken his hint and walked the last half block in a state of meditative grace, falling in step with her escort. His thumb as he held her hand swept back and forth against sawed-off black velvet. If she was a CIA whore, she would try to worm the secrets of the financial counterculture out of him. He would tell her how to overprint studio voices, bootleg Rod Stewart, control thirty-two-track recording, make money sometimes, feel smart, discover the essential difference between Jew and Greek, Saint Paul and Paul McCartney, winners and losers and Zen biders of time. They were suddenly practicing the resolution of silent conflict through silent agreement. Bowers was smiling. He was thinking: Here we are, two ancient numbers, and we're a veritable museum of kiddie courting reflexes.

"So here's my pad. You'll find it comfy. I cleaned up since Emmet Grogan came and camped last week, I had to sweep them out, hosed it down and everything. Somebody put a foot through one of my speakers. I think you'll find it cozy. I tole you I had to tend to something, just take me a minute."

•

Her cats.
She had to tend to her cats.
Her little pussies, quite a lot of them.

Otherwise the place was bare—a pallet on the floor, a skeletal stereo rig beached like a crumpled helicopter, a pile of records in a Sunkist crate, the floorboards painted in battleship gray, the walls whitewashed and one lonely footprint on the ceiling—the abominable peg-legged spiderman of the Tenderloin? There was also a fern in the corner near the window which gave on the alley, and its leaves were sharp, green, comb-like, unwounded by fire. There was a snapshot of a child in a greenish oxidized tin frame, stuck in the dirt, brown at the bottom, leaning against the stem of the plant.

The place was clean, silent, and still, except for a pile of newborn kittens in the corner. They made little peeping noises as she fussed and tended to them. What the devil made her think she was needed? Mama lay sleepily alongside, blinking in her dream of maternity as the pink muzzles nipped at her.

Well, it was nice of Cordelia to be needed by somethings. She looked up. Christ, just like Judge Crater, a night for the years slipping off. She was fifteen years younger. She looked sixteen with her contagion of motherlove for these cats.

"Say, Sam, you ever make it with kitties all over you?"

He wasn't sure.

"It's nice and warm, Sam." When she bent over, her cutoff velvet pulled up just above the T formations of her behind, and his eye followed up her strong back, over the shoulder, down—Sam leaning to look—and there was the box of newborn kitties. They squirmed and nestled like pink furry maggots. No, he had never made it with a bunch of kitties. "Won't they get smashed?"

"Won't we be careful?" she inquired.

Tender crisp little kitty bones and pink flesh all over them both. "Guess we will be," he said.

Somehow this hell's angel needed to make a love guaranteed for tenderness by the chaperonage of seven newborn pussies. She picked up the mama and kissed it and nuzzled it a lot and locked it in the kitchen. "There," she said. She returned and stood looking at the kittens. Then she looked at Sam. Then they began. It was anxious, but nice. It was slow and easy, but sweet. Her lips moved perhaps too rapidly when she talked—she explained too much—but when he kissed them, they were firm and pleasant. They were nice soft warm firm pleasant lips which Sam liked kissing. She didn't have to shut up. She just had to shut up once in awhile. He kissed her again and again and she was miraculously still. She seemed to sink and slide into the mattress, and without speaking, blessedly without a word, she asked, she implied, she made it clear that it was important to kiss her again and again and he did. Warm larval stirrings all over and around them. Mewlings, and on her mattress pitched on the floor, one highpitched shrieking meow of relief.

Neither slept. In the little light of dawn the ceiling of the Tenderloin flat began to glow like a screen before their wide-open eyes. She let the mama cat into the room and then she snuggled back alongside him. The janitor rattled down the alley, dragging a trash can. She told him the janitor worked nights at the P.O., feeding the zip-code machine. The kittens stirred contentedly. They milked. In their pussycat ganglia they imagined it would be like this to be born in San Francisco.

The ceiling was as good as a fireplace for dreaming at dawn. They dreamed, they touched, she clasped his hand, it wasn't necessary to talk but Cordelia did anyway.

She stated that she liked him a lot and did he mind that their relationship began in this sordid, cat-haunted flat?

He answered, begging to differ with her, that their relationship began near a carefully-singed fern and a superior court judge on the front stoop of a legal benefit and he liked her a lot for her spirit, pluck, and conversation.

Um, she replied. She showed him a torn match cover on which she had scribbled: *J.C.C. Rm. 864, Jack Tar, Wed checkout*. She tried to be prudent.

He stated nothing much. Perhaps he dozed. Not to be jealous of Judge Crater. When he came back to Alpha-wave life, or perhaps it was Beta—he didn't go out on dates with his machine—

she was trying to draw conclusions. She had a fabulous, modified-feminist way of turning real life into open discussion.

"Now that I'm in love," Cordelia said, "true love at last, you know what? I think I'll give up the Life. Peddling your ass is okay when you're young and fancy free, but it's time to get serious now. I got a brain. I got a imagination. I got a way with words. I sort of got probation for a first offense."

"What'll you do next?"

"You'll support me a little cause you like me." He nodded. That's right. "So it's sort of like a scholarship. I'm not going to be just another chick, live off my man, let him buy me my cat food and kitty litter. No, buster. Prepare myself for the future, and do a little good for the world, besides. Not so much to earn money, hell, you got plenty of that. But as a warning to other women."

"You're going to work in a VD clinic?"

She sprayed a look of heat and energy all around him. A whiff of sadness. A perfume of tender bitterness. A fallout of longing and desire. A complication.

"How I was brought up in cactus, lost my education through impatience and my own hostility, ran the risks of victimless crime and cared only for my kitties, but through them, learned the value of true love and now I have a chance, just a chance, depending both on myself and one other, to make it on through," she said. "I'm going to find me a writer and tell him my sad story. How I'm bound and determined to make union for all the other hustlers and get on national nighttime teevee and bring a little dignity to my profession. How it really was for us in the days before I got organized. How we are still waiting for justice but we won't wait forever."

He listened, a thirty-two-track sufferer, an arranger, a hearer out. She had no man. She gave up her chance for her very own Superior Court judge. She was lonely. In this empty flat with its battleship-gray painted slats, its whitewashed walls, its fern in a redwood pot, its hungry kittens, she came to the end of her act. She pulled the rumpled sheet over them like a tent, she put her hands on his shoulders—none of that outrageous horny and stagy groping—she looked into his sleepy, suddenly wide-awake, worried eyes. "Just give me a kiss like you mean it, Sam. Don't stiffen on me. I don't care what sex you are, what you like, what you think you are, I'll even work for you, I can pay my own way. I don't need anybody, I got used to it since I was brung up with the cactus, it was raining all the time in Seattle, I was the nutty one even in that state campus of mine, even with the spooks and faggots they thought I was nuts, so just mean it, Sam, be nice, be nice for once, I'll even shut up for you, be nice to me, someone—"

He put his mouth against hers on that mattress on the floor. Larval kittens came to squirm against the long warmth of bodies. This overage kid had his work cut out for him. "Okay," he said.

"I got no friends worth mentioning. I got a daughter makes a lot of trouble, Sam. Cindy. I got a lot of friends not worth mentioning."

"You are *defended*," he said.

She grinned and suddenly sat up—a brown sturdy lady thumping her mattress. "Ah, that's right. Now you've got it. So you know me through and through, don't you, Sam?"

18

CORDELIA WAS REALLY ARTICULATE, a wonderful subject for a formerly psychopathic, now merely cool-hearted sociologist. I mean, with me she talked a lot. With others she talked little, and for some, action was all they required. With Sam Bowers she came to talk just as much as she felt like talking. This difference made my sinuses ache. It made me heartsick. It made me want to die, but so weak I couldn't carry out my wish. I carried out my work instead.

"You let me down," she said. "That's all right, Al, people do, but *you let me down*."

"I wasn't supposed to."

Her smile was huge and happy.

The hum of a motor on a long automobile trip with a person you like a lot. Intimacy exists. You turn off the radio. You just ride the highway. You touch. Fences, billboards, meadows, cows. The throb of the internal combustion universe penetrates both your bodies. The highway swerves; the trip ends. Maybe amnesia replaces that feeling of souls touching which you don't mention. But that close swimming together, that throb and sway, that silence, that endless moment existed.

Didn't it?

Not if I didn't take charge of Cindy. Instead, I had my thesis.

Someone else had Cordelia. I had not gone far enough with her to lose her. I practiced patience too long. I feared my impulses too much. It was only natural. Please.

But what right had she to ask me to care for her child? I only wanted to pick up a little love. She was Cindy's mother, by God! I wasn't even a stepfather. She thought my desire gave her the right to ask this of me.

And now she was silent. I had answers for all that flood of her words. I listened. Her silence was unanswerable.

I had had my chance.

This sadness. This loneliness. This loss.

•

The women marched in an orderly line in front of the Fairmont Hotel on Nob Hill. Barbara, Rose Ann, Rachel, Sharon. "End Discrimination! End Slave Wages! End Forcible Payoffs! Make the Streets Safe for Walking! Freedom and Justice for All!" A crowd was watching. Trucks were illegally parked. Cables snaked across the street. Police were keeping order. "Sisterhood!" stated a large banner held up by two women. The pickets were moving slowly. The law states: *Keep it moving.*

A woman I didn't know carried a sign that said: "We Rent Only What We Own." She was blinking in the watery San Francisco morning sunshine. She was up early today.

A black Cadillac slid across the sidewalk toward the police sergeant with his walkie-talkie and his radio hooked to his belt. The sergeant waited. The people inside the Cadillac waited. There was a child in the automobile. Benito, Calvina, haggard old Leopold at the wheel, Marietta. Sergeant Sheean recognized the next mayor and stepped forward, haunches squeaking in his high boots. She showed him a paper with a judge's seal on it.

The cop's belt began crackling with radio instructions. One of the doors of the Cadillac flew open. Marietta extended a hand like a claw to catch the person in flight. The sergeant blew his whistle to gather the other policemen toward him. His face was rosy. At last there would be some real action around here.

Marietta's hand didn't come near the body hurtling toward Cordelia. She withdrew it from the dangerous outside world and the gray-tinted window slid up. Cindy ran weeping toward her mother.

The police advanced in a line toward the group of strikers. They expected no trouble. Cordelia had one arm around her daughter. She looked straight at the police. She looked straight at the camera's eye. She hoped someone could make clear the message she was bringing to the world. She was telling it as best she could. As the police sergeant touched her arm and her daughter sobbed and a cameraman ran toward her, hobbled by his equipment, taping the moment of arrest, she raised the two fingers which mean victory. I could see her teeth hilarious in the morning light.